# "LIST~~~~~~~~~~~
# NUMBER ONE. IN TWO MINUTES—
# AT EIGHT O'CLOCK—WE WILL
# KNOCK OUT YOUR RADAR.
# INSTRUCTIONS WILL FOLLOW."

Then she heard the dial tone.

"Did he tell you who they were? Any name?" Malone pressed.

"He called himself Number One."

"Take it easy, Captain," Wilber counseled. "It's just eight now and everything's fine."

He pointed at the nearest radar set and they looked.

At that moment all the electronic "blips" on the screen disappeared.

"If you like a real thriller, this is for you . . . the suspense continues to the final page. This one is worth reading."
—Abilene *Reporter News*

"A thriller! The story moves along at a rapid-fire pace."
—Asheville *Citizen*

Other Tor Books by Walter Wager

BLUE LEADER
SWAP

# WALTER WAGER

# 58

# MINUTES

**TOR** ®

A TOM DOHERTY ASSOCIATES BOOK
NEW YORK

A TOR Book
Published by Tom Doherty Associates, Inc.
49 West 24th Street
New York, NY 10010

Cover art by Dan Osyczka

ISBN: 0-812-51036-4     Can. ISBN: 0-812-51037-2

Library of Congress Catalog Card Number: 87-622520-4

First Tor edition: July 1989

Printed in the United States of America

0  9  8  7  6  5  4  3  2  1

*This book is dedicated to*
JEROME S. MORRIS,
*attorney, philosopher and friend*

# 1

DECEMBER 21.

5:09 P.M. on the western edge of the churning Atlantic.

It was cold on the island. Light snow was fluttering from a blue-black winter sky, but the men and women peering down from the 86th floor of the famous skyscraper didn't really mind.

The view from up here was still spectacular. It was also familiar. Many of the tourists on the Empire State Building's open observation deck nodded in approving recognition as they stared at the great city. The promise had been kept. The skyline looked just the way it did in the movies. Even through the shimmering curtain of frozen white crystals, this was clearly the legendary metropolis they'd come from a dozen U.S. states and nine foreign lands to see.

This was New York—the power place.

This was the celebrity city against which others were measured. Admired, envied and despised, it was more than a collection of dynamic innovators and achievers known around the world. This cocky and controversial city itself was the celebrity—a vital and cosmopolitan creature that couldn't or wouldn't stand still.

It was moving right now. Some 1,050 feet above the streets, the tourists heard the insistent hum of rush-hour crowds and traffic—the municipal background music of bustling Manhattan. The visitors could almost *feel* the surging energy below. Suddenly the fabled skyline began to change before their eyes as swirling snow blurred the dramatic panorama. Soon scores of office towers and tall apartment houses were visible only as exotic clusters of lights, suggesting giant Christmas trees in the growing darkness.

Many of the men and women on the observation deck raised cameras to try to record this extraordinary illusion. Other tourists eyed it intently through coin-operated telescopes mounted on the parapet. There was something almost magical about this glittering sight, and they would talk about it when they returned to their distant homes.

Nine miles due east of the Empire State Building, someone else was watching the snow fall. He too was a visitor to this city. A thin-faced man in his late thirties, he'd been a visitor everywhere for more than a decade. He traveled so much he rarely recalled that he'd once had a home. When he did remember, it often made him angry.

Now he was seated on a tweed-upholstered armchair in Room 206 of the Queens Skyway Motel, staring at the television set as the local news continued. Frowning in concentration, he listened carefully to every word spoken by the perfectly barbered meteorologist on screen.

". . . low pressure north of us. Let's take a look at the latest satellite photos."

The pictures of the cascading snowflakes vanished. A large multishaded map of the United States and southern

Canada abruptly took their place. It was marked with three large curved arrows. From north, south and west, they swept toward the east coast region between Washington and Boston.

"As you can see, the snow that's falling here now is only the beginning of our problems. There's another load of snow heading our way from the south, and the jet stream is bringing us a juggernaut of icy Arctic air. Add to that some really nasty electrical storms in Pennsylvania that could get to us early tomorrow evening. Of more immediate significance, the National Weather Service is predicting very heavy precipitation for our entire area during the next twelve to fifteen hours," the dapper meteorologist singsonged briskly.

Then he reappeared on the screen.

"It looks as if they're right," he continued seamlessly. "Our own computer analysis shows that much of the tri-state region can expect at least a foot of the white stuff by noon tomorrow, and—don't blame *me*, folks—Mother Nature could sock it to us with as much as sixteen inches."

The man in Room 206 sat rigid and unblinking.

He was completely focused on this weather report.

It was, literally, a matter of life or death for thousands of people.

That didn't bother him. Death was a part of his business—the part he liked best. He enjoyed killing with a variety of weapons, including the P-15 semiautomatic in the holster under his left armpit. Tonight he'd use a new method.

"The five P.M. temperature in Central Park was twenty-four degrees Fahrenheit. It's going to drop to twelve or thirteen by midnight."

Now the weatherman was sharing a split screen with pictures of cars moving through the snow down a wide highway.

"Driving conditions are deteriorating steadily. Traffic on the New Jersey Turnpike is being limited to thirty-five miles an hour. New York State Police have issued Traveler's Advisories for the entire Governor Dewey Throughway. Bottom line? We're facing the first major snowfall of the winter and it could be one of the nastier storms in recent years."

The man who enjoyed killing smiled.

This was *perfect*.

As the weather report ended, he got up and walked to the closet. Ignoring the banal banter ricocheting between the meteorologist with the fine haircut and the pretty anchorwoman, he reached into the closet and took out a silvery aluminum suitcase. He had bought it after some thought. Thieves at airports sometimes razored open soft-sided luggage to loot the contents. He could not run that risk.

He put the metal container on the bed, opened the top button of his shirt and slid a hand in to grasp the suitcase key on the chain around his neck. The eighteen-carat gold loop had been a gift from an Italian millionaire's passionate daughter who hated imperialism and her father. She was dead. It was her own fault. If she had followed instructions on how to handle the bomb, she would not have been blown into seven pieces outside the American embassy in Rome.

She had moaned a lot during sex, he recalled as he unlocked the suitcase. It took only a moment to trip the hidden catch that released the false bottom. Then he took out the upper section filled with shirts and set it down beside the valise.

Each thing in the secret lower compartment was held in place by a padded clamp welded to the metal shell. He had chosen every item carefully on the basis of years of covert combat in many countries. These were the tools of his lethal trade.

A stubby Czech submachine gun—the 10.6-inch Skorpion—plus a shoulder holster and a dozen twenty-round clips of ammunition.

A bulletproof vest, a gas mask and four small incendiary bombs.

A disassembled 460 Weatherby Magnum rifle with eight-power telescopic sight and heavy-load, high-speed bullets that could drop an elephant or take off a quarter of a man's head.

A pair of walkie-talkie radios, three time fuses, a remote-control radio-detonator and a night-vision scope with light intensification power of 35,000.

Two snub-nosed Heckler and Koch VP70Z pistols and a pouch filled with eighteen-round magazines for the 9-milli-meter weapons.

Screw-on silencers for the submachine and handguns, three L2A1 antipersonnel grenades with a "kill circle" of ten yards and a plastic bag containing a neatly trimmed black wig.

He scanned his tools and nodded.

It was time for the next phase of the operation.

He put on the bulletproof vest. Then he took from the closet and donned a khaki-green Loden coat. Made of sturdy and tightly woven cloth, the waterproof garment was highly efficient in retaining body heat. Efficiency was important to the man in Room 206. It was one of his obsessions.

He returned to the open suitcase, unclamped and loaded a 9-millimeter pistol and slipped the weapon into the right pocket of the coat. A few seconds later, he put one of the L2A1 grenades in the left pocket. It wasn't that he expected any particular trouble. He routinely carried a grenade as a prudent precaution when he ventured outdoors.

There was another factor: the imminence of battle. The dangers of combat did not trouble him. They were exhilarating. Though he'd never told anyone, they aroused him more than any woman ever had. But they also made him tautly cautious. The closer this man got to armed confrontation, the more wary he became. In less than three hours, he would launch the biggest and most complex attack of his violent career. He certainly wasn't going to take any chances now.

After reattaching the false bottom, he locked the suitcase and deposited it in the closet. Then he paused before the large mirror to adjust the curly brown wig that he'd worn since leaving Madrid twenty-three days earlier. Next he put on the horn-rimmed eyeglasses, studied his appearance and finally nodded. With the elementary camouflage of the false hair and equally fake spectacles, he didn't look much like the photo on the Interpol "alert" reports.

The damned TV set was still on. Reflected in the mirror, the sincere anchorman, who had even better teeth than the ruthlessly perky blond "newscaster" beaming beside him, was burbling abut the new doll that was "definitely this year's *hottest* gift for the kiddie crowd—and very big bucks for the stores."

Grunting in contempt, the man who enjoyed killing flicked off the set. As he left the room, he pulled up the hood of the coat to cover three quarters of his head. He couldn't rely absolutely on the wig and glasses. The less of his face that people saw, the smaller the risk of being recognized. He only had to fool the Americans for another four hours.

The plan was good and the timetable was definite.

By 9:45 P.M., 10:15 at the latest, he'd be out of the country.

When he reached the motel's crowded lobby, he heard the infuriating music pouring from invisible loudspeakers. He despised Christmas songs as much as he loathed the holy day itself. From the age of eighteen, he had detested every religion and the priests, rabbis, nuns, monks and mullahs who were all enemies of the masses. He'd often told the Russians how wrong they were to let even a token shred of religion survive anywhere in the Soviet Union. They'd smiled patronizingly and ignored him.

He walked out the front door and his stomach knotted in tension. It was completely automatic. In his trade, he never knew what or who was waiting for him. Ambush was a constant occupational hazard. A hail of bullets could tear his hand off at any moment. The body armor wouldn't help him if they aimed high. Local police might not, but that was exactly what the FBI's coolly practical shooters would do.

He wouldn't blame them. It was the professional thing to

do. In their place, he'd do the same. He already had—in five countries.

He looked around, saw nothing threatening and relaxed— a little. But he was never totally relaxed. It wasn't only his mind that was always aware of the danger. By now, his *body* knew in some fierce visceral way—an animal's survival instinct. He hadn't really slept well for years, and his stomach hadn't been right for more than a decade.

The price of fame, he thought sarcastically. Then he walked through the falling snow to his car. The Americans were obsessed with fame, he brooded as he reached the vehicle. They all wanted to be on television and see their names in newspapers and *Time* magazine—to be celebrities. Tomorrow he'd be the main celebrity in this media-sick society. They'd all be talking about him.

And they would fear him.

He'd like that.

He hated the Americans most of all. They were the most powerful of the imperialists, and their intelligence networks were leading the global search for him right now.

He got into the car, inserted the ignition key but did not turn it. Instead, he connected and adjusted the seat belt. He never drove a car without wearing a seat belt. He was only going nine blocks, but statistical studies had established that most auto accidents happened within half a mile of where the trip began. He believed in statistics.

He checked both the side and rearview mirrors—twice— before he started the motor. Everything seemed to be going well. He was on schedule, the equipment was in place and the rest of the assault group was ready. He had the coins, the radio cube and the slip of flash paper. There were only a few things left to do—simple acts that wouldn't take more than twenty minutes.

Then he would give the order to attack.

# 2

SOME SIXTY YARDS in front of the motel lay a wide and busy highway. As usual, it was covered with a constant stream of vehicles flowing on to nearby Kennedy Airport, outer Queens and the "bedroom" communities of suburban Nassau County beyond the city limits.

Expecting the worst of his fellow humans in everything, the man who enjoyed killing always drove defensively. To-night he was especially wary as he guided the Volvo sedan onto the multilane expressway. Rush-hour traffic surging from the great city's commercial center was building rapidly, and visibility was declining in the mounting snowfall.

He had anticipated those conditions.

He had factored both of them into his timetable.

With windshield wipers flicking and clicking like twin metronomes, he drove three hundred yards in the slow outer lane to the turnoff. After leaving the highway, he cruised right for five blocks into an area of tree-lined streets and three-story private homes. There were a few neighborhood stores, one a small grocery named Arthur's. The telephone booth on the corner beside it was the reason he'd come here.

Though he had seen no sign that he was under surveillance, he certainly wasn't going to dial *these* numbers from the motel. That would be as stupid as making more than two calls from the same booth—a dangerous violation of the basic rules.

He parked the Volvo and looked carefully in both directions. There were hardly any pedestrians in sight, and only an occasional car loomed through the fluttering snow. Entering the booth, he caressed the grenade in his pocket as if it were some magical totem or religious talisman.

It was merely a habit. He certainly didn't believe in good luck or that primitive God rubbish. Still, for a moment, he felt a visceral surge of confidence and power.

Then he pulled from his shirt pocket the slip of fast-burning flash paper on which he'd written the first three numbers. He'd memorized the other three. He was the only member of the assault team who knew all those. It was safer for the entire group that way.

He took out a fistful of coins, studied the piece of paper and dialed the first number.

202 . . . 936 . . . 1212.

After a few seconds of preamble, he finally heard the words that he was waiting for.

". . . another two inches in Washington by midnight as the new storm sweeps across the District of Columbia into Maryland."

He dialed again.

617 . . . 936 . . . 1234.

"Heavy fog continues to blanket greater Boston. Driving conditions will remain hazardous until early morning."

It was time to move on. Following his security rule

against more than two calls from one phone, he got back
in the Volvo and drove nine blocks to the next booth on his
list.

412 . . . 936 . . . 1212.

". . . at Pittsburgh Airport. Major thunderstorms are rolling through Allegheny County. Freezing sleet is following
right behind them with forty-mile-an-hour winds."

The outer perimeter was secure for at least six hours.

That was more than he needed.

The attack could proceed.

Satisfaction gleamed in his left eye as he put more coins
into the phone slot. Nothing showed in the right eye. It was
artificial, a replacement for the one lost in a 1981 shootout
with French antiterrorist police. He'd killed three of the
leather-jacketed troopers before escaping into the Paris
dawn. A month later he cremated the woman who betrayed
him. She had screamed for a long time in the burning car
before the fuel tank exploded.

He wasn't thinking about her as he dialed the first of the
numbers that he'd memorized. Concentrating on tonight's
operation, he was again scanning the street warily, peering
through the snow for any sign of danger. He let the telephone
ring four times, hung up and redialed the same number.

It belonged to a pay phone on the wall of a South Bronx
garage. The man who picked it up was a stocky twenty-eight-
year-old Latin. He had strong convictions and considerable
experience with explosives.

"Is Mr. Enrique Velez there?"

"No. This is his cousin, Jose," the man in the garage replied.

Challenge and countersign correct. The conversation immediately switched to Spanish, an exchange of short staccato
phrases like bursts from an automatic weapon. After twenty
seconds of curt communication, there was a brief silence
while the mustachioed bomb expert studied his wristwatch.

Then he adjusted it, carefully moving the larger hand forward one minute.

"Bueno . . . adios," he said and hung up the phone.

He turned to make a thumbs-up gesture to another young Latin male leaning against a white minivan ten yards away. Paco Garcia smiled back at his older brother. They had always been very close. That was a matter of official record in the files of the Federal Bureau of Investigation. The FBI had been interested in Juan and Paco Garcia for five and a half years.

Paco Garcia unlocked the rear door of the van and took out a pair of tan, twenty-six-inch Samsonite valises. They were heavy, and he set them down on the garage floor immediately. He opened his lips to call out the defiant slogan of The Movement but he stifled it. Their orders had been blunt and specific. They were to say nothing political—not even here. They were to assume that they were under visual and electronic surveillance at all times.

They couldn't even embrace as they usually did before an operation. There might be a hidden camera. Paco Garcia shrugged, lifted one of the cases and placed it on the front seat of a blue Ford. Juan Garcia deposited the other on the floor of the front compartment of a green Omni. Both cars had four-wheel drive and snow tires. The orders on that too had been precise and unequivocal, and one did not defy *his* commands.

*He* was utterly vicious, Juan Garcia reflected soberly. For a moment the husky Puerto Rican wondered about the others involved in this operation and what they were doing. They had never met. It felt unnatural to fight as part of an army of strangers, but there was no time to dwell on that now. Each of the brothers had almost an hour's drive to his target. The younger brother opened the garage door, and the two cars glided out into the night.

The man who enjoyed killing was already on his way to

the third telephone booth. He had to follow the rules. Taking chances would be stupid. Pausing at a red traffic light, he recalled a Russian proverb: "All the brave men are in prison." The Russians were wrong. Those men were dead. The litany of the U.S. Air Force test pilots had much more truth: "There are old men and bold men—but no old bold men."

After searching several minutes for a parking space, he found one. Then he walked back three blocks to the booth to make the next call.

Four rings . . . hang up . . . dial again. Now he was speaking to a swarthy man in the Atlantic Avenue section of Brooklyn where so many immigrants from the Middle East lived. They talked in Arabic, a tongue the man in the telephone booth had learned when he'd been an instructor at a "covert warfare" training camp in Marxist South Yemen. The man he was speaking to had been one of his best students. The brief and guttural conversation ended with another synchronizing of watches.

The last of this group of calls was to a small warehouse in Queens some two miles from the snowswept phone booth. It was an earnest bespectacled Japanese in coveralls who answered. He was seated on a swivel chair in front of two large metal racks. The three shelves on each were crammed with sophisticated radio equipment and electrical gear. There were also six television sets.

He was a small man with a large anger. Takeshi Ito, five feet four inches tall and a week from his thirty-first birthday, was an electronics expert on loan from the fanatical Japanese Red Army. His technical skills were crucial to the success of this operation.

"I'm calling to remind you about the party tonight. It starts at eight."

"No problem," Ito replied.

"Good. Dammit, my watch has stopped. What time have you got?"

Ito looked at the electric clocks on the rack. One ran on wall current and the other was battery-powered. Trained as an electrical engineer, he believed in backup systems for everything. He watched the sweepsecond hand move.

"It's . . . five forty-one, straight up," he said.

"Thanks. See you later. Don't be late."

"I never am," Ito answered truthfully.

When he heard the click and the dial tone, Ito put down the phone to glance at the video screens. They were as important to his survival as the 9-millimeter submachine gun on the ammunition box at his feet. Connected to television cameras mounted high on the exterior of the warehouse, they provided continuous surveillance of the street out front and the rear alley. He studied the screens for half a minute, squinting to see through the falling snow. Everything seemed quiet and normal outside.

The man who had telephoned Ito felt exuberant as he walked back to the parked Volvo. The operation was moving forward. Nothing could stop it now. In two hours and nineteen minutes, war would come to the United States.

It would be both a shock and a lesson to the complacent Americans. They hadn't endured a war in their homeland for more than a century. Their wives and children had felt safe behind two oceans for a long time—a dozen decades.

That would end tonight.

They would learn the meaning of fear.

All the other major powers—Britain, Russia, China, France, Germany, Japan, India and Italy—had been bombed and battered in bloody battle. Now it was America's turn, he exulted silently.

He patted the grenade in celebration.

The plan was perfect, the equipment was excellent, the handpicked personnel he'd assembled were ideal for this unique assault. He hadn't told any of them what the real goal was or who was paying for this extraordinary operation. All they knew was that they were liberating political prisoners and each member of the attack group would receive $1 million.

That part of what he'd told them was true. Most of the rest was a lie, but that didn't matter. They'd collect the $1 million each and disperse to deliver the money to their various organizations to fund their own future operations.

He'd get a lot more.

$5 million.

He deserved it. He had conceived the plan and how to camouflage the real objective. That deception was extremely important to the enormously rich and famous man who was investing some $11 million in tonight's attack. That sum did not bother him. The only thing that counted was that the objective be achieved and in a way that did not point to him.

In his own field, the man who would get the $5 million was also prominent. Britain's MI5, France's SDECE and "Police National," the American FBI and CIA, West Germany's internal security apparatus, Israel's Shin Bet and Mossad, a dozen other intelligence organizations and millions of newspaper readers and television viewers around the world were aware of his violent activities.

The middle son of a leftist German magazine editor and a plump Austrian schoolteacher had come a long way since he was expelled from Ludwig-Maximilians Universität in Munich for "political hooliganism." He wasn't just another ranting revolutionary student anymore, he reflected as he saw his car up ahead. Even though he wasn't a sports, television or music star, he'd killed enough people to make the media take him seriously.

He was one of the three most notorious terrorists alive.

He was feared and "wanted" in many lands.

He was Willi Staub.

# 3

6:10 P.M. in affluent midtown Manhattan.

The winds were growing stronger. Erupting like tantrums, gusts swirled the snow on the fashionable East Sixties street into irrational pirouettes. Not being ballet fans, the two young policemen guarding 12 East 65th Street merely stamped their half-frozen feet and hoped that they wouldn't pull diplomatic protection duty again soon.

As the brass plate on the five-story building announced, number twelve housed the Consulate of the Islamic Republic of Pakistan. Pakistan meant Land of the Pure, according to Sergeant Schwartz, who had sent these same patrolmen to protect the Soviet U.N. Mission on East 67th Street for two rainy weeks in November. Cops on that assignment had heated guardhouses to shield them from bad weather, but

16 WALTER WAGER

there was a much greater risk of being caught in a riot or a bombing.

Tonight there was some kind of a party going on at 12 East 65th Street. Cars and limousines had been unloading dozens of people since five o'clock. Stoically enduring the steadily building snowfall, the two red-faced patrolmen could see knots of well-dressed men and women eating, drinking and chatting away cheerfully. Framed in the ground-floor windows, they seemed to be having a good time. It wasn't cold in there. Several of the smiling women were wearing sleeveless cocktail dresses, indicating that it was at least seventy degrees in the big room.

"*Shit*," one of the policemen swore softly as another blast of icy air swept in from Central Park half a block away.

"*Shit*," the other foot patrolman agreed.

At that moment, the door to 12 East 65th Street opened. A welcome wave of warmth rushed out and a tall, sandy-haired man followed. Blue-eyed, bare-headed and wearing a Burberry overcoat, he walked with the gait of an athlete. He had been one for more than a decade. For two years, he'd been voted best quarterback in the Ivy League.

Neither of the young policemen recognized him. But when he paused to fasten the top button of his dark coat, there was something in his eyes that made them feel that they were being judged. They were. For no reason they could name, both of them stood straighter and nodded in silent salutation.

For a few seconds, he considered telling them that it was just another reception—duller than most because the conscientious Moslem hosts did not serve hard liquor. Deciding that it would be condescending, Frank Malone simply nodded back and strode east on 65th Street.

Trying to ignore the snow, he thought about the reception as he walked toward his car. He had nothing against diplomats, but he'd only gone to the party because his job required him to maintain certain lines of communication. Diplomats were no worse than any other bureaucrats. No, the administrators were much more depressing. They were as pompous as the lawyers, Malone thought as he crossed Madison Avenue.

It was ironic, and he almost smiled. He'd been admitted to both the Harvard and Columbia Law schools, but had not gone. Though he knew many people who had become rich attorneys, Frank Malone could not say that some of his best friends were lawyers. One was—a sophisticated black woman who wrote excellent briefs and even better poetry.

Aware that the snow could add at least 20 minutes to his ride to the airport, Malone marched on to Park Avenue. Electric bulbs beamed from the evergreens on the divider that separated the north-south traffic, and uniformed doormen outside luxury apartment houses glowed with the serenity of individuals who have a strong union and cast-iron expectations of substantial Christmas gratuities.

Malone continued east to Lexington Avenue and turned north. When he reached 66th Street, he saw his parked car. Beside it stood a thin young man wearing a jaunty cap, a down-filled short coat, tweed pants and brown cowboy boots. He was trying to unlock the dark-green sedan's front door.

Malone unbuttoned his overcoat a moment before he accelerated his stride. He stopped five yards away from the man as he'd been taught to do. Any closer could be dangerous.

"That's my car," Malone said.

Now he saw the ring of keys in the stranger's hand.

"You're making a mistake," Malone said calmly.

The man spun around and opened a large button-knife. The blade was five inches long.

"You only get *one*," Malone announced.

As the car thief rushed forward to stab him, Malone drew his Colt .38 pistol and smashed it against the wrist of the hand holding the knife. It was all one fluid motion—swift, precise and effective. The wrist was broken. Screaming in pain, the thief dropped his weapon but clawed for the gun with his other hand. That frantic effort ended when Malone slammed the Colt against the left side of his head.

Dazed and gasping, he fell to his knees. His vision was blurred and he heard nothing. The only thing he knew for certain was that he hurt. He didn't feel the blood oozing from the two-inch gash in his temple. He wasn't aware that it was dripping down to stain the snow. Shaking his head and making sounds that were almost animal, he resembled some hybrid man-beast creature from a "mad scientist" movie of the 1940s.

"Pay attention. I'm only going to say it once," Malone told him.

Trying to focus, the battered thief peered up at him. It was a look of raw hate.

"I'm a police officer. You're under arrest."

Now the groggy man was trying to struggle to his feet.

"You have the right to an attorney. If you don't have one, you may request that one be provided."

"You son of a bitch!"

"Watch your mouth," Malone advised. "Anything you say can and will be used against you."

"Screw you!" the car thief replied hoarsely.

"Save your breath. You have the right to remain silent, and I wish you would. I don't have any time to waste tonight."

Now the man on the sidewalk could see again. His eyes brightened when he noticed the open knife gleaming a yard away.

"Don't even consider it," Malone said and picked up the weapon by its blade to avoid smudging any fingerprints on the handle.

A chubby woman walking her Saint Bernard saw him, knife in one hand and pistol in the other. She saw the bloodied man on the sidewalk too. Without blinking, she guided the big dog in a wide circle around them and continued north. Malone closed the knife, wrapped it in a handkerchief and put it in his coat pocket.

The car thief finally managed to stand. His face was a bitter grimace as he swayed in the gusting snow. The pain was still terrible.

"You broke my wrist!"

"It was nothing personal," Malone replied. "Let's go."

He gestured toward his car with the short-barreled Detective Special. When they reached it, he searched his prisoner for other weapons before handcuffing the man's uninjured wrist to the rear door. Then he unlocked the front door and slid behind the steering wheel to use the two-way police radio.

The patrol car that he summoned arrived three and a half minutes later, and the pair of uniformed men who got out eyed him with a mixture of respect and curiosity. They had heard about Captain Frank Malone. He was a much decorated hero, the youngest captain in the NYPD and its pistol champion. He was known as a first-class commander, defending his people when they were right and sparing no one who was wrong.

When the two patrolmen reached his car, Malone slid out and identified himself. Summarizing what had happened, he handed over the cloth-wrapped knife and unlocked the handcuffs.

"Get him to a doctor as soon as he's been booked," Malone ordered. Then he reentered the green sedan and drove away down Lexington Avenue. The thief began to swear bitterly.

"What are you cursing about? You're a *very* lucky man," the taller patrolman said.

"First I pick a cop's car and then I get my wrist busted. What's so lucky about that?"

"You're lucky the cop was Frank Malone. A lot of others would have blown you away if you came at them with a blade."

"You'd be in a goddam body bag right now, Jack," the other radio patrolman agreed.

That ended the conversation. The car thief said nothing as they led him to their cruiser. He was still silent six minutes later when they herded him into the station house. Frank Malone was less than a mile away, guiding the green sedan onto the 59th Street Bridge that would take him over the East River to Queens.

# 4

ALTITUDE: 39,200 feet.
Airspeed: 548 miles an hour.
Flight number: BA 126

Thundering westward through the blackness some seven and a half miles above the North Atlantic, the big British Airways jet was exactly on schedule. The silver and blue Boeing 747 had left London eighteen minutes late, but skillful flying had closed that gap. Barring unforeseen problems, BA 126 would touch down at New York's John F. Kennedy Airport in ninety-five minutes.

The flight had gone well thus far. There had been no bumpy turbulence, no difficult passengers complaining about the food or getting drunk, no infants wailing while furious adults tried to sleep, no irritatingly amorous travelers trying to seduce the flight attendants and no heart attacks, diabetic crises or women going into labor. With nearly three quarters of the journey over, almost everyone aboard—crew and passengers—was in fairly good spirits.

Among the less enthusiastic minority was a graying, patrician-looking man seated up front in the First-Class section. First Class had been Sir Brian Forsythe's natural habitat and life-style long before he became the head of the United Kingdom's mission to the United Nations. The handsome son of a hard-drinking baronet, he knew Britain's elite. He was one of them.

Like the custom-made clothes he wore, his credentials were inpeccable. He'd won the Latin medal at Harrow, a Distinguished Flying Cross in the Royal Air Force and an "honors" degree in history from Trinity College, Cambridge. His intelligence and "Old Boy" connections weren't the only reasons that he'd later risen swiftly in the Foreign Office. Beneath that elegant manner and upper-class accent, Forsythe had the toughness and practicality of a street fighter. A man of high principle and no illusions, he'd developed into one of the most effective diplomats serving Her Majesty's government today.

HMG—the concise usage of generations of British civil servants—usually sent Forsythe where the trouble was. He had never hesitated or resisted. A gentleman did his duty, and did it well. That was the Forsythe code. It had been since the twelfth century.

He had survived riots in Teheran, an assassination attempt in Cairo, three years of ugly futility in Saigon, Washington's steamy summers and pushy press corps, malaria in East Africa and forty-one months of terrible food and worse weather in Moscow. Shrewd, patient, hard as steel and always *pleasant*, he'd earned the respect of ally and adversary alike—even the wary Russians.

After thirty-three years with the Foreign Office, he knew the game well.

But he wasn't sure that he wanted to play it anymore.

Someone had changed the game in recent years. It had become vicious and violent, a brutal thing much closer to war than diplomacy. Political murders, terrorist attacks and naked military aggression were replacing international law almost everywhere. Barely sixty hours ago, bloody fighting had erupted in the Near East again. That was why Sir Brian Forsythe was on BA 126 en route to New York for an emergency session of the U.N. Security Council.

Another orgy of righteous oratory, he thought as he refocused on the speech he was holding. When he reached the last paragraph, he took out his fountain pen . . . paused . . . struck out a phrase . . . and wrote two words above it. Then he finished reading and sighed.

"Is something wrong, Ambassador?" the tall woman seated beside him asked anxiously.

"Hardly anything. As usual, Miss Jenkins, you've done a splendid job. I'm fortunate to have such an able special assistant."

Ellen Jenkins beamed. This soft-spoken woman's expertise in both Soviet and Arab affairs had earned her many commendations during her fifteen years with the Foreign Office, but Forsythe's approval was especially important to her.

It wasn't because he was her boss and one of Britain's top diplomats. Career considerations were not involved. This was something more elemental. Sir Brian Forsythe, admired at the Foreign Office for his sensitivity in negotiation and grasp of people, had no idea that the wide-eyed woman he worked with nearly every day was in love with him.

She had been for almost two years. She hadn't admitted it to herself until his wife died nineteen months earlier, but, deep within her, she had *known*. She had hidden it from everyone. The Oxford-educated son of a baronet couldn't possibly care for a Welsh butcher's daughter who'd studied at an unimportant "red brick" university devoid of tradition or status.

And there was another gap between them—eighteen years. People might smirk and jest about a "father fixation," and the fact that she looked even younger than her age would only emphasize the meaningless numerical difference. Class, education and age were not the only reasons that she concealed her feelings. She had her Welsh pride too.

There was no way she could tell him.

That was unthinkable.

It was much safer and wiser simply to acknowledge his compliment about the speech.

"That's very kind of you, Sir Brian," she said and immediately regretted her compulsive modesty.

"I'll try to do your text justice," he promised and drained his champagne glass. "I'd like to go out on a high note."

"Out?"

"There isn't much time. I'll be sixty in June, and that's the retirement age."

Six months. She had tried so hard not to think about it. When he retired, she'd probably never see him again.

"Couldn't they make an exception for a valuable senior diplomat?" she asked in as calm a voice as she could muster.

"I'm not sure that I'd want them to. Don't worry, Miss Jenkins. The chap who takes over may be much better."

Unable to stop herself, she shook her head in disagreement.

"Oh no, Sir Brian!"

"I appreciate your loyalty, but no one's irreplaceable."

She struggled for the courage to tell him.

"In any case, HMG has rules," he continued as a blond stewardess approached with an opened bottle of champagne. "I've lived by those rules for over half my life."

"May I, Sir Brian?" the smiling stewardess asked.

He thanked her, and she began to refill his glass.

"Now let's talk about something more interesting," he said. "Stewardess, please tell us about that old lady who attracted so many journalists at Heathrow. Her dreary clothes seemed Russian."

"Bull's-eye, Sir Brian," the pretty flight attendant complimented. "She's seventy-six, I'm told, and she is Russian. Her name is Mrs. Olitski."

"Sarah Olitski is a Jewish widow who has become a *cause célèbre* for several U.S. politicians and two New York City newspapers that detest each other," Ellen Jenkins said crisply. "They've all been trying to get her out to rejoin her only living relatives who are, I believe, residents of Brooklyn."

"The Kiev Grandma!" Forsythe recalled. "It was on the BBC last night that she'd left Moscow. She must be delighted."

"Not entirely," the flight attendant said as she filled Ellen Jenkins's glass with chilled Mumm's. "In point of fact, Mrs. Olitski is rather distressed about *something*, but we don't know what it is. She doesn't speak a word of English."

Then she paused before she asked the question.

"Do you happen to speak Russian, Sir Brian?"

"Not as well as Miss Jenkins. She has a remarkable gift for languages. Is it five . . . or six?"

Embarrassed by his disclosure, Ellen Jenkins unbuckled her seat belt.

"I'd be glad to help if I can," she said and rose to follow the stewardess.

Sarah Olitski sat twenty-two rows back, wearing a tired woolen babushka over her hair and an expression of acute tension. When Ellen Jenkins asked in Russian how she was, a torrent of words poured out in urgent reply.

"It's a human and not a political problem," the Welsh diplomat told the stewardess. "Mrs. Olitski needs to use the lavatory. I'll show her the way."

When they returned to the gray-haired exile's seat a few minutes later, the older woman squeezed Ellen Jenkins's hand and spoke again.

"Could you *possibly* get her a *glass* of tea? It's the Russian custom," the Welsh woman explained.

The Kiev Grandma beamed and squeezed Ellen Jenkins's hand once more when the glass of tea arrived. Then the older woman thanked her, sipped the tea and closed her eyes in contentment. When she opened them, she uttered another burst of Russian and Ellen Jenkins replied softly.

Then she started back with the flight attendant toward the First-Class compartment. As they reached it, Ellen Jenkins turned sideways to let a portly stockbroker pass. In doing so, she inadvertently brushed against a well-dressed young man in the aisle seat.

"I'm *terribly* sorry," she said in reflex courtesy.

He didn't answer. Clutching a black attaché case with both hands, he scowled at her in open hostility. Ellen Jenkins noticed something else in his eyes as well. It looked like fear.

She apologized again, as she had been brought up to do, and continued toward the First-Class section with the stewardess.

"Did you notice his leather case, Miss Jenkins?"

"Yes. Why?"

"That's what he's so bloody nervous about . . . won't let go of it for a second. Even takes it to the loo with him," she confided with a wry giggle.

For a few moments Ellen Jenkins wondered what might be in the attaché case. Then her mind turned, as it did so often, to Sir Brian Forsythe. She felt a sudden tightening in her throat, and it took a strong effort to speak when she sat down beside him twenty seconds later.

# 5

*NOSE HIGH* like some huge predatory bird, the swept-wing transport knifed through the sky like a supersonic dagger. Racing above the South Atlantic from Morocco, it was the fastest and most expensive passenger plane on the planet. The 747s and DC-10s, the L-1011s and Soviet Ilyushins were all bulky buses in comparison.

1,350 miles an hour.

Only the highest performance military aircraft could match it.

There was no airline name or designer-crafted logo on the side of this exceptional machine. It did not belong to any of the globe-girdling air carriers or famous multinational corporations. This Concorde was the private property of one of the wealthiest men on earth.

He was Prince Omar, eldest son of the king of Tarman. An

insignificant land of semiliterate Bedouins, drifting dunes and sand fleas until forty years ago, Tarman was now one of the richest of the Arab oil states. With more than $6 billion a year in petroleum income, the royal family could afford almost anything. King Raschid, who traveled with a large retinue, had a 747 of his own as well as a fleet of smaller planes and helicopters.

Prince Omar, heir to the throne and thoughtful foreign minister, preferred the smaller and much swifter Concorde. A sophisticated man with a degree in management and international trade from Stanford University in California, thirty-eight-year-old Omar had a shrewd sense of both politics and business. The Concorde screeching toward New York from Rabat, where the Tarmani crown prince had conferred with the Moroccan monarch, was both a jet-propelled pleasure dome and an airborne executive suite.

This was no holiday or shopping trip. While the damask-and velvet-draped bedroom at the Concorde's rear housed two perfumed wives—one third the number that accompanied his father on journeys—Prince Omar was working right now in his ultramodern and handsomely furnished office.

"As you instructed," he dictated to his male secretary, "I will make it absolutely clear to the American secretary of state that our position has the support of both our Moroccan and Saudi brethren."

He stopped to phrase the final sentence carefully.

"Following Allah's sacred precepts, I believe that we will be able to stop this bloodshed within two or three days. . . . Put that in my personal code and have it radioed to my father immediately."

As the respectful secretary left, Omar pressed a button on the elaborate control panel built into his elegant desk. The large computer screen five feet away instantly began to display a running report on the latest London market quotes on gold and oil. He touched another button and the current values of the world's major currencies stutter-stepped into sight.

Omar studied them soberly and knowledgeably. He understood exactly how these numbers affected his family and his country. He knew almost as much about interest rates and wheat futures as he did about the Holy Koran. Neither libertine playboy nor fundamentalist fanatic, hawk-faced Omar of Tarman was a versatile contemporary executive—simultaneously prince and tycoon.

While Omar swiftly analyzed the implications of the newest surge in the value of the dollar, his secretary was busy thirty feet away in the office suite's data center and communications room. More than $2.6 million had been spent on this high-tech facility, and it was all visible. There were two large computers; an Associated Press teleprinter for news; a pair of state-of-the-art word processors, one with Arabic typefaces and the other for Western tongues; an ultramodern and highly sophisticated coding machine and two powerful radio transmitters equipped with scramblers.

This section of the Concorde was never left unguarded. Even when the plane was on the ground, two armed men were always on duty to prevent any tampering or bugging. Every week, the entire aircraft was "swept" by electronics experts for concealed eavesdropping devices. Right now, four members of the prince's own security team carrying West German MP-5 submachine guns were on duty.

A pair of Tarmani Army sergeants were busy at the word processors, while a trio of lieutenants—all wearing automatic pistols—manned the radios and the cryptographic gear. Within half a minute after the prince's secretary handed over the message, the encoding began.

A dozen yards away in his private office, the hawk-faced prince flicked on the speakerphone on his desk. With stock prices still parading across his computer screen, he tapped a button on the communications control panel to talk to the pilot in the cockpit.

"When do we reach Kennedy, Captain?"

"We should be landing in approximately forty-two minutes, Your Highness."

Omar thanked him and turned off the speakerphone.

He glanced at the massive gold Rolex on his right wrist before looking at the wall clocks showing the time in five key cities around the world.

Forty-two minutes?

That would be three minutes after eight in New York.

# 6

*THEY* would kill to stop her.

She had known that long before she boarded Aerovias Flight 16.

Lima . . . Quito . . . Bogota . . . Caracas . . . San Juan . . . and, in another forty minutes, New York.

Clutching her rosary, the determined young woman in seat 37A stared out the window at the stars. She didn't see them—or anything else. She wasn't blind. She was looking inward, concentrating totally on her crucial mission.

She had to complete it.

This was a matter of principle.

That was what gave her the strength to face the terrible danger. Her heart had been pounding wildly at the airport as she waited for Flight 16. Her mouth had been so dry that she could barely speak. If they had suspected what she'd con-

cealed beneath the gray nun's habit, she'd be spread-eagled
on one of their interrogation tables now.

Naked . . . bloody . . . screaming as they hurt and de-
filed every part of her twenty-nine-year-old body.

They did such things—routinely and expertly. Just thinking of it made her shudder, and she turned her head in unconscious reaction. When she squirmed in her seat, the
pouch taped to her skin just beneath her breasts chafed her
and she winced.

Seeing her discomfort, the dapper steward hurried toward
the pretty young nun. Product of a religious home, Enrique
Arias was always respectful toward members of the Catholic
clergy. The fact that she had the lovely face of a cherub
helped accelerate the macho steward's stride.

"Is there anything that I can do for you, Sister?" he asked
solicitously.

"I'm all right."

"A pillow—that will help you," he said and reached up to
provide one from the overhead bin. As he walked away, he
found himself wondering why such an attractive female had
chosen celibacy. After all, ordinary-looking women could do
this noble work just as well.

She closed her eyes, but opened them wide a dozen seconds later. She couldn't afford to relax. She was still in danger. There might be a plainclothes policeman on the plane,
watching her. She would have to stay fully alert until the
Aerovias 767 landed and she entered the terminal at Kennedy.

Then she would complete her crucial mission.

She would help strike an important blow against the op-
pressors—one that would be noticed around the world.

Some 385 miles to the northwest, Paco Garcia was driving
the blue Ford carefully down the New Jersey Turnpike. Visibility wasn't good in the falling snow, but he'd been here
twice before in the rehearsals that Staub had ordered so he

knew exactly where he was. Traffic in this storm was only half the normal flow, and that helped too.

He saw the blinking lights and grinned.

There was the target—sixty yards ahead.

When he reached it, he pulled the Ford off onto the shoulder and turned off the engine. The target was a microwave relay tower capped by a round dish and adorned with lights so that pilots would see it. The roar of a big jet overhead confirmed what Paco Garcia had noticed on his first reconnaissance here. Newark Airport was only three miles away.

Garcia took the heavy suitcase from the car, cursing its weight and the blowing snow as he trudged toward the tower. Shuddering in the cold wind, he swore at Staub for planning an attack for late December in the middle of a storm.

What the hell was so special about *this* tower?

Why did the assault have to be tonight?

Completely obsessive about security, Staub hadn't explained the entire operation to the Garcia brothers. He'd told them about the money, their FALN comrades who would be liberated and the targets that Paco and Juan Garcia were to destroy—when he gave the order. That was another thing the one-eyed European was insistent about: absolute control.

When Paco Garcia neared the base of the tower, he set down the suitcase and opened it. With blowing snow pelting his face, he took out the two explosive charges and their timers. Having scouted and studied the metal structure earlier, he knew precisely where to place the explosives. He was an expert with mines and explosives, having learned a great deal during three years as a combat engineer in the U.S. Army.

He began to tape the first charge into place on one of the main metal supports. Concentrating on this and unable to hear much beside the storm, he didn't notice the car that pulled up behind his Ford. Like the microwave tower, it was crowned with a flashing light. It was a State Police cruiser.

Spotting the sedan by the side of the highway, the two uniformed troopers had stopped to see whether he required help. Assisting motorists in distress, especially in temperatures well below freezing, was one of their responsibilities.

When they found that the Ford was empty, they looked around and saw Garcia at the foot of the nearby tower. In the black winter night and swirling snow, it was difficult to make out what he was doing. It never occurred to them that he was an armed professional terrorist making war on the United States of America.

"Hey, Mister! You okay?" one husky trooper shouted.

"Need any help?" the other called out loudly.

And they kept walking toward him.

Paco Garcia turned and saw the two uniformed men.

Talk or shoot? He had only seconds to decide.

He reached down into the suitcase, grasped a silenced MAC11 submachine gun and swung it swiftly. The policemen never even reached for their holstered pistols. Garcia fired in short accurate bursts, putting half a dozen heavy 9-millimeter slugs into each of them.

They had no time, no chance. In five seconds they were corpses. Battered by the automatic weapon's terrible torrent of bullets, they reeled and spun under the impact. They were dead before they hit the snow.

Garcia looked at the ruined bodies for several seconds, decided not to take any chances and put another burst into each. Unlike Staub, he got no pleasure from killing. Sometimes the liberation of his native island required it, he reflected as he put down the submachine gun.

Then he finished rigging the two charges and set their timers in accordance with Staub's order. His brother was doing the same thing at two other towers, and for all Paco Garcia knew, somebody else might be planting explosives at a fourth and fifth.

He clapped his hands together a few times for warmth, picked up the suitcase and hurried back to his car. He didn't slow down when he passed the corpses, but he looked at them. The 9-millimeter slugs had torn big holes. The snow for a yard around the bodies was dark with blood.

It was their own fault, Paco Garcia told himself. If they hadn't stopped to help him, it wouldn't have happened. He'd explain that to his brother when they met at the rendezvous. He didn't want Juan, who had such firm views on how "unnecessary bloodshed" would hurt the FALN's image, to be angry with him.

He put the suitcase in the Ford. Then he realized that there was one more thing to be done. The flashing light on the police car might attract attention. The longer the bodies remained undiscovered the better it would be, so he had to turn that light off immediately. He did it with two bullets from the automatic pistol that he drew from a belly holster.

He wiped the melted snow from his face when he entered the Ford. Warm air poured from the heater as soon as he turned on the motor, and he shivered. Well, he'd be away from this imperialist land and its awful weather in a few hours—with his brother, their freed comrades and the money. He and Juan would be heroes.

There was no time to think about such things now. He had to meet Juan and transfer to the white van. As he drove onto the highway, he couldn't help wondering why they'd been ordered to paint the name of that hospital on the van. He'd find out when they met Staub.

It wouldn't be long.

The operation would begin very soon, when the charges knocked down the towers.

That would be in thirty-six minutes.

# 7

LIGHTNING flashed on the horizon.

The boom of thunder reached the large L-1011 airliner five seconds later. Then more jagged bolts ripped the night sky and another cannonade sounded swiftly.

The senior pilot on TWA Flight 22 wasn't the least bit troubled. Captain Lawrence Pace had more than thirteen thousand hours of multiengine jet experience, a thorough knowledge of this well-built plane and solid confidence in the competent people and impressive electronic gear of the sophisticated U.S. airways guidance and control system.

"What have we got up ahead, Tom?" he asked calmly.

The navigator rechecked the weather radar screen.

"I think we've outrun it, Captain," he reported. "Some turbulence a few miles down the road . . . heavy rain all the way in . . . nothing to sweat about. New York Center should pick us up in about nineteen minutes."

Pace nodded comfortably. The Federal Aviation Administration staffed its New York Center with some of its best air traffic controllers. These able veterans would bring TWA 22 into JFK with no trouble at all.

At that moment, Pace smelled the Ferré perfume and smiled. Samantha Wong, the sleek and wordly Chinese-American flight attendant who intrigued so many pilots and even more passengers, had arrived with his caffeine-free herb tea. Ferré was her trademark.

"Thanks, Sam. How're we doing back there?" he questioned.

"*We* are working our tails off. It's wall-to-wall people," she replied as he took the cup.

"Full house?"

"Not an empty seat; two hundred and sixty-five thirsty people and a box."

"What's in the box?" he asked between sips.

"A *kidney*, Captain. It's flying First Class—with a courier—for a transplant operation."

Pace shook his head.

"Don't think I ever hauled a kidney before," he said.

"Got to be a first time for everything."

"Is that a proposition, Sam?"

"Don't hold your breath, Captain," she advised and left the cockpit. When she entered the First-Class section, she heard the entertainment business shop talk that was so familiar to her after 174 flights between Los Angeles and New York.

"Four million two in the first week . . . It's *definitely* going platinum . . . Very high concept . . . *Perfect* for Eastwood . . . Those network bastards . . . *Great* foreign sales . . . So we're getting three new writers . . . The kids will *love* it!"

Making her way past the development deals, miniseries,

tax shelters and dirty jokes, she saw the white box. At first
glance it looked like a picnic cooler. It was about fourteen
inches long, twelve high and six wide. Made of Styrofoam, it
was bound with metal strips and had a pair of sturdy handles
double-riveted for extra safety. It was hard to believe that
there was a living kidney inside.

The bearded man in the seat beside it appeared to be in
his late twenties. Wearing a plain sport shirt, corduroy trousers and low work boots, he was busy reading a thick paper-
back book. As she came nearer, she could see the title—
*Chemical Warfare Today*. Suddenly he looked up and their
eyes met.

"Excuse me. I didn't mean to stare," she apologized.

"Lots of people do. I suppose you want to know how we
keep it alive."

She hesitated and nodded.

"It's in a chilled slush," he said curtly and returned to
reading.

"I didn't intend to disturb you, Doctor. Can I get you
anything?"

"No," he answered without looking up.

Embarrassed and annoyed, she remembered the flight attendants' maxim as she walked away: There was always one
nasty son of a bitch on every flight. No reason it couldn't be a
rude young physician. It wasn't that rare for doctors to be
abrupt and patronizing—especially with women.

There were plenty of pleasant passengers aboard, too, she
reminded herself as she entered the Economy-Class section.
The middle-aged black man in the uniform of an air force
major—the one talking to the pretty little girl—had impressed her with his amiable courtesy from the moment he
boarded the plane. He was the absolute opposite of the gruff
kidney courier.

"Is there time for another cup of coffee, Miss?" he asked
with an appealing smile.

"No problem. We won't land for half an hour. Would the young lady like a soft drink?"

"Orange juice, *please*," the tanned eight-year-old replied. Somebody was raising this long-haired girl with manners, Samantha Wong thought as she turned and headed for the galley.

The steady rain continued. It kept beating at the windows in heavy sheets. Looking out at the downpour, the girl frowned in concern.

"There's nothing to worry about," the uniformed man beside her said. "We've got a fine crew and an excellent aircraft. Rain's no problem for this machine."

"I've never flown before," the child confessed.

"Well, I have," he answered and pointed to the shoulder patch on his jacket.

"Stra . . . Strategic Air Command," she read aloud. "I guess you know about airplanes."

"A fair amount."

"I'm not afraid," she announced, "but it's good to hear an expert say everything's all right."

"Everything's fine."

Now he noticed her studying the silver metal oak leaves on his shoulders.

"Those mean I'm an officer," he said in answer to her unspoken question. "I'm a major."

"My daddy's an officer, too. He's a captain."

"Which branch of the service?"

"The New York City Police Department. He's going to meet me."

In the nearby galley, Samantha Wong poured coffee as she told another flight attendant about the rude man with the Styrofoam box.

"He's got the manners of a thug."

"Maybe he is one, Sam," the heavy-hipped redhead said.

"Don't be silly, Irene. He's just another arrogant young doctor."

"Have you seen his license? He *could* be a dope courier. That box wasn't opened by airport security. Who knows what's in it?"

Then the senior pilot's voice sounded from the loudspeakers. Captain Pace asked everyone to fasten their seat belts. There was turbulence ahead.

# 8

KENNEDY AIRPORT—¼ MILE

Malone merely blinked as he saw the sign on the right side of the Van Wyck Expressway. The bulk of his attention was divided between driving carefully through the storm and listening to the flow of coded messages on the police radio. Though his car was equipped to pick up a wide range of commercial AM and FM stations, he always listened to the police frequency.

It was more than a job or a custom.

It was his natural habitat.

He'd been born into this world. He was a third-generation New York cop. In 1914, a thirteen-year-old boy named Patrick Joseph Malone had migrated to New York with his family from a small town fifty miles south of Dublin. Pat Malone became a U.S. citizen and a policeman—happy to be both.

The firstborn of his eight children, Michael Peter Malone, was even more delighted to join the force in 1945—a month after he left the Marine Corps with three Purple Hearts for wounds received in the Pacific.

Tough and enthusiastic, Mike Malone proved to be a first-class cop. He really was one of "New York's finest." It seemed as if he had both a gift and a passion for this work. Nothing bothered him. Nothing frightened him. Other cops talked with affectionate admiration about Big Mike Malone . . . his shrewd knowledge of street crime . . . his awesome appetite and matching thirst for beer . . . his directness . . . and his courage.

It wasn't only his boldness and swift skill with a pistol that made holdup men, burglars and other thugs shun his beat. Quick-witted and intuitive, he had the instincts of a hunter and used them well in the urban jungle. It was almost as if he could "smell" where the criminals were.

Having survived the bloody fighting on Guadalcanal and Iwo Jima, he confronted armed hoodlums without hesitation. Mike Malone made far more arrests than the ordinary foot patrolman. His extraordinary list of "collars" was noticed, so nobody in the NYPD was surprised when he was eventually promoted to detective and assigned to the Safe and Loft Squad.

Nobody was that surprised by the way he died either. He didn't change that much when he became a plainclothes detective. He was still a hard-driving street cop and ex-marine at heart. One winter night at a stakeout behind a fur warehouse, he went charging up an alley after a fleeing burglar. Big Mike Malone died with two bullets in his heart. Despite a determined and extended investigation, his killer was never caught.

Frank Malone had been a skinny twelve-year-old when his father was shot down. Now, twenty-three years later, he still remembered the terrible night clearly. That was why he hated snow. It had been in a storm like this that his father was murdered. It was the snow that had blurred his father's view of the alley. It was the snow that helped the faceless, nameless hoodlum kill him.

Frank Malone would never forget how small his six-foot-one, 195-pound father had looked in the casket. New York had given Detective Michael P. Malone another citation for valor and an inspector's funeral. Hundreds of cops from six states had been there. Both the police commissioner and the mayor had come to express their condolences to the widow, her five children and the seven television news cameras.

Then the municipal "death benefit" checks began and the media attention ended. Another cop was killed, then two more . . . three firemen perished a few months later. Before anyone knew it, the late Detective Michael P. Malone became last year's hero. Within eighteen months, only the family, a few neighbors and friends and twenty thousand policemen and women remembered. They didn't forget their dead. It was a tribal thing.

Shortly after Frank Malone's seventeenth birthday, his pious mother received a startling letter. Her thousands of sincere Hail Marys and Our Fathers had reached the Lord, who sent help through an organization she'd never heard of. The Jerome Mintzer Foundation had been created by some Jewish millionaire, a merchant prince whose generous gift threw off enough income to fund complete college educations for five or six children of police killed in the line of duty. One of those grants was now available.

Frank Malone, Latin scholar and one of the top quarterbacks in the high schools of the Brooklyn diocese, had been hoping for a football scholarship somewhere. Now he startled his mother by applying to Harvard. There he excelled both academically and athletically, and he learned about a much larger and more diverse world than he'd known.

Good-looking, amiable but disciplined and highly intelligent without a trace of arrogance, Frank Malone was popular with faculty and students of both sexes. It didn't hurt that he threw a football as accurately as his father had wielded a pistol, playing a key role in two winning seasons. His instincts were nearly as good as his father's, and his thinking was better. It was both fascinating and thrilling to watch him coolly pick apart the other teams' defense.

"This policeman's brilliant son has the mind of a safe cracker and the agility of a cat burglar," one sportswriter reported. "He should do well as a tax lawyer."

But Frank Malone didn't go to law school or any other graduate studies that could have kept him out of the armed forces. He went to Vietnam, won a Silver Star for gallantry and turned down a "regular" commission and career. When he got home a month after the city once known as Saigon fell, he declined job offers from the Central Intelligence Agency and a conglomerate headed by his Harvard roommate's uncle.

He had other plans. They startled everyone. He applied to be trained as a New York City policeman. With the help of his father's friends, he was accepted quickly and graduated from the academy at the head of his class. During all the months there he never spoke about his father, college, his experiences in Nam or why a Harvard Phi Beta Kappa would want to be a cop. His mother had thought he did it out of family pride, but she wasn't entirely sure.

JFK INTERNATIONAL

He saw the sign and turned off onto the curved multilane road that led to the huge airport's various terminals.

He'd been happy as a rookie, enjoying the camaraderie and the work. He moved up the ladder steadily. On the way up, he disarmed pipe-wielding maniacs, talked down would-be jumpers, caught vicious rapists, broke up arson rings, arrested muggers and burglars and drunken drivers, busted two of the city's senior dope dealers and earned a reputation as an excellent homicide detective.

He'd been shot by fleeing bank robbers. In three violent

confrontations, his .38 Special had dropped criminals trying to kill him. Those men had all survived.

The word spread through the department.

Frank Malone didn't shoot to kill.

Some said that he was such a good marksman that he didn't have to.

Others had different opinions.

Everyone respected him as a cop's cop who didn't lie, grandstand or play departmental politics. Now he was commander of the New York Police Department's elite antiterrorist unit, an unusual assignment for one of the youngest captains on the force. One reason he'd been given the complex and highly sensitive job was his record of solid achievements. Another was the sophisticated style that let him get along so gracefully with foreign diplomats, self-important public officials and legislators and even the sometimes difficult FBI people. Only last week, the commissioner had complimented his "human relations."

Sheila Malone didn't rate them that highly, he reflected as he peered through the snow for the turnoff to the International Arrivals Building. He'd met her the week she'd come east to study at The Actors Studio. After nine years of wedlock she had realized that her husband really meant to stay a cop despite the danger and mediocre salary. She had returned to her parents' luxurious home in the fashionable California community that Frank Malone called The Amaretto Ghetto—Malibu by the Sea.

That had been eleven months ago. She had taken their daughter with her to provide "a more stable childhood" than the girl could expect in the home of a man "foolish enough to risk his life every day." Kate Malone hadn't seen her father since early July, and he was on his way to meet her at Kennedy when she got off TWA Flight 22.

He was worried.

Not about his wife's recent application for an annulment

to end the marriage. He couldn't think of anything to do about that. He had tried to hold things together, but they'd been growing apart for several years. What troubled him was the separation from his only child. It hurt him deeply, and she must be suffering, too. Though he told himself that it wasn't his fault, he was wracked with all the anxieties and ghostly guilts of every caring nonresident father.

She was coming in for Christmas—seven days together. Was this what it was going to be like? A week together now and then? Would she blame him for the separation? Would she blame herself as children often did? Would pain and helpless anger . . . time and distance . . . drive them apart forever? Would she someday call another man father?

It had happened to two of Frank Malone's friends. He'd seen it tear them to pieces, he recalled grimly as he swung the green sedan into the parking lot. Looking at his watch, he saw that he was ten minutes late for his appointment in the control tower. That wasn't too bad for this weather, and he could still get over to TWA's terminal in time.

When he parked the car and stepped out into the falling snow, his stomach tightened involuntarily. He was known for his cool logic and self-control, but he couldn't help his body's reaction. *It* remembered the night that Detective Michael Malone had been shot down in that alley. Maybe it always would.

Captain Frank Malone shrugged and walked through the slow stream of cars to the entrance of the International Arrivals Building. As he reached the safety of the sidewalk, he noticed the small white panel truck directly in front of the main entrance. That was a No Parking area, so the truck had to be something special. Now he saw the name MOUNT SINAI HOSPITAL lettered on one side of the vehicle, and nodded.

It must be here on some medical mission.

It was perfectly all right to park a hospital vehicle here for a while.

There couldn't be any crime in that.

# 9

MALONE didn't notice them when he entered the terminal.

He wasn't expecting danger here.

The first thing that seized his attention was the colorful array of many nations' flags on the glass-walled balcony atop the escalator. The second was the bustling crowd and its noise.

Scores of people waiting for relatives and friends to come through Customs filled the large high-ceilinged chamber. The sibilant French of tall, elegant black women from Haiti, the staccato dialogue of two knots of earnest Koreans, the laughter of a cheery Colombian family and the hard-edged syllables of a cluster of young Swedes collided with the rhythms of Russia and the loud nasal tones of New York.

The Dixie drawl of four well-fed executives in boots and

wide-brimmed cowboy hats and the pulsing Yiddish of a
dozen Hassidic Jewish men in traditional black fedoras
added to the cosmopolitan wall of sound. Only a handful of
bored-looking limousine service drivers, each clutching a
small sign bearing the name of those they'd come to meet,
stood silent in the milling throng.

A few moments after Malone walked into the building, he
paused beside the information booth on his left to take a cigar
from his jacket. Standing beneath a big, multicolored, Calder
mobile hanging from the roof, he lit the dark corona and
puffed on it.

He still didn't see them.

Then his restless policeman's eyes swept the crowd
again.

There they were.

Two of them were chatting only a few yards from him.
Wearing what looked like a Sony Walkman headset, another
loitered in front of the ground transportation counter. A
fourth, near the escalator, was attired in the visored cap and
dark suit of a chauffeur.

*Four?*

There had to be more than that.

They took no chances. There must be others whom he
didn't know lurking nearby, all armed and ready to strike.
There could be shooting here very soon. Glad that his daughter would arrive at another terminal, Malone zigzagged his
way to the escalator. According to the instructions he'd received, these moving metal steps were the most direct way to
his rendezvous in the control tower.

When Malone got off the escalator, he recognized another
one of them twenty yards away. The barrel-chested man in
his forties scanning the throng below was Thomas Jefferson
Gill, head of the New York City office of the U.S. Drug Enforcement Administration. The four plainclothes operatives
whom Malone had spotted downstairs worked for Gill, and

T. J. Gill didn't come out to Queens in snowstorms for minor "busts."

It had to be something big—a major dope ring.

Gill was speaking with a neatly dressed brunette in her early thirties who had to be another agent. They looked like a typical middle-class couple from the suburbs, not federal police. The glossy Bloomingdale's shopping bag that she carried was a nice touch. It probably concealed a walkie-talkie and a stubby Ithaca Model 37 "Stakeout" shotgun, Malone calculated as he approached them.

He stopped a yard away. He didn't face them directly.

"How's it going, T.J.?" he asked softly.

Gill warily turned his head three inches, recognized Malone out of the corner of his eye and looked away again.

"What the hell are you doing here?" he challenged in an irate whisper.

"Just passing through. Something going down?"

"Something *federal*. Good-bye, Malone."

Then a surge of sound from below made them glance down at the ground floor. Flanked by the Hassidim and four other men holding up large pictures of an old woman, U.S. Senator Joseph Bono stood talking with a tall man and a woman in an ankle-length fur coat. A pair of teenagers and a boy of nine or ten fidgeted beside them, and a platoon of newspaper and wire service reporters and photographers leaned forward to listen.

Half a dozen radio correspondents were thrusting their microphones toward the senator. Two television news crews were setting up their equipment, and a third was pushing closer through the crowd. Now another TV news team hurried in through the front door.

Startled, Gill shook his head in silent anger.

Malone recognized the photo that the Hassidim held, but decided there would be no point in telling the DEA executive that the senator and media mob were here to witness the poignant reunion of the Kiev Grandma and her U.S. relatives. Gill wouldn't care. Whatever their reasons, their presence was an added complication Gill didn't need.

They might "spook" the "mule" or those who came to meet the dope courier.

They might inadvertently obstruct the surveillance or arrest of the key drug dealers.

They might even be taken as hostages or—caught in the line of fire—shot.

In any of a dozen ways, they could wreck a delicate and important DEA operation that involved thousands of man and woman hours and great personal risk.

"Jesus . . . Jesus . . . Jesus," Gill sighed urgently.

It was difficult to tell whether it was an appeal or an imprecation. Frank Malone didn't have the time to ask.

"See you," he said and walked away quickly to the right.

He turned past a cluster of bored people watching small coin-operated television sets bolted to their plastic chairs. They were "killing" time. Malone wondered why they didn't appreciate how precious it was . . . how little they had. Then he realized that he was thinking about death again. He often did when it snowed.

Now he reached the glass door to the open bridge that linked the million square feet of the sprawling three-story International Arrivals Building to the forty-five-by-sixty-foot control tower that was the highest structure at the airport. Capped by a radar dome, it was nearly four times as high as the adjacent terminal. When Malone strode from the warmth out onto the stormswept span, his pace accelerated immediately. It didn't slow until he reached the well-heated lobby of the tower.

"Help you?" the uniformed security guard in the booth asked alertly.

"I'm supposed to meet Lieutenant Hamilton of the Port Authority Police in Mr. Wilber's office. My name's Malone."

The guard glanced at a clipboard on his desk.

"Can I see some ID?" he asked.

Malone produced his gold badge and NYPD card.

"Sixth floor, Captain. Elevator's back there."

There was a list of the tower's "tenants" on the wall beside the elevator door. Every floor was occupied by some unit of the Federal Aviation Administration, but there was no indication of where the air traffic controllers worked. That was almost surely a security precaution, Malone reasoned. The fewer people who know the precise location the better.

That was simply common sense, he reflected as he got into the elevator car. There really wasn't much chance that anyone would attempt to storm the controllers' facility. There had to be more "security" systems or guards upstairs, and there must be alarms to summon the well-equipped Port Authority Police, who maintained a strong force on the airport itself. While the FAA handled air traffic and safety, the joint Port Authority created by the states of New York and New Jersey took care of "security" as the overall operator of the three major local airports.

The guard had phoned up from the lobby. When Malone emerged from the elevator at the sixth floor, two men were walking down a short corridor toward him. They appeared to be in their forties. One was about five feet ten inches tall, fifteen to twenty pounds overweight and smiling. His features suggested one or more Irish ancestors.

The other man was bigger—and harder. Wide-shouldered and muscular, he stood six feet four and there wasn't an ounce of fat on him. He was black, sharp-eyed and handsome. There wasn't anything resembling a smile on his face. His expression was cool and impersonal.

"My name's Malone. Is Lieutenant Hamilton here?"

"I'm Hamilton," the powerfully built deputy commander of JFK's Port Authority Police replied. "This is Pete Wilber."

"Welcome to the Kennedy Tower," the smaller man said.

"He runs it," Hamilton announced.

Wilber took a leatherette case from his shirt pocket, extracted a business card and gave it to Malone.

Peter O. Wilber was the air traffic manager for the Federal Aviation Administration here. His address was Kennedy Control Tower, JFK International Airport, Jamaica, New York 11430. There was a phone number that Frank Malone guessed was unlisted. He was right.

"Thanks," Malone told him. "Sorry I'm late."

Hamilton ignored the apology.

"Let's get to it. As you know, *primary* responsibility for security at Kennedy belongs to the Port Authority," he reminded in a casual-blunt assertion of territory, "but other government agencies are involved. We always cooperate fully, and, of course, we expect them to do the same."

Malone managed not to smile at the barely disguised warning.

"Of course," he agreed and puffed on the cigar.

Then his eyes wandered to a nearby desk.

"There's an ashtray in my office," Wilber said. When they were seated in the FAA executive's large room at the end of the corridor, Frank Malone tapped the ash from his corona and Hamilton resumed the briefing.

"We *think* our security procedures are good. We *know* they're probably not perfect. At the very least, there's always the question of human error. Will somebody get bored or careless? Will someone panic?"

Malone nodded in approval. Hamilton's style was a bit abrasive, but he was a realistic professional.

"So you run tests," Malone reasoned.

"That's what we want to talk to you about," Hamilton answered as Wilber took a cigar from his desk drawer. The Port Authority lieutenant glared when Wilber lit it.

"This is *my* turf, Ben," Wilber reminded cheerfully. "Tell him about the test."

Hamilton opened a window several inches before he continued.

"After each security test we do a critique. We've been through a number of them, and maybe a fresh set of eyes and a new mind might notice something we don't. We'd like you to come to the next critique session."

"Sure, when is it?"

"I don't know," Hamilton said. "We never get advance warning about when or what the test will be."

"The folks in Washington call the plays," Wilber explained. "Some bright people in the FBI and FAA figure out a clever stunt and spring it on us. Could be a simulated hijacking, a multiple hostage situation, sabotage of the fuel trucks or ten other things."

"I think there might be one coming *soon*," Hamilton said.

"It's about time," the FAA tower chief agreed. "Every major U.S. airport catches one or two a year. We haven't had any for seven months, so they could drop a test on us any minute."

"Tonight?" Malone asked.

"I doubt they'd spring one in this weather," Wilber replied. "We've got the people and equipment to handle a storm with no great sweat, but Washington knows we wouldn't want any *extra* problems on a messy night like this."

Frank Malone's eyes narrowed in concern.

"Something bothering you, Captain?" Hamilton questioned.

"My daughter's flying in from L.A. in that storm right now."

"Nothing to worry about," Wilber assured. "A whole army of highly skilled people has been working on her flight from before it even took off. They're first-class, and so's the hardware. Our navigational and air traffic control gear is the most sophisticated in the world. It's an all-weather system, Captain, and a damn good one."

Now Hamilton rose to his feet and waved away a spiral of offending cigar smoke.

"Then it's set. I'll phone you when we schedule the next critique," he said. "Is there anything else to discuss before I go?"

Wilber shook his head.

"I've got a question. No, *two*," Malone said. "Am I right that there's never been a major attack on an American airport by a team of professional terrorists?"

"Not *yet*," Hamilton answered evenly. "What's the other question?"

"What kind of weapons do you have here to deal with such a raid?"

"Handguns, shotguns and submachine guns. There's an armored car, too."

"Tear gas? Masks? Bulletproof vests?"

Hamilton nodded.

"Is there any special reason you're asking, Captain?" he questioned slowly.

"I wasn't reflecting on your planning," Malone told him. "I was thinking about a warning that came in from the FBI today. They've heard a rumor that some foreign terrorist group may hit the U.S. mainland with a major operation."

"*Soon?*" the big Port Authority lieutenant asked.

"Very soon. It's just a rumor, but they've killed a lot of people at airports abroad. I don't suppose that an attack on a U.S. airport would be entirely out of the question, would it?"

"Not *entirely*," Hamilton answered in a voice edged with irony. "You're a very tactful man, Captain."

"Thanks, Lieutenant. I'll be waiting for your call."

Hamilton didn't answer. He departed without saying a word, and Malone turned to the FAA executive behind the desk.

"He's a very good cop," Wilber said in answer to the unspoken question.

Then Malone looked at his wristwatch. It was ten minutes to eight.

"My daughter's plane lands in fourteen minutes—if it's on time."

"We can check on that upstairs," Wilber suggested. "It'll only take a couple of minutes, and you'll get an overall view of the airport."

"Okay," Malone agreed. "It's TWA Flight twenty-two from Los Angeles."

Walking to the elevator, Wilber began to talk about how the U.S. air traffic control system worked.

"It's a very careful hand-off operation, high-tech and high-skill. When your daughter's plane got near the edge of the area our Los Angeles Center has under radar control, it was handed off to the Denver or Albuquerque center—depending on which route it took. Then more hand-offs from center to center as it flew east. There's also a network of navigational radio stations to help the pilot keep to the flight plan he filed in L.A. before being cleared to take off."

"Sounds good," Malone said as Wilber pushed the elevator button.

"*Good* won't cut it. It has to be just about perfect—all the way. When her plane was about a hundred miles from here, it was handed off to New York Center. That's out on Long Island near Islip. It controls the metropolitan area's three biggest airports: JFK, La Guardia, Newark."

The elevator arrived. They entered and Wilber poked the button marked "8."

"New York Center's job is to bring the plane in to about fifty miles from here," Wilber continued. "At that point Flight twenty-two will be handed off to the TRACON at Westbury."

"The *what?*"

"*Sorry,* Captain. TRACON's our acronym for terminal radar approach control. You asked about attacks on airports.

Well, you can rest easy about the TRACON. Armed guards, wire fences, alarms—nobody's going to try anything there."

The elevator door opened.

"Going back to your daughter," Wilber said as they stepped out, "the TRACON team will direct her plane—direction . . . altitude . . . speed—to within six miles or so of Kennedy. Then our controllers in this tower guide it down to the right runway, direct it to the appropriate taxiway off the runway and shepherd it to full stop on the apron at the TWA terminal."

The FAA veteran pointed to the nearby stairway.

"Come on," he invited. "You can see for yourself."

Malone followed him up two flights of steps to a metal door.

"Security," Wilber said curtly.

He inserted a plastic card containing coded circuits into the electronic lock, and the heavy portal opened. They then ascended ten more steps to the command post for the five-thousand-acre airport's air traffic control.

"We call this The Cab," Wilber told him.

The large room had eight sides, each with two big windows made of quarter-inch-think, double-wall, tinted anti-glare glass. Though the falling snow reduced visibility somewhat, Malone could scan the wraparound panorama of runways, taxiways, parked aircraft and hangars, terminals and other buildings.

He noticed three multijet transports—their wing and tail lights blinking insistently in the black winter night—lined up on a taxiway awaiting takeoff clearance. Another was swooping in to land. On a different runway off to the left, a fifth airliner was touching down.

Now Frank Malone's eyes swung around the chamber in which he was standing. The decor was Federal Functional. The black fiberboard cealing was punctuated with air ducts to suck out tobacco smoke. Cocoa-colored plastic wastebaskets dotted the well-worn brown-orange carpet that spread wall-to-wall. A cluster of telephones hung on wall-brackets beside a watercooler.

On the far side of the comfortably heated room were two teleprinters, silent for the moment. At the high desk near them, a dark-haired woman, facing away from Malone, was busy on another phone. She stood straight in well-tailored slacks, her posture radiating strength and energy. Men noticed that figure and presence, Frank Malone thought.

There were eight more people—seven male and one female—working in The Cab. Several of them were facing the four radar sets. Most of the controllers sat on brown plastic swivel chairs, but others in The Cab preferred to stand. Their attire was informal and comfortable—not a jacket in sight. Jeans and corduroy pants, sport shirts and turtlenecks, running shoes and loafers seemed to prevail. In a white shirt, suit and tie, Wilber was clearly an outsider as he spoke into a phone on the other side of the room.

Those studying the green radar screens wore ultralight headsets with miniature microphones built into the ends of thin white plastic tubes no thicker than soda fountain straws—the whole rig attached to expandable accordionlike wires connected to consoles before them. The controllers' ages appeared to range between twenty-six and forty. Some looked like solid suburbanites. One lean young controller with longer hair and a floral printed shirt didn't. He had the cool taut air of a savvy rock guitarist rather than that of a civil service technician.

There was no tension or worry in these faces, just total concentration. They were working swiftly and deftly, and they knew exactly what they were doing. The storm might be adding pressure to their work, but it certainly wasn't intimidating them. Malone felt better watching them in action.

Listening was something else. The controllers at the radar screens were all talking—very fast. They squirted out gusts of words and puzzling phrases in startling singsong eruptions. Watching Wilber speak on the phone across the room,

Frank Malone tried to understand what the balding controller a yard away from him was saying.

It wasn't easy.

"Eastern eighteen Heavy. Turn Right. Taxi via Zulu and Hotel. Hold short of two-two right and remain on this frequency."

Malone had no time to decode this. The controller seated a yard away was pouring out more instructions at a startling pace.

"American thirty-five cleared to land. Runway two-two left. Empire ninety-two, would appreciate first available turnoff after landing, please. United fifty-two. Wind two-zero-zero-one-four. Gust one-nine. Cleared for takeoff. Clipper five-six-three Heavy. Caution. Wake turbulence departing, heavy jet runway two-two right."

Now Wilber hung up the phone and started toward Malone. The controller whom the detective had been listening to was still machine-gunning instructions into his microphone. His colleagues at the other radar sets were also speaking very quickly and constantly, providing a seamless curtain of background sound.

"All right, gentlemen," the controller beside Malone said briskly into his microphone as Wilber approached. "Everyone waiting for departure clearance on twenty-three-ninety can monitor one-one-nine-point-one."

"He's telling them to shift radio frequencies," Wilber said. "No problem with your daughter's flight. Trans World twenty-two Heavy shouldn't be more than a few minutes late."

Malone sighed in relief before he asked the question. "Heavy?"

"A jumbo. Seven forty-seven or DC-ten or L-ten eleven, like the one your daughter's on. What do you think of The Cab, Captain?"

"I've never heard anyone talk so fast."

"There's no choice," Wilber told him. "All the major airports handle a tremendous volume of traffic—and it's growing. We're responsible for those planes in the air and on the ground. We've got nine miles of runways and twenty-two miles of taxiways to supervise in addition to what's flying. It takes a ton of directions to cope with all that, so both controllers and pilots have to speak quickly to avoid frequency saturation."

"I suppose that shorthand they talk helps."

Wilber nodded and gestured toward one of the radar sets.

"So does the hardware," he said. "We've got Airport Surveillance Radar to monitor what's flying within thirty miles of here, Airport Surface Detection Radar to control what's moving on the ground, Instrument Landing Systems, Approach Lighting Systems and a lot of other gear. And we've got damn good professionals to work it."

Now he saw the trim woman at the desk hang up the phone.

"First-class supervisors, too," he continued. "I'd like you to meet the watch supervisor who runs this shift. Smart, fast, cool—nothing ever bothers her. Annie, could you spare us a minute?"

She turned at the same time that Malone did. She took two steps toward them and stopped. Wilber immediately realized that he was wrong about his watch supervisor. Something was bothering her right now, and it wasn't anything small. He'd never seen her like this before.

She was staring at Frank Malone.

She seemed to be very angry.

# 10

"*SOMETHING WRONG?*" Wilber asked.

"No," she replied curtly.

She was speaking to Wilber, but she was looking at Frank Malone.

"Annie, if this is a bad time . . ." Wilber resumed.

"It isn't."

Even though she'd graduated at the top of her class from the FAA controllers' academy in Oklahoma City, Annabelle Green hadn't risen to become one of the few female watch supervisors by talking sharply to her bosses. There was something more than anger in her tone, Wilber decided. Whatever it was, this wasn't the moment to inquire.

Not with an outsider present. Part of the public still wasn't *entirely* sure that the "new" controllers hired after the 1981 strike had enough experience, and newspapers kept questioning whether there were nearly enough of them. The inflated stories about nervous pressure and emotional burn-out didn't help either. The last thing the air traffic manager for JFK needed was to have a senior New York City police officer see a watch supervisor pour out her problems or discontent.

Short and sweet.

That would do it.

Wilber would make a quick introduction and hurry Malone away to meet his daughter's flight.

"We've only got a few seconds, Annie. I'd like to introduce Captain Malone of the police department."

She didn't answer. It was Malone who spoke.

"How've you been, Annie?"

"You know the captain?" Wilber asked.

Still staring, she shook her head.

"I once *thought* I did," she replied. "He wasn't a captain then."

Now Wilber recognized the other ingredient in her bitter expression. It was *hurt*.

"I was just a dumb college kid," Malone recalled soberly. "That was a long time ago."

Then he looked at his watch.

"I'd *really* like to talk with you, Annie," he said, "but I have to go now."

"You always did," she answered and walked away to check a message clattering in on one of the teleprinters.

Peter Wilber didn't ask the question until he and Malone were at the bottom of the stairs from The Cab.

"I don't mean to pry, but what was *that* all about?"

To his surprise, Frank Malone suddenly remembered it clearly. He saw it in small disconnected bursts, like badly edited film clips. Walking hand in hand on the bank of the Charles . . . making love—her first carnal experience . . . her silent weeping when he left.

"She's still beautiful," Malone said.

"And mad enough to spit. What the hell did you do to that woman?" Wilber asked a moment before opening the metal security door.

"It's what I didn't do—stay. Instead of going to law school and staying with her, I enlisted and went to Vietnam."

"*Enlisted?*"

Malone didn't seem to hear the question.

"I heard that she was married," he said.

"She's a widow—a very peaceful one until two minutes ago."

"I didn't plan this," the detective reminded him.

"I know. Jeezus, you're the only person I've ever seen rattle her—in four years. And you did pretty well stirring up Ben Hamilton, too."

"It's a *gift*," Malone answered. "Just last week the commissioner complimented my terrific 'human relations.' "

Wilber recognized the sadness beneath the irony.

"I don't want to get into your private life, Captain . . ."

"It's kind of messy," Malone said and pressed the elevator button.

"You realize that she doesn't *really* hate you?"

"Let's talk about security. I'm better at that," Malone said.

"My business if safety, not security. Radar not guns."

"Okay, how safe is your radar? What happens if a plane crashes into the tower or somebody fires a rocket into The Cab? Or blasts the tower with three hundred pounds of plastic explosives?"

"We're still in business," Wilber replied confidently. "Our whole U.S. air traffic control operation is based on backup systems to deal with just about anything. Kennedy, La Guardia and Newark have overlapping radar coverage. So even if this tower was totally destroyed, the planes would be landed safely."

"If the runways haven't been bombed or dynamited,"

Malone said and pushed the elevator button again impatiently.

"Worst-case scenario, right?" Wilber tested.

"I've got worse than that. Could it happen?"

"It never has—anywhere—in peacetime, Captain."

Terrorists and guerrillas were waging war around the world, Malone thought grimly, but many intelligent people such as Peter Wilber hardly noticed it. It hadn't come to their cities—yet.

"Humor me," the detective urged. *"Could* it happen?"

"It's theoretically possible," Wilber admitted and then he smiled. "We've got a system to deal with that, too. Pilots have to file flight plans, and every airliner's flight plan includes an *alternate* airport to be used if the plane can't land at the scheduled destination. If an airport's out of service, its tower radios inbound traffic to divert to the alternate. You want the rest?"

"Why not?"

"Every airliner is required to carry extra fuel for that. Part one twenty-one, Federal Aviation Regulations. It takes one gallon of jet fuel to haul four, so tankering that nonrevenue fuel reserve boosts the prices of airline tickets a bit. Any more far-out scenarios, Captain?"

"Listen, I'm doing my job," Malone said. "It isn't that different from yours. We're both in the life-and-death business. Your system is terrific, but people made it and people run it, so it can't be impregnable. And I'm only *half* paranoid. There *are* terrorists out there."

Wilber shrugged.

"If you don't have any more questions, Captain . . ."

"Just one," Malone broke in as he jabbed the "down" button for the third time. "Is there something wrong with this damn elevator?"

Seven and a half miles away in the warehouse, Takeshi Ito was listening to a radio. It was a special set that could pick

up both police calls and conversations between airport controllers and pilots. It was tuned to the frequency of the FAA's
TRACON at Westbury.

Ito had no trouble understanding the rapid-fire dialogue.
He was used to it.

The Red Brigade electronics expert had been eavesdropping on these conversations for weeks. The Americans made
it easy. There were plenty of stores selling these sets to hob-
byists who enjoyed listening to official transmitters on these
relatively inexpensive transceivers.

Delta 59 was being handed off to the JFK tower. Pied-
mont 47 was told to descend to 18,000 feet. BA 126 was ordered to hold at 14,000. Trans World 22 Heavy acknowledged
a new heading, and U.S. Air 31 was handed off by New York
Center to the TRACON five seconds later. The voice from
Aerovias 16 sounded Hispanic. Then Ito heard a French-ac-
cented pilot from Tarman 2, followed by clipped tones from
JAL 93 that Ito identified immediately. That was the speech
of a fellow Japanese talking English. This was probably Japan Air Lines' nightly cargo flight from Tokyo, the earnest
engineer decided.

Ito had a cousin who flew as a JAL navigator. It didn't
matter whether his cousin was up in that jet, of course. The
Cause was much more important than any obsolete notions of
family. Takeski Ito was the New Japanese Man, free of those
primitive traditions. History, custom, ritual meant nothing to
him. He had no past, and no one could stop him from seizing
the future. If they tried, he'd kill them.

He wasn't thinking of any of this now. He was concentrating on the flow of radio messages. When the phone beside
him rang, he looked at the clock before he raised the instrument to his ear.

It was 7:57.

"Three minutes," Staub said.

"Check," Ito confirmed.

"I'll be in touch," Staub told him and hung up. He was standing in a phone booth four miles from the Kennedy control tower. He wasn't wearing the Loden coat anymore. He had changed to the attire of a priest before he checked out of the motel half an hour earlier. The black shoes, black clerical garb, black raincoat and hat were appropriate, he reflected. Black was the color of death and mourning, wasn't it?

All the charges were in place.

All his people were in position.

Glancing from the phone booth, he saw the Arab waiting at the wheel of the truck ten yards away. Achmed was the one he knew best. That was why Staub had chosen him to be his driver and bodyguard tonight. If there should be an armed confrontation, Achmed wouldn't panic. He had courage, and he was almost as good a shot as Staub.

Not that anything could go wrong tonight.

His carefully designed assault was brilliant. So was the backup.

It would all come as a shattering surprise, he gloated and studied his wristwatch again.

Forty seconds.

# 11

*IT WAS* a mistake.

He should never have agreed to do it, the man with the black leather attaché case thought grimly.

All the other passengers near him in the First-Class section of BA 126 seemed to be relaxed. A few appeared to be bored. The man with the leather case was acutely uneasy.

No, there was no point in lying.

He was afraid.

It had been bad enough last time, but this was much worse. He could feel the danger all around him. He had thought that he could do it. He had trained for this, and they'd assured him that he'd have no problem. He'd been a fool to believe them.

He was going to die.

He knew it.

His heart was pounding and his mouth was dry. He could hardly swallow. His stomach was knotted. Now he felt it convulse in another spasm, and he barely managed not to throw up. Wide-eyed and sheeted with perspiration, he silently cursed his stupidity.

He forced himself to remember the training. It all seemed confused now. Suddenly he heard the blond flight attendant's crisp cheery voice over the loudspeakers.

"Ladies and gentlemen, please fasten your seat belts and extinguish your cigarettes. In a few minutes we'll be landing at New York's John F. Kennedy International Airport."

She continued talking, but he only half heard the words. Whatever she was saying so briskly didn't matter. Another wave of dizziness blurred his vision. The coppery taste of terror filled his mouth as he battled against the panic. One numbing thought swept through his mind again and again, as if on a continuous tape loop. His life was about to end.

In The Cab atop the Kennedy Tower, the controllers were busy guiding seventeen aircraft in the sky and on the ground. Long-haired J. J. Seigenthaler had gone to the eighth-floor "staff lounge" for a cup of coffee, but the others were coping well and he'd be back in ten minutes so someone else could take a break.

This should have been a relatively stress-free period for The Cab team—the heavy traffic period that made 4:30 to 7:30 P.M. a pressure cooker was over—but the snow was creating new complications for both the pilots and the controllers, and the FAA specialists in The Cab felt it. Annabelle Green almost welcomed it. The continuing need to concentrate intensely made it impossible to think about Frank Malone. It had been a shock to see him, and she didn't want to deal with that now.

It was disturbing that he could still move her so.

Was it the man or the memory?

She had tried to answer that when he left The Cab. Then she had realized that she'd never know, for she wouldn't ever

see him again. The wedding ring on his left hand guaranteed
that. Frank Malone had always been a man of quiet principle.
That was one of the reasons she'd fallen in love with him.

She had nearly wept after he left The Cab. It was the
planes that had saved her. They had forced her back to the
reality of here and now. Escaping into the safety of her responsibilities and work, she had regained her self-control
and focus. Within half a minute after he'd gone, she was the
competent supervisor again—moving across the room,
checking with her team, considering details and making decisions.

She was functioning smoothly when the telephone rang.
The others were "working" the planes, so she answered it.
That was part of her job.

"Kennedy Tower," she said.

"Listen carefully," Staub ordered in a voice disguised
with an Hispanic accent. "This is Number One. In two minutes—at eight o'clock—we will knock out your radar. Instructions will follow."

Then she heard the dial tone.

For a few seconds she wondered whether it had been a
very bad joke or some lunatic. Whatever it was, there were
specific, standard procedures for what to do in such a situation. There had been a threat to interfere with the safety of air
traffic, and it was the watch supervisor's duty to signal an
immediate "security" alert.

In the adjacent International Arrivals Building, Wilber
and Malone were descending the last few steps to the
crowded ground floor. Looking down, the detective noticed a
man in the white garb of a hospital attendant and guessed
that he was the driver of the Mount Sinai van parked outside.
Off to the right, the throng of reporters ringing Senator Joseph Bono had grown larger. Now Bono saw Malone on the
stairs and remembered meeting him at a breakfast honoring
medal-winning police heroes. As a good politician should,

the senator waved and Frank Malone gestured back politely in obligatory response.

"Mr. Gregory Kincaid . . . Mr. Gregory John Kincaid. Please call extension two-two-two-two," the overhead public address system rasped.

Wilber froze.

"Gregory John Kincaid. Call extension two-two-two-two," the metallic voice repeated.

"Security alert in The Cab," the FAA official translated.

"Let's go," Malone responded immediately.

They ran. Pushing startled people aside, they raced up the steps against the flow of descending men and women. They sprinted past the DEA supervisor and his female aide to the tower lobby. Recognizing Wilber, the uniformed guard let them by without delay.

"What is it?" Wilber asked when they entered The Cab fifty seconds later.

"A man just phoned that they were going to knock out our radar at exactly eight o'clock," Annabelle Green reported.

"Is that possible?" Malone asked swiftly.

"No," Wilber answered, "but you did the right thing, Annie."

"I went by the book."

"That's the right thing," Wilber told her. "There's nothing to worry about. It was probably some crank."

"Is The Cab number listed?" the detective asked.

She shook her head.

"Did he tell you who they were? Any name?" Malone pressed.

"He called himself Number One."

"Take it easy, Captain," Wilber counseled. "It's just eight now and everything's fine."

He pointed at the nearest radar set and they looked.

At that moment all the electronic "blips" on the screen disappeared.

# 12

*WILBER* stared at the nearest screen in stunned disbelief.

"Hey," the controller at that radar said with a puzzled frown. "I've lost them."

Annie Green didn't waste time talking. She hurried to check the three other screens.

"We've lost them all," she told Wilber and Malone. "*Every* plane on *every* screen—on the ground and in flight— has vanished."

"That's impossible!" Wilber insisted.

Now other controllers were speaking, swearing, questioning. They were all talking when the watch supervisor's firm clear voice cut through their words. They immediately stopped to listen.

"I'm declaring a radar emergency," she announced in a tone of complete calm and authority. "It may be sabotage.

We'll find out—second. First we start standard emergency procedures, right now. Stanley, call for technicians to check the equipment. Betsy, notify the TRACON to alert the Newark and La Guardia towers we need help. Ground Control, hold all planes at the gate or on taxiways."

She was cool and precise. Wilber nodded in professional approval.

"Those working inbound traffic, radio them at once that we have a temporary problem with the ASR-seven," she continued swiftly. "They're to maintain altitude for a few minutes until we shift to nonradar landing procedures."

"*Perfect*," Wilber commended and turned to Malone as the controllers hurried to carry out her instructions. "We can bring those planes down by ILS—Instrument Landing System—and radio if we have to. I told you that we had good backup systems, Captain."

"I bet he knows that, too," the detective replied.

"*He?*"

"The man who called."

The telephone rang. Wilber started to reach for the instrument.

"Don't! Let Annie take it," Malone said quickly. "She knows his voice."

The air traffic manager shrugged in assent, and she picked up the receiver.

"Don't waste your time, *puta*," Staub taunted before she could say a word. "You can't fix it."

She pointed to the receiver in her other hand and nodded. Then she held up a single finger.

It was the man who called himself Number One.

"Your radar's down, and we're taking out your ILS and radio next," the terrorist announced.

Malone and Wilber saw her flinch.

"Why are you doing this? What do you want?" she demanded tensely.

Click. Dial tone.

"He didn't answer," she reported a moment later.

"He wants us to sweat. Terrorists have standard procedures, too," Malone said, "and keeping the authorities uncertain is one of their basic tactics. What did he tell you?"

"They're going to take out our radio and ILS next."

"That's crazy," Wilber judged scornfully.

At that moment, the woman controller whom Annabelle Green had assigned to alert the TRACON walked toward them. She was shaking her head in distress.

"We won't be getting any help from La Guardia or Newark," she said.

"Why not?" Wilber asked incredulously.

It was Frank Malone who answered.

"Their radar's down, too," he thought aloud.

She nodded.

"How the hell did you know that, Captain?" Wilber asked.

"All I know is that we're up against professionals who must be familiar with your whole operation, including the backup systems. If that's true, your radio and ILS might go any minute."

It was shocking but logical.

"You could be right," Wilber said. "Annie, we'd better switch to ILS procedures immediately. And advise the TRACON to divert any traffic more than twenty miles out."

Then he saw the concern in Frank Malone's eyes.

"Don't worry, Captain. We'll get those planes down all right," Wilber said.

Annabelle Green moved quickly from controller to controller with word to start instrument landings now. There was quiet urgency in her voice. She knew that Frank Malone was probably right. He was almost always right, she remembered as she walked back to report to Wilber.

"They should have the first one down in three or four minutes, Pete," she said.

As she spoke, she wondered whether they had three or four minutes before the next attack. If Malone was correct, it might come at any moment.

"Fine," Wilber replied. "Now that that is moving along—"

Then it happened.

It was invisible. No one in The Cab could see it. The controllers speaking to the inbound "traffic" were the first to know. They heard it over their headsets.

They grimaced.

It hurt their ears.

One controller immediately lunged for the volume control dial. Another pulled off his headset to end the pain. The Kennedy air traffic manager and tonight's tower watch supervisor had thirty-one years of FAA experience between them. Neither Peter Wilber nor Annabelle Green had ever seen anything like this.

"What is it?" he called out loudly.

Before any of them could answer, Annie Green suddenly pointed off to the left. Through the falling snow, the people in The Cab saw a pillar of orange-red piercing the black night. Its exact shape was blurred by the curtain of snow, but its location was unmistakable.

"Oh, my God!" Wilber gasped.

Malone turned to Annie Green.

"The ILS gear?" he asked.

She nodded.

The glow grew larger. Within seconds, the building housing the key equipment of Kennedy Airport's instrument landing system was a roaring pyre.

# 13

*THE SHOCK* in The Cab was almost tangible.

No one spoke or moved for several seconds.

Then Annie Green stepped forward purposefully. This was her watch. It was her responsibility as supervisor to know exactly what was happening. She grasped the headset the controller had tugged off and raised it swiftly to her ear. Frowning in acute discomfort, she forced herself to listen for ten seconds before she put it down.

"Major electrical interference. Extremely strong," she reported.

"Could it be temporary? The storm?" Wilber asked.

"They're *jamming*," Frank Malone said flatly.

"That's what it sounds like, Pete," she agreed.

Wilber thought of the decades of engineering and billions

of dollars that made U.S. air traffic control the most advanced in the world. Outsiders such as this well-meaning police captain wouldn't understand its awesome complexity and sophistication. Whoever was naive enough to challenge it and whatever they were doing to attack it, the system could cope with the assault.

Every possibility had been considered.

There were procedures for dealing with equipment breakdowns and other communications crises.

"Okay, maybe they've screwed up this frequency for the moment," Wilber said in a loud determined voice, "but we've got others. The pilots know them. Switch to the emergency frequency and tell those planes to divert to their alternates."

*Now* the policeman would see how wrong he was about the vulnerability of the system, Wilber thought as the controllers adjusted their radios to Kennedy's primary emergency frequency. Wilber was startled a few seconds later when they pulled off their headsets and turned.

"Same damn thing," one of the controllers said.

"Try the other emergency frequencies!" Wilber ordered impatiently.

They did—one by one.

It took the controllers nearly a minute to test all the secondary and tertiary emergency frequencies. After that they swept up and down the airwaves probing every frequency that might reach the radio bands built into modern airliners. Then one controller shook his head and another simply turned to give a thumbs-down gesture of defeat.

"The ILS and the radio—the son of a bitch kept his promise," Malone said.

"It's impossible," the veteran air traffic manager insisted. "*Nobody* can blot out all of our frequencies."

"*Somebody* just did," Malone replied bluntly.

Then he thought about TWA Flight 22.

Before he could catch his breath, he wasn't a skilled, sure

police captain anymore. He wasn't the tough and clever head
of the elite antiterrorist unit.

He saw his daughter's face, and suddenly he was just a
desperately concerned father. While Mike Malone had been
widely admired for his lusty lack of fear, it was no stranger to
his son. Frank Malone was fighting its numbing embrace
right now . . . silently, secretly. His face gave no hint of the
struggle within him. It had been a long time since Frank
Malone had let such feelings show.

After a dozen bitter seconds, the fear vanished.

Intense anger took its place. Malone felt a surge of rage at
the threat to the life of his only child, and he was furious that
some faceless terrorist had frightened him. The effects were
instantaneous. Suddenly Captain Frank Malone was functioning at full and fierce efficiency.

With their electronic eyes, ears and mouths devastated,
the baffled controllers sat helpless at their consoles. They
didn't know what to do. Malone did. He had to learn three
things before he could counterattack.

The scope of the terrorists' attack.

The purpose of the operation.

The identity of the enemy.

"Annie, we've got to find out whether it's just here or
they're hitting airports in other cities, too," he said. "That
will tell us how big a force we're up against. It could give a
clue as to what those bastards want."

"Shall we start with the East Coast?"

"Sure. Boston to Washington. Try Pittsburgh and Chicago too. I have a hunch it's only where the weather's bad."

She turned, looked at the phone on which Number One
had delivered his warnings and shook her head.

"Keep that line open," she told the others. "He may call
in again."

Then she instructed the controllers to use other phones
and the teletype to query other airports.

"And if they are under attack?" Wilber asked.

"Then we're fighting a major enemy—maybe a government."

"The Russians?"

"Who the hell knows?" Malone answered impatiently and pointed to the row of six phones on the wall beside the water cooler. "Can I reach my office on any of those?"

"Try the third from the left."

They were emergency hot lines—direct connections. The one on the far left was marked PONY POLICE, a link to the Port Authority cops on the airport. The next one was beige and was labeled FBI. The yellow instrument beside it was designated NYC POLICE–NYC FIRE. Twenty seconds after he picked it up, he was speaking to one of his men in the antiterrorist unit at Police Headquarters in downtown Manhattan.

"Sergeant Bolivar."

"This is Captain Malone. I'm in the air traffic control center on the tenth floor of the Kennedy Tower. We've got a critical situation," he announced and swiftly described it.

He ignored the sergeant's startled curse.

"I need a dozen men, full combat gear, out here, right away," Malone continued. "I want everyone else in the unit—*everyone*—standing by in cars waiting for instructions. I don't know yet what these bastards will demand, or where they'll want delivery."

"Anything else, Captain?"

"Contact the precinct nearest here. Tell them to rush over every radio unit and foot patrolman they've got. I don't give a damn if they strip the streets. When people waiting in the terminals here find out what's happening, we'll need at least a hundred men for crowd control."

"A hundred men . . . in a snowstorm? I'll *try*," the sergeant vowed.

"Tell the commissioner's office we're facing a major disaster. That should get us lots of cops," Malone predicted. "Send another hundred to La Guardia, and phone the Newark police to roll extra units to their airport."

He heard Bolivar suck in his breath tensely.

"Captain, I know your daughter's up there. I don't know how to say this."

"Try straight."

"Do you think . . . would you want ambulances?"

*And hearses.*

Bolivar didn't speak those words, he didn't have to. As professionals in the life-and-death business, both policemen knew that this situation could produce many casualties. The killed or crippled or burned could run as high as a thousand.

"Good idea," Malone replied in as cool a voice as he could muster. "Ambulances and emergency medical teams. Some fire trucks wouldn't hurt either. I'll be in touch."

Next Frank Malone phoned the Port Authority Police on the airport.

"What's up?" Lieutenant Benjamin Hamilton asked. "I'm just heading home for dinner."

"Better make it breakfast," Malone advised and described the crisis.

"Our emergency plan goes into operation immediately," Hamilton responded. "We'll have a command post set up in fifteen minutes."

"In The Cab," Malone urged. "This is where they've been calling. The Cab has hot lines, teleprinters, radio—the best communications gear at Kennedy."

"We're equipped to run a CP here," the Port Authority lieutenant said firmly, "and our people are well trained for defense of this airport."

"Against a normal bomb-or-gun attack. This is *different*," Malone reasoned. "We're in a nasty new kind of combat. This is an air traffic war, so we'd better fight it from the air traffic control center."

"Maybe. The Cab does have the best view of the whole airport," Hamilton thought aloud.

"Exactly. In military terms, it's the High Ground. That's just about the only advantage we've got."

"And it may not be worth much in an electronic battle in a snowstorm," Hamilton calculated.

"It may be worth *nothing*," Frank Malone admitted, "but you and I are going to nail these bastards anyway."

There was neither arrogance nor desperation in his voice. His tone was one of simple naked fact. Whatever the odds, the obstacles or the price, it would be done.

"How soon will you be here?" Malone asked.

"About eight minutes."

As Malone hung up the telephone, he heard Annie Green call out his name.

"What is it?" he asked.

"We checked with all those towers," she replied, "and I spoke to Miami and Los Angeles as well. Not one of those airports has any radio or radar problem."

So it was only here.

Nobody was starting World War III.

A local attack ruled out any attempt to cripple the United States.

It couldn't be a foreign government—not even the hate-filled regime in Teheran. This certainly wasn't a Russian operation.

So now Frank Malone knew who it *wasn't*.

He still didn't know who it was, or what they wanted.

Without those answers, it would be much harder to find them and their jamming equipment. Until he did, the thousands of people in those airliners—including TWA 22 Heavy, would be helpless hostages in the sky.

Those big jets were burning fuel every second.

What the hell were the terrorists waiting for?

Why didn't they call with their demands?

# 14

"*KENNEDY TOWER*, this is BA one twenty-six Heavy," the British Airways captain said in the rich burr of his native Glasgow.

The ear-jarring interference continued. The red-bearded Scot suffered it for a dozen seconds before he tried again.

"Kennedy Tower, this is BA one twenty-six Heavy."

He winced at the torrent of inhuman sound. After several moments, he shook his head and pulled down the earphones.

"Nothing but *bloody* noise," he grumbled.

The pilots of some other large jets circling nearby were also attempting to communicate with The Cab.

"Kennedy Tower, this is Tarman two Concorde requesting landing instructions."

"Aerovias sixteen to Kennedy Tower."

"Kennedy Tower, this is TWA twenty-two Heavy."

There was no reply.

The only thing the fliers heard was the battering clatter of the relentless jamming. With each plane isolated by Takeshi Ito's electronic wall, none of the pilots suspected that something invisible and "impossible" was threatening their lives.

So they weren't afraid. They were skilled and sensible professionals with thousands of hours of multiengine flying time. This was a big storm, but they had dealt with worse ones. Soon the competent JFK controllers would answer and bring them down safely as they always had.

But the seconds ticked away and there was no word. There was no indication of how long the delay would last. The passengers would blame the pilots for the lateness, of course. The men in the cockpits began to feel annoyed—and a little uncomfortable.

In The Cab below, Annie Green leaned over the teleprinter as it rattled out a message from the FAA's New York Center. Malone was looking intently at the telephone near her. The terrorists would call with their demands at any moment. Wondering what they'd ask, he turned to stare up at the sky, searching the snowy night in some irrational effort to find TWA 22.

After a few seconds, he swung his glance to the hot-line phones. His eyes swept from the black instrument labeled WHITE HOUSE to the beige one marked FBI. Holding primary responsibility for U.S. internal security, the Federal Bureau of Investigation was supposed to be informed *immediately* about any terrorist incident.

Malone could not wait to find out who the attackers were or what they wanted. He had to notify the antiterrorist unit in the FBI's Manhattan office that the battle had begun—*now*. Like the FAA and other government units, the Joint Task Force on Terrorism that united the NYPD and the FBI had its procedures too. Malone reached for the hot-line phone linked directly to the Bureau.

Another telephone rang a few yards away.

It was the one on which the terrorists had spoken earlier.

There was a sudden silence in The Cab. Everyone realized that this could be Number One again. Malone pointed a finger at the watch supervisor.

"If it's the same man, I think it's time I talked with him," Malone told her.

Annabelle Green nodded and picked up the telephone.

"Kennedy Tower," she said.

She listened for five seconds before she nodded again.

It was the man who had called before.

"Excuse me. Frank wants to talk with you," she announced and quickly handed the phone to Malone. In the booth six miles away, Willi Staub was startled and suspicious.

"Who's Frank?" he demanded angrily.

"The person you'll be speaking with from now on," Malone replied.

"*To*, not *with*," Staub corrected arrogantly. "I'll talk, Stupid, and you'll listen."

Malone refused to respond to the provocation. He'd never let a terrorist or any other criminal trick him into an ego struggle. Staying cool and focused was critical, a key factor in the unspoken invisible battle for psychological dominance. Malone decided to take control by saying nothing.

"You hear me?" Staub erupted impatiently.

"Yes."

"Then listen good. You know how many planes are trapped up there and how many people are in them. We know that we'll destroy them if you don't give us what we want."

"What's that?"

"The liberation of seven prisoners of war from your filthy imperialist prisons!"

As Staub spoke, Malone carefully weighed every word, every inflection, every tone. This was standard procedure in dealing with terrorists. The tiniest sliver of information could be extremely important.

There was *something* in the way Number One spoke.

What the hell was it?

"Seven? Who are they?" Malone asked evenly.

These names would be crucial.

Now he'd know who was behind this attack.

"Comrades Thomas Makumbo and Simba Brown of the Afrikan People's Army; Julio Sanchez and Carlos Arroza of the FALN; Sandra Geller, Arnold Lloyd and Ibrahim Farzi."

Malone recognized the names instantly.

Black revolutionaries Makumbo and Brown had killed two bank guards in a Queens robbery.

Arroza and Sanchez were Puerto Rican extremists arrested for half a dozen fire bombings.

Chubby Sandra Geller was awaiting sentence for driving a getaway car in the March 13th Brigade's attack on an armored car, and former CIA man Lloyd was going on trial the following week for selling poison gas to the piously homicidal ruler of Soraq. Tarzi had tried to murder Jordan's U.N. delegate.

These names did not supply the answer. They seemed to suggest some sort of coalition, but didn't indicate who was controlling this complex operation. That was as unusual as the attack itself. Terrorists' demands almost always identified them. This list didn't.

"All seven must be brought to Kennedy at once," Staub continued.

There was *something* beneath the Hispanic accent. It was a minute trace of central or northern Europe. Even though Frank Malone couldn't pinpoint the country, he felt a little better. This was the first step toward identifying the son of a bitch who threatened the survival of Katie Malone and four thousand others.

"I'm listening," the detective said.

"Have a long-range jet ready for immediate takeoff."

Where were they going?

The destination might tell what the names had not. Malone decided not to ask. He'd say nothing to hint at resistance or·pursuit. In this war of deception and disguise, he'd let Number One believe that their surprise attack had won them complete dominance.

"I'll try," Malone said, "but all this may take a while."

"You don't have a while, Stupid. Until that jet's out of U.S. airspace, we won't let a single one of your planes land. They're burning fuel fast, so you'd better hurry."

"Now wait a minute," the detective began.

"Not a *second*," Staub broke in harshly. "I'll call back."

When Malone heard the dial tone, he hung up the phone and started across The Cab to the hot lines. On the ground floor of the International Arrivals Building sixty yards away, Sidney Stern rechecked the positions of the television news crews and their cameras. Senator Bono's press secretary, a thirty-nine-year-old workaholic with less hair than his employer but just as much ambition, saw that the CBS correspondent was taping "human interest" comments from a rabbi, the NBC unit was getting a wide-angle crowd shot of the throng and the ABC producer was tapping his wristwatch.

As a dedicated civil servant, Stern understood the reason for the newswoman's concern. In fact, he shared it. This was a very serious situation. If BA 126 was much later and the snow continued to slow traffic, the welcoming of the Kiev Grandma might not make the eleven o'clock news at all.

# 15

IN THE CAB, Malone scooped up the beige phone that was a direct link to 26 Federal Plaza in lower Manhattan.

"FBI," a midwestern male voice announced crisply.

"Carl Wheeler," Malone said.

There was no such person in this unit of the Federal Bureau of Investigation. The name was the code phrase for the Antiterrorist Task Force, an elite group whose office was manned around the clock . . . 365 days a year.

"Wheeler," a Task Force agent said five seconds later.

"This is Captain Frank Malone, New York City Police. We've got an emergency, and I'm calling an alert."

"Numbers?" the FBI man requested as he tapped a button on the computer terminal beside his desk.

Malone recited the digits on his Social Security card and

his badge before giving his birth date. The federal agent studied the computer screen and noted the correct match.

"What kind of alert?" he asked quickly.

"Heavy Metal. Repeat—*Heavy Metal.*"

Washington had established four levels of alert.

Heavy Metal was the highest and most urgent: imminent danger of major loss of life to terrorist action.

"What's the situation, Captain?"

"Critical," Malone replied and swiftly spelled out the crisis.

"Four of the seven they want delivered to Kennedy are in federal custody here: Ibrahim Farzi, Carlos Arroza, Julio Sanchez and Arnold Lloyd," Malone told him. "Phone the attorney general in Washington immediately."

"This could take a couple of hours to organize," the FBI man warned.

"We don't have *a couple of hours.* Every minute counts. Tell him there may be four thousand people up in those planes, and he's got to save them *now.*"

"I'll call. Isn't there something else we can do?"

Malone hesitated. He looked around The Cab, eyed the FAA team and made his decision. He could not discuss his plan. The risk was too great.

"I'll get back to you," Malone said curtly.

Moments after he hung up Malone was speaking on another "hot line" to Sergeant Grady in the police commissioner's office.

"The PC's not here," Grady reported.

"Find him. He's got to reach the mayor. We'll have a goddam massacre if you don't."

He explained what was happening and identified the three prisoners who had to be driven from the municipal jail to JFK at once. As Malone named them, he saw the long-haired controller return from his coffee break. The young controller stopped dead in his stride as he noticed that none of the others were "working" aircraft. He'd never seen The Cab like this.

"What's happening?" he asked Annie Green.

Frank Malone didn't wait for her reply.

"Get them out here *fast*," he told Grady. "Radio cars up front; sirens all the way."

"In this storm?"

"Do it!" Malone ordered harshly and slammed down the phone.

Then he gestured to Wilber.

"Come on," Malone said as he hurried toward the stairs. The FAA executive blinked in surprise but followed immediately.

"Where are we going?" he blurted when he caught up with Malone at the elevator door a floor below.

"Your office," Malone answered as he pushed the button to summon the car.

The gleam in the police captain's eyes was cold and sure, and Pete Wilber recognized it at once. It was the completely focused and purposeful look of a man who knew exactly what he was doing.

Wilber wondered what it was, but decided not to ask. If he didn't explain now, he had a reason. It was probably—like Frank Malone—clever, complicated and practical. The grim-faced detective would spell it out only when he was ready, not a second before.

Both men remained silent as the elevator arrived. Neither uttered a word until they reached Wilber's office. Malone unbuttoned his jacket as he sat down, and Wilber saw the holstered .38 Police Special as the detective picked up the telephone and dialed swiftly.

"Washington, D.C.," an information operator announced.

"The Pentagon, please."

There were several moments of silence before the soulless recorded voice of a computer's memory bank replied.

"Five . . . four . . . five . . . six . . . seven . . . hundred."

Malone broke the connection and dialed the number. Some forty seconds later he was speaking to an army colonel in a subbasement of the huge headquarters building near the Potomac. Floor-to-ceiling maps of every region of the world covered one wall of the large subterranean chamber where seventy-two uniformed men and women worked at computers, teletype machines and other communications gear.

Electronically "swept" every month for concealed "bugs," this was a "maximum security facility." Military police with automatic weapons guarded every door, and no one could enter without Top Secret clearance. This blastproof, gasproof, germproof bunker was the interservice Operations Center. The burly middle-aged colonel to whom Malone spoke was the duty officer.

It was a short conversation.

"We're under a major terrorist attack," Malone reported after he identified himself. "They've crippled our airports, and we urgently need immediate military assistance."

"How big is the terrorist force?"

"I don't know. It doesn't matter. I need an air force plane—right away."

"A *plane?* What for? I'll have to get a senior officer to authorize sending a military aircraft, so you'd better give me the complete picture. Then I'll tell him—"

"No time," Malone interrupted. "I'll tell him myself. While I'm doing that, you can check the facts with the FBI in New York."

*You* and the facts, the duty officer thought.

"Okay," he agreed.

Since the 1941 sneak attacks on Pearl Harbor and the Philippines caught the U.S. armed forces napping, there has always been a flag rank officer—a general or admiral—on duty at the Pentagon to deal with emergencies. Tonight it was a rangy and prematurely gray air force officer with one star on each shoulder and very recent memories of commanding a B-52 wing based south of Miami.

"General Sloat," he said. "What the hell's going on?"

Malone told him how a thus far unidentified terrorist group had knocked out the radar, radio and instrument landing systems for the three major airports serving New York and Newark.

"We've got dozens of airliners trapped up there in a four-star snowstorm," Malone concluded.

"And they're running out of fuel," Sloat reasoned aloud.

"Exactly. That's why I need one of your aircraft immediately."

"You want to call in an air strike in a snowstorm? On an unfamiliar target? That could kill hundreds of civilians nearby if the bombardier is just three seconds off, dammit."

"Not if you do it my way. I'm talking about a special kind of air strike. *No bombs.* I want one of the Sentries from Langley."

Brigadier General Sanford Sloat frowned in an unpleasant mixture of surprise and concern. The Sentry was a modified Boeing 707-320B transport plane that carried several pieces of highly classified equipment. Officially designated the E-3A Airborne Warning and Control System, it flew at more than five hundred miles an hour. That made it—in Pentagon and NATO parlance—"a mobile and survivable surveillance and command platform" that offered no fixed target. Even the most accurate Soviet intercontinental ballistic missiles couldn't hit it.

The E-3As were state-of-the-art war machines that cost $150 million each. They were worth it. Russian intelligence had made repeated efforts to find out how they worked, and almost everything about the Sentries and their operations was Top Secret.

Who had told this stranger that there were E-3As at Langley Air Force Base in Virginia?

Was the man on the telephone really a New York cop or a daring KGB agent on some devious mission?

Whoever he was, what else did he know about this security-shrouded weapons system?

"How could a Sentry help?" Sloat tested.

"You know damn well," Malone replied angrily. "Don't play games with me, General. You can't afford it. If those planes go down, you're going down with them."

"What does that mean?"

"It means I'll be on all three networks tomorrow telling the country you could have saved those people—and let them die."

"That's insane!"

"Civilians . . . men, women and children . . . *thousands* of them."

Shaken, the general managed to regain his self-control.

"Even if I get an okay, it'll take time to collect a crew and fuel the bird," he reasoned earnestly. "Then there's over an hour flight in a major storm. I can't promise that we'll deliver an E-3A in time."

"I don't want your promise. I want that plane!"

Then Malone hung up the telephone.

"Not a word about this to anyone," he told Wilber.

"For the same reason you came down here to call?"

"I thought you'd figure it out," the detective said coolly. "Nothing else made sense. *Why* don't you trust our people in The Cab?"

"Because I know that this operation was meticulously planned by a very clever son of a bitch," Malone said. "If Number One is as careful and tricky as I think, he'd have an inside man."

"Or *woman?*" a female voice behind them asked.

Annabelle Green stood in the doorway with a large audiocassette in her hand. Malone wondered when she'd arrived and how much she'd heard.

"Or woman," he agreed. "What are you doing here, Annie?"

"I came to give you this," she said as she handed him the cassette."

Wilber nodded in recognition and approval.

"All radio and phone talk to and from The Cab is recorded," he explained. "Number One's voice is on this tape."

"That could help," Malone said. "Thanks, Annie."

"Don't go overboard, Frank," she advised in a voice aglow with sarcasm. "The spy could still be me, right?"

"We'll talk about it later," he told her.

"You haven't changed at all," she said bitterly and left.

Wilber shook his head in disbelief.

"You know her, Captain," he reminded. "You know she couldn't work with those maniacs."

"I know who she *was*, not who she *is*. A lot could have happened to her head in thirteen years."

"She's no terrorist," the FAA executive insisted.

"Maybe not. Maybe she's in love with one of them. Widows can be lonely and vulnerable. Maybe it isn't politics or love. Maybe it's blackmail or hard cash. If career navy and CIA men can sell out their country for money, why not air traffic controllers?"

"*Maybes* aren't good enough," Wilber said firmly.

Not in your world, the detective thought. It was different where Frank Malone fought his war. In that dark land of pious psychotics and viciously virtuous assassins, deception was the state religion and *maybes* were the national currency.

"Spare me the goddam sermon," Malone replied grimly, "and find Number One on this—now."

Pointing to the cassette player atop a file cabinet, he handed Wilber the recording. The FAA official frowned as he put it in the machine and pressed the fast-forward switch. A shrill babble gushed from the cassette player.

Wilber stopped the tape, played it at normal speed for several seconds and accelerated it once more. He repeated this again and again. The room was filled with samples of many voices. None of them was that of Number One.

Ignoring the cataract of sound, Malone thought about what he'd do when Wilber found it. Having analyzed reports from many countries on hundreds of terrorist assaults, the detective knew that a key reason for their success was complete surprise. If his counterattack was to work, it had to be equally unexpected. The longer he kept his battle plan to himself the better.

His strategy was simple.

He would strike at the terrorists with their own weapons: not guns but modern electronics.

His tactics would be like theirs: multiple complex and sophisticated attacks.

He'd use the same methods the army had taught him in Vietnam: search and destroy. It didn't matter that this war was half a world away from Indochina. This black night and fierce snowstorm were only another kind of jungle, and he was a first-class jungle fighter. That was why he had survived and others hadn't.

There was one thing that was different about this fight.

The armed struggle for Indochina had raged on for years.

This war would be won or lost in less than ninety minutes.

He couldn't afford to make a single mistake. There'd be no way to turn back the clock or try again.

Frank Malone looked at his wristwatch. It was 8:19. He wondered how much time he had. How soon would the first airliner fall from the sky?

Another thought suddenly filled his mind.

Would that plane be TWA 22 from Los Angeles?

# 16

*SOME NINETY MILES SOUTH* . . . thirty seconds
later.

"Philadelphia Tower to all aircraft. New York Center reports Newark, La Guardia, Kennedy and Westchester are
closed by heavy snow and electrical storms causing radio
interference."

This was the story FAA headquarters had just teletyped to
Cabs across the country. The purpose of the rapidly impro-
vised fabrication was to avoid, for as long as possible, panic
in the skies and on the ground.

There was also another reason.

It might be possible to contact and peel free some planes
on the outer edge of the jamming area where the electronic
assault was weakest.

"Aircraft inbound to Newark, La Guardia, Kennedy and

Westchester must divert immediately," the man in the Philadelphia Cab continued. "Proceed directly to alternates speci-
fied in your flight plans. Please check in now for altitude
assignments."

It wasn't only FAA teams at Philadelphia's airport and
others near the electronically besieged New York City area
that were relaying the order to divert. From the towers of
nearly two hundred municipal and armed forces airfields in
every part of the nation, controllers were broadcasting similar instructions. So were their colleagues in Canada, Mexico
and the Caribbean.

In Miami, Montreal, Chicago and Boston, airliners already on taxiways were ordered to return to terminals and
unload their passengers. In Atlanta, St. Louis, Toronto and
Nashville, irate travelers waiting to board planes grumbled
when delayed departures were announced. At Los Angeles
International, a graying grandmother who wrote a syndicated
column on manners expressed her indignation in a stream of
loud and startling obscenities.

It was quieter in Wilber's office in the JFK Tower.

The only sounds there came from the cassette player.

"Delta one-zero-three, turn left on—"

Click. Fast-forward gibberish. Click.

"United sixty-five Heavy to—"

Click. More babble. Click.

"We will knock out your radar."

"*That's him!*" Malone erupted and reached for the telephone.

He dialed the FBI office in Manhattan. Within moments
he was talking to the antiterrorist agent with whom he'd spoken earlier.

"This is Malone. I need the secure line to Washington."

"The Bureau?"

"No, Sea Sweep."

The secret U.S. Navy unit code-named Sea Sweep was
the American intelligence community's joint library for all

data on global terrorism. Its computers held millions of pieces of information from counterespionage and police organizations around the world. Sea Sweep might have the answer, Malone thought as he waited.

Well, *one* of the answers.

"Two two hundred," a male voice said suddenly.

Standard security procedures. No name, just part of a phone number.

"I want the senior officer on duty," Malone announced.

He heard three long buzzes.

Then a woman, crisp and midwestern, spoke.

"Data Control."

"This is Captain Malone of the New York Police Department. We have a *critical* situation, and I need an immediate audio probe."

"Your account number?"

"Don't have one, but you can phone General Sloat at the Pentagon for authorization."

"I need an account number," she said firmly.

"This is an emergency—Heavy Metal—not a test. We've got a couple of thousand people in goddam mortal danger. Call the FBI if you want confirmation."

"I'm sorry, Captain, but I must have an approved number."

"You're going to be a *lot* sorrier. I'm taping this conversation," Malone lied. "If one person dies because you won't bother to make a call, the tape goes straight to the U.S. attorney."

"What are you talking about?"

"*Ten* years for manslaughter. You'll get your fucking number. You'll be *wearing* it."

"That's preposterous. I don't make the rules, Captain."

"But you'll do the time," he predicted. "When those pictures of the heaps of bodies hit the newspapers, *somebody's* going to jail—and it won't be any admiral. You're *it*, lady."

Silence.

"It might be *fifteen* years," he threatened.

She coughed uneasily before she replied.

"Since it's an emergency," she said stiffly, "I could check with the FBI *while* we run the probe. If they authorize use of their number, you'll get the results."

"*Right away*," he pressed. "I'm ready to roll the tape of the man's voice we need identified. You record all your phone traffic, right?"

"Roll your tape," she ordered curtly.

He placed the receiver next to the cassette player and started it. While the tape rolled, he asked Wilber for the numbers of the phones in this office and The Cab. As soon as the terrorist's first conversation with Annie Green ended the detective turned off the player and recited both numbers to the Sea Sweep officer so she could call back.

"Thank you, Captain," she said in a tone of frigid hostility. "You realize that we may not have that man's voice in our audio file. Even if it's there, the distortion of a voice delivered over a telephone line could make identification impossible."

"Give it your best shot."

"We always do," she replied righteously and hung up.

As Malone put down the phone, he wondered whether he'd just lost the element of surprise. Number One was a professional at this game and a careful planner. If he knew the FAA system so well, he'd probably scouted the offices too. This room or phone could be bugged.

Number One might have heard the call to Sea Sweep.

He could be listening now.

There was no time to search for cunningly concealed microphones. Malone had other things to do, all desperately urgent. He decided to do them elsewhere.

"Let's go," he said abruptly and started toward the doorway.

"Where? Why?" Wilber asked. "I'd like to know what the hell's going on here."

"I'll tell you when I find out," Malone promised. "Right now I've got to talk to somebody downstairs. Come on."

They took the elevator to the ground floor and hurried through the swirling storm across the open bridge to the International Arrivals Building. Both men were brushing melted snow from their faces as they passed the federal narcotics agents on the balcony.

When Malone and the FAA executive reached the top of the stairway, the detective looked down at the noisy crowd in the large chamber below. He scanned the journalists and Hassidim, the Russian woman's family and scores of others here to meet inbound travelers.

"There's our *somebody*," Malone said and pointed at a well-dressed man in the throng.

He was standing where he often stood—near a television news crew. He looked assured, sincere and maturely handsome. Barely five feet nine, he radiated the authority of a *big* man.

"That's Senator Bono!" Wilber exclaimed.

"Has been for eleven years. Where's the toilet?"

"In the right corner there, at the back."

"Meet you inside in three minutes," the detective said and hurried down the steps. He zigzagged through the crowd warily, trying to avoid any press people who might recognize him. When he spotted a lanky Associated Press photographer who knew him, Malone instantly turned his head.

He found himself looking at Bono's "media assistant" five yards away. Sidney Stern's brow was furrowed in concentration and he was walking quickly. When Malone gestured to him, the publicist waved back but didn't slow down until the detective blocked his way.

"Nice to see you, Captain," Stern said mechanically as he tried to pass. Malone didn't let him.

"I have to talk to him right away," Malone announced.

"If you'll call the office in the morning—"

"*Now*, Sidney. It's life and death for a lot of people . . . in this state . . . tonight. He can help save them."

"This is for real?"

Malone nodded.

"We're fighting the clock," he warned the balding press aide. "I'll meet him in the john in two minutes."

"The *john*?"

"Don't argue with me, Sidney. Do it!"

Senator Joseph Bono entered the men's lavatory of the JFK International Arrivals Building a minute and forty seconds later. Stern was with him. Bono glanced around the toilet, shrugged and looked Malone squarely in the eye.

"Life and death for a lot of people?" he asked bluntly.

"Including Mrs. Olitski," Malone replied. "You might help save them."

"I'm listening."

Malone described the crisis and Number One's demands.

"Unbelievable!" Bono said softly and shook his head.

"Don't take my word for it," the detective told him. "This is Pete Wilber. He's federal. He runs the tower here."

Wilber gave his FAA identity card to Bono, who studied it carefully.

"It's *true*," Wilber blurted. "I don't know how they did it, Senator, but they did."

Bono sighed as he returned the ID card.

"How can I help?" he asked.

Malone took a quarter from his pocket.

"Phone the White House immediately," he said and handed Bono the coin. "If we don't nail these bastards in time, we have to deliver the people they want. Four of them—Farzi, Arroza, Lloyd and Sanchez—are in federal custody in Manhattan. Ask the president to rush them out here at once."

"The president may not do it," Stern warned. "He just made one helluva speech against any deals with terrorists."

"And I supported his position the next day," Bono recalled soberly.

"*Life and death,*" Malone challenged. "Will you make the call?"

Senator Joseph Bono looked at himself in the big mirror, adjusted the knot of his tie and turned to his media expert. Stern scooped a handful of change from his jacket and gave the money to his employer.

"It costs more than a quarter to call Washington," Stern said.

"You're pretty damn sure of yourself, Sid," Bono told him.

"No, I'm sure about you, Joe."

"*It'll work,*" Malone predicted. "The president will listen to you, Senator. You're his friend."

"Presidents don't have friends," the graying politician replied. "I'll call him though. Anything else, Captain?"

"We'd like to keep this situation secret as long as possible."

The senator shrugged and smiled.

"Business as usual, Sidney," he said cheerfully. "Let's go talk to the president and con the media."

Bono and Stern left first and went to the nearby row of phone booths. While the senator was speaking to a senior White House aide a minute later, Malone and Wilber were going up on the escalator. The detective looked down and frowned.

"So much for secrets," he said ironically.

More people were surging into the International Arrivals Building. There were at least a score of them—all but one male and most of them in uniforms. They looked bulky in their bulletproof vests. Five carried submachine guns, while others held shotguns and sniper rifles with the assurance of familiarity. Among those bearing walkie-talkies was a tall and muscular black man who was clearly in command: Lieutenant Benjamin Hamilton of the Port Authority Police.

The initial reaction of the startled civilians was shock. Guns, even in the hands of the police, meant danger. What kind? How serious? For several moments the crowd grew much quieter. Then there was a rising surge of sound as scores of worried people asked those questions aloud.

Other shaken men and women stared silently at the heavily armed Port Authority force. It was the submachine guns and bulletproof vests that chilled the waiting relatives and thrilled the press people. These police were clearly equipped for battle.

With whom?

Why?

The reporters reacted instantly to the sight of Hamilton's combat-ready unit. Aroused by the prospect of a major shoot-out that would make a much "hotter" story than some old woman rejoining her family, graduates of distinguished journalism schools shoved people aside and bulled forward to demand answers from Hamilton.

He knew what he had to do.

He had to keep the secret for as long as possible.

Hamilton ignored the shouted questions as if he didn't hear them. He looked straight ahead as he led his unit toward the elevator. Avoiding eye contact, Lieutenant Benjamin Hamilton coolly pretended that he didn't see the arm-waving reporters. He didn't blink or break stride when two of them called out his name.

Irritated but undiscouraged, the television crews, radio teams, print journalists and photographers all pressed forward through the crowd. Hamilton hurried on steadily, moving ahead with a graceful style that made Frank Malone wonder where he'd played football. Hamilton was almost at the elevator when a pretty Haitian woman backed into his way, forcing him to stop. The surging media mob closed in immediately.

# 17

SOME FOUR MILES SOUTHWEST and three thousand feet up, Kenji Tokoro squinted as he tried once more to peer through the billowing white wall of tumbling snow. The earnest copilot of the Japan Air Lines cargo plane had flown through plenty of bad weather before, but nothing quite like this.

It was quiet in the cockpit of the big Boeing.

For a moment Tokoro felt isolated and uneasy.

Then he turned his head, just two inches, to sneak a discreet look at the middle-aged man in the seat beside him. Tokoro had great respect for Captain Shigeta. It wasn't only because the bespectacled commander of the 747 was an older person, although that was not unimportant. Captain Shigeta was also a very experienced and excellent flier.

There was no uncertainty in his face, Tokoro thought admiringly. As usual, Captain Shigeta was serene and in complete control of the situation. Neither the blinding storm nor the unusual communications problem ruffled him. It was definitely an honor to fly with such a mature man who exemplified Japanese dignity, patience and efficiency so well.

Tokoto felt proud and reassured as he turned his head away.

There was nothing to worry about with Captain Shigeta in command.

Flying a thousand feet above the Japanese 747, the senior pilot of TWA 22 Heavy from Los Angeles wasn't nearly as contented. His stomach, bloated and burning, was bothering him again. Bitterness about his damned alimony payments had been gnawing at Lawrence Pace's belly for months, and the hot sauce that he'd carelessly tossed on the *chimichangas* at lunch in the Mexican restaurant near Burbank had obviously been a mistake.

Being stuck up here in this lousy snowstorm only added to the TWA pilot's discomfort and tension. It could have been worse, he reflected sourly. Having been bothered by similar gastric distress several times recently, the practical captain of the L-1011 was ready to cope. He had the solution in his pocket.

Of course, he didn't want the others in the cockpit to see him take out the bottle. There was no telling what sort of stupid gossip might start if they noticed him swallow the tablets. They might not believe that these were just an ordinary antacid remedy, and there could be troublesome rumors that fifty-one-year-old Lawrence Pace had an ulcer or shaky nerves. Envious of his seniority, the younger crewmen might say almost anything.

Pace *knew* that he wasn't sick. He took good care of his body—aside from an infrequent lapse with Mexican food—combining a balanced diet of sprouts, wheat germ, bran, fish, and fresh vegetables and a meticulous program of daily exercise. He opened the small bottle in his pocket, shook out two tablets and warily raised them to his lips.

As he began to chew the tablets, he looked across and saw his copilot watching. Had he noticed? Annoyed, Captain Lawrence Pace wanted to swear.

In the Pentagon's Operations Center, General Sloat did.

"Son of a bitch!" he cursed into the phone. "An *hour* to get the bird airborne?"

"And at least forty-five minutes more to fly to Kennedy, which could be *real* hairy with all those planes up there playing blindman's bluff," the colonel at Langley Air Force Base warned.

105 minutes, Sloat thought and looked at the wall clock. It showed 8:31.

The E-3A from Langley couldn't reach JFK before 10:16 at the earliest, and that could be too late.

"What do you say, General?"

Sloat hesitated. There would be a terrible loss of life—and political hell to pay—if an E-3A crammed with Top Secret gear collided with a civilian airliner.

"General?"

It could all be for nothing. Nobody knew what kind of jamming the terrorists were using. Malone's idea might not work anyway.

"What's the word, General? Go or no?"

"Go!" Sloat said defiantly.

105 minutes.

Maybe they could save a few of the trapped planes.

That would be better than none at all.

# 18

*WATCHING* from the balcony, Malone saw Hamilton speaking to the encircling ring of journalists. After about twenty seconds, the Port Authority lieutenant suddenly turned and pointed directly at Frank Malone.

What was Hamilton doing?

The reporters looked up at Malone. Three photographers swiftly squeezed off pictures of the detective, and a pair of television cameramen raised their minicams to videotape Captain Frank Malone through power-zoom lenses.

What was Hamilton telling them?

The Port Authority lieutenant stopped talking and waved pleasantly up to Malone. It was a startling but friendly gesture that called for a response. Malone forced himself to smile as he waved back. When Hamilton resumed speaking and tapped his wristwatch, the circle of reporters opened to let him proceed to the escalator.

"What the hell was that all about?" Malone asked as Hamilton led his heavily armed unit onto the balcony half a minute later.

"The routine security test that the FAA called for tonight," Hamilton answered evenly. "You know, the one that you came out here to observe."

"Oh, *that* one. Is there anything else I'm going to do?" Malone asked while they walked toward the control tower.

"Not till nine forty-five. That's when we're supposed to brief the press on how well the exercise went."

"Very creative," Malone said admiringly.

"You helped. Their seeing the city's top antiterrorist cop lent credibility to my fable."

Then Malone remembered, and sighed.

"Your fable could have bought us over an hour," he thought aloud.

"*Could* have?"

"More cops, a lot more than a test would need, are on the way."

"It really wasn't that good a fable," Hamilton said with a shrug. "How much time have we got before they arrive?"

"Not enough. It's going to get messy downstairs."

"Jesus!" Wilber blurted. "What are you going to do?"

"I'm going to nail Number One and get those planes down," Malone answered.

They were approaching the two federal narcotics agents. T. J. Gill and the slim woman with the Bloomingdale's bag scanned the platoon of Port Authority police warily, worried that the uniformed intruders might make always edgy dope dealers cut and run. Gill frowned as he whispered to the female operative. Then she stepped forward to ask the question.

Frank Malone spoke first.

"Terrorists," he said bluntly as he strode past.

Only her eyes showed her surprise—and anger.

"DEA on stakeout," Malone told Hamilton and Wilber while they walked on toward the bridge. "It's big. I made seven or eight more downstairs."

Salvos of wind-driven snow silenced Malone as soon as they stepped onto the stormswept span. When they reached the shelter of the ground floor of the control tower building, they stamped their feet and brushed the wet flakes from their outer garments.

The guard behind the desk peered at them in amazement.

He'd worked at the Kennedy Tower for nearly four years, and he'd never seen any Port Authority police in this kind of battle gear. These men looked like an assault unit, one of those SWAT teams who appeared on television. Here they were, live, only a few yards from him.

They seemed very big in their bulky flak jackets, and dangerous. The guard felt uneasy. Then he recognized Benjamin Hamilton's familiar face.

"Is it a drill, Lieutenant?" the guard asked uneasily.

Hamilton shook his head.

"This is for real," he replied.

"Shit," the man behind the desk whispered.

"Just go about your business," Hamilton ordered and turned to his team.

"Sergeant, seal off this building. Nobody comes in from the arrivals terminal."

Then Wilber pointed at the glass doors at the other side of the lobby. Beyond those portals was a bridge to the airport's chapel.

"And nobody from there either," Hamilton added.

At that moment, they saw a dark figure on the span to the house of worship. In instant reflex, five submachine guns swung to cover the faceless stranger beyond the doors and half a dozen police reached for their pistols. The quickest— the first to draw—was Frank Malone.

The heavyset man who entered was dressed in black.

Fedora, overcoat, pants, socks, shoes—all black.

The police stared for several seconds.

Then they lowered their weapons.

"Sorry, Father," Hamilton apologized to the priest. "We thought you might be someone else."

"Is something wrong?" the cleric asked earnestly in a deep bass voice.

"I'm afraid so," Hamilton answered. "For your own safety, it would be wise to leave this building immediately."

The priest studied the armed men and sighed.

"We live in violent times," he said slowly. "Well, if you should need me, I'll be downstairs in the terminal."

The clergyman walked out into the storm. Then Malone realized that he still held his .38 Police Special, and returned it to its home in the shoulder holster. For a few seconds he wondered what his devout mother would say if she'd heard that he'd pointed a loaded gun at a Catholic priest.

Crossing the span to the International Arrivals Building, the man in black allowed himself to smile. It was all right to do so in the swirling snow. No one could see. He knew he had to be extremely careful about showing his pleasure. It could be dangerous for people in his business to reveal any of their emotions. That was something Willi Staub had learned a lot of corpses ago.

The bulletproof vest chafed as he pushed through the storm. It was 16 degrees Fahrenheit, and the slashing wind was getting meaner by the minute. Staub felt warm and good. With his priestly garb and practiced American speech, he had penetrated the enemy positions and studied the defenders. He had observed their numbers and weapons. More important, he had seen the tension and uncertainty deep in their eyes.

*They had no plan.*

*They had no idea of how to resist his.*

He'd recognized one of them. Staub had seen his photo in a newspaper. The tall, sandy-haired man commanded the city's antiterrorist police. His boyish face was typically Irish, good-looking in a crude way but basically unsophisticated.

*Malone?*

Yes, Captain Frank Malone.

Staub had been surprised when Ito first reported that Malone was in the Kennedy Tower. Now it was time to call the Japanese again for the latest news on what the enemy was doing in The Cab. It probably wasn't anything to worry him.

*They had no plan.*

He was still in control.

# 19

*THE TELEPRINTER* was clattering as Wilber led Malone and Hamilton into The Cab. Annie Green stood beside the stuttering machine, reading the incoming message and taking notes on a clipboard pad.

The controllers watched her silently. Three were seated. Two others were on their feet, sipping coffee. The young one with the longish hair puffed on a 100-millimeter cigarette. They all looked grim.

The teletype halted for a few seconds. Then it began to cough out another message. She nodded, scrawled something on her pad and nodded again a moment after the machine stopped. Her eyes swept down and up and down the column of numbers again. Then she turned and saw Malone.

Their eyes locked for a few seconds before she broke free.

It would be easier to talk to Pete Wilber. He wasn't dangerous. He couldn't hurt her.

"The printer's been going like crazy, Pete," she said with more energy than she felt. "Washington, the TRACON and eighteen . . . no, nineteen . . . airlines. I've been adding up the score."

"What does that mean?" Malone demanded impatiently.

"Washington's trying to peel off every plane it can reach," she announced, looking at Wilber. "They've succeeded in diverting eleven of them."

"How many are still up there?" the FAA executive asked.

"For the three airports? It's forty-six, if my addition's right."

"Is TWA twenty-two one of them?" Malone asked.

She scanned the pad.

"Yes," she answered coolly. "Is there something special about it?"

"Captain Malone's daughter is on board," Wilber explained.

Annie Green flinched.

"Oh, my God!" she gasped.

Now she looked directly at Malone. She had to.

"I didn't know, Frank. I *really* didn't know," she said in a choked voice.

"How could you?" he responded evenly. "How much time have those planes got?"

This was *his* child. How could he be so damn calm and rational?

"Fuel figures are still coming in," she reported, "and the estimates on what those loads translate to in flying time could be off a bit. But so far the lowest seems to be some Arab prince's Concorde—sixty-seven minutes. The next three are an Aerovias seven forty-seven with sixty-nine, British Airways one twenty-six Heavy with seventy-three and a Japanese freighter with seventy-six."

Annie Green glanced at her pad again.

"No word yet on TWA twenty-two," she said.

Something gleamed in Malone's wide blue eyes. It wasn't fear.

"We better start gassing up that long-range jet Number One asked for," the detective decided.

"We did," she told him and looked at her wristwatch. "A DC-ten will be ready for takeoff in about thirty-five minutes."

Suddenly the teletype began to clatter again, and she hurried to the machine to monitor the new message. She studied it for several seconds. Then she turned to Malone and shook her head. The report coming in concerned some other plane. There was still no word on TWA 22's remaining fuel.

Now one of the hot-line phones on the wall rang.

It was the yellow one, the direct link to Police Headquarters.

The detective grabbed it.

"Is Captain Malone there?"

"Speaking."

"Please hold for Commissioner Shaw."

Frank Malone didn't like Bruce Allan Shaw. The dapper man who ran the New York Police Department was too clever, glib and ambitious for Malone's taste. The previous PC had been much less of a wheeler-dealer.

"Captain Malone?"

"Yes, Commissioner."

"Exactly what's going on out there?"

"The radar's gone, the radio's jammed, the Instrument Landing System's been wrecked and there are forty-six planes up there that we can't get down."

"I see."

"They don't. They're flying blind and they're running out of fuel. Are those three prisoners on the way here?"

"I've discussed this with the mayor. We're gravely concerned about this situation," Shaw said pompously.

"*Gravely* is the right word," Malone told him bluntly.

"We'll have three or four thousand corpses to bury pretty soon. The first plane will drop in sixty-seven . . . no, sixty-six . . . minutes."

The teleprinter stopped. Everyone else in The Cab was watching and listening to Malone.

"Is that *exact* enough, Commissioner?" he asked bitterly.

"I . . . I'd better get out there," Shaw announced.

"What about those three prisoners?"

"It's a matter of principle," Bruce Allan Shaw said piously. "The mayor and I feel it would be immoral to cave in to these thugs."

In an election year, Malone thought.

"Captain, it would only encourage other terrorists to—"

"The president just called," Malone interrupted ruthlessly. "He's ordered immediate delivery of the four in federal custody to Kennedy. They're on their way."

"The president?"

"He said he didn't want to be responsible for the murder of thousands of innocent civilians."

That would dump the guilt for the loss of all those lives on the mayor of New York—and his police commissioner.

"Humanitarian considerations come first, of course," Shaw said smoothly. "That's always been my basic policy. Yes, I'll come out to the airport with them."

And talk righteously to the press later, the detective thought.

Public relations usually prevailed over principle—around the world. Hell, shrewd public relations *was* a principle these days.

"As soon as possible, Commissioner," Malone urged.

"You can count on me, Captain. I never let my people down."

The teletype began to stutter as Malone hung up.

"He's going to bring them out himself," the detective announced.

"You sure?" Hamilton asked.

"Absolutely. He's already writing his speech," Malone replied.

Wilber looked uneasy.

"*When* did the president call?" he wondered aloud.

"About five minutes from now."

"Captain, I think that I underestimated you," the husky Port Authority lieutenant admitted. "You just bare-ass lied to the PC—and the mayor. He's gonna tell that fable to the mayor, you know."

"Screw the PC *and* the mayor," Malone said.

"I think you just did," Hamilton told him.

Then they heard a noise.

It was faint, but growing louder.

It sounded mechanical and insistent—demanding attention.

It was coming from down below, not from the runways but from the network of feeder roads that brought cars, station wagons and taxis to the terminals. After a few seconds, Malone and Hamilton recognized what it was.

Sirens.

They walked to a window on the side of The Cab from which the noise was coming and peered down through the curtain of snow. Through the quivering white curtain they saw an armada of New York City police cars. The turret lights on top were flashing as they drew up to the International Arrivals Building, and their sirens ripped the night.

"Ten, eleven, twelve," Hamilton counted. "There goes the neighborhood."

Malone didn't smile at the black lieutenant's jest. *Somebody* should have told the local precinct to order a silent approach. The *somebody* was Frank Malone. This was his own damn fault. The rest of the blue-and-whites carrying cops to JFK's other terminals would arrive with screaming sirens, too.

Patrolmen would pour into the buildings.

That would start it.

Everyone in those terminals, including the journalists whom Hamilton had deceived, would quickly realize that some terrible crisis was at hand.

Confusion, rumors and fear would sweep through the buildings like a vicious virus. The truth could not be concealed any longer. The people in the terminals would have to be told that the three airports were under electronic attack, and that thousands of passengers on inbound flights were in mortal danger.

Then it would happen—wild and ugly.

Nothing and no one could prevent it now.

"Panic time," Frank Malone said grimly.

"Panic time," Hamilton agreed.

Not just here, Malone thought. The reporters would be on the telephones in seconds. Within minutes, news of the ingenious terrorist assault would spew from thousands of wire service teleprinters and radio stations to shock the nation. Maybe that would jolt the federal government into rushing the other four on Number One's list to Kennedy.

There was something *wrong* with that list.

Something about that list didn't *fit*, Malone thought as he watched the uniformed police piling out of their cars.

And there was a reason that it didn't fit. The tricky son of a bitch who had planned this complex operation didn't do anything without a reason. Malone considered the seven names again.

Thomas Makumbo.

Simba Brown.

Julio Sanchez and Carlos Arroza of the Fuerzas Armadas Para La Liberación Nacional.

Sandra Geller.

Arnold Lloyd.

Ibrahim Farzi.

What the hell was it?

Was it what was on the list or what wasn't?

At that moment, the machine behind him stopped and Annie Green spoke.

"Frank, can I talk to you for a minute?"

Was it news about TWA 22?

His heart beat faster as he turned and walked toward her.

# 20

SHE SAW the caring in his eyes as he approached, and shook her head.

"No, there's no word on your daughter's plane yet. It's something else."

"What?"

"I had an idea about the jamming."

"How to stop it?" he asked.

"Well, how to find where it's coming from."

Once they knew where the transmitter was, they could destroy it. They might even take prisoners in the attack— terrorists who could provide crucial information.

But the enemy must not learn that they were hunting down the transmitter. Who was the enemy? Was the enemy here in The Cab now?

Malone took her shoulder and gently turned her so she faced away from the controllers. For a moment she was startled. He hadn't touched her for so long. Then she understood and sighed.

It wasn't affection at all.

It was Captain Frank Malone on official police business.

"What's the idea, Annie?"

"There's almost no traffic out of here at night, but a lot of planes come in and park to be cleaned and refueled for early morning departures. Sometimes one of the men cleaning the cockpit accidentally brushes against a switch, and inadvertently knocks on the radio. It happens during daytime cleaning, too."

"I'm listening."

"You'd find that hard to do if you were a pilot approaching JFK and some transmitter in an empty plane on the ground was messing up the frequency. That happens a couple of times a year. This is a huge airport, Frank. We may have eighty or ninety planes—sometimes more—parked in different places."

"And the problem is to find out which plane parked where is jamming the frequency," he reasoned.

"Exactly, Frank. We have a great deal of traffic and this airport has certain assigned frequencies. The pilots monitor them, and we really can't afford to have one of the standard frequencies out of action, as we see tonight."

"What do you do?"

"We call in outside help: the Coast Guard. At their base on Long Island, they've got a couple of search-and-rescue helicopters equipped with directional finding radio gear to locate ships in distress. They've got excellent equipment and very good crews."

"Good enough to fly over this immense airport and pinpoint precisely which parked plane is screwing up the frequency," he thought aloud.

"Absolutely. They just home in on the signal. We've

never asked them to do it in a major storm before," she said. "I don't even know if they'll fly in this weather."

"Let's find out."

"I'll call them right away."

"The hell you will. I think it might be safer if you and I were the only ones who knew we were trying this," he announced softly.

"How do I reach them—telepathy?" she asked irately.

He pointed at the printer.

"You've gotten paranoid, Frank, but you're still smart," she admitted.

As she began to type on the printer's keyboard, Malone watched the controllers' faces cautiously. They were looking at her but their expressions showed no emotion. The detective's eyes swept around the room several times before he noticed that Pete Wilber wasn't there.

Now an answer was stuttering in on the machine.

She read it and turned.

"They'll try, Frank," she reported.

"Fine. By the way, where's Wilber?"

She scanned The Cab swiftly.

"He was here a minute ago," she said. "Probably went down to use the john."

*Maybe.*

Was it only coincidence that Wilber—a senior official— was working unusually late on this extraordinary night?

Why hadn't the FAA veteran, who had many more years of experience than Annie Green, thought about the control tower tape or the Coast Guard helicopter?

How long had it been since Peter Wilber went through a security check? Had he ever had one?

Where was he right now?

What was he doing?

Was he talking to Number One?

# 21

LESS THAN a hundred yards away, Willi Staub was annoyed. He had planned to call Ito five minutes earlier, but all the phone booths on the first floor of the International Arrivals Building had been occupied. Irritated that he was behind schedule, he dialed the number of the warehouse, hung up after four rings and dialed it again.

The cautious Japanese engineer picked up the telephone but didn't say anything. He wasn't taking any chances, wasn't exposing anything—not even his voice. He waited for Staub to speak first.

"Extension six," Staub said—as the agreed password.

"I'll try it for you," Ito responded in countersign.

"What do you hear from The Cab?"

"The city will deliver the three packages," Ito reported,

"but there's no word on the other four. Your friend, Frank, has asked for them—urgently."

Staub didn't give a damn about the trio in city hands.

It was the four in federal custody who mattered.

He wasn't going to tell that to Ito or anyone else. To do so might expose the basis of the entire operation and compromise the rich and powerful man who had ordered it. That would endanger Staub's $5 million fee—and perhaps Willi Staub himself.

"How about the birds?" Staub asked.

"They're getting tired and thirsty. They might start dropping in about sixty-three minutes. It sounds as if Frank's worried about that. His daughter is involved with the birds."

"Wonderful. Do you think that will make him cooperative?"

"It should, but I wouldn't count on it. Would you?"

"I don't count on anything I can't touch," Staub said candidly. "Is Frank trying to reach me?"

"Yes, but he doesn't know how to spell your name so he can't find your number."

"Too bad," Staub mocked. "Maybe I'll call him."

In twelve minutes, according to the plan.

Takeshi Ito didn't say that aloud. You couldn't know who might be listening on a wiretap.

"By the way," the electronic warfare specialist said, "your friend in the trucking business phoned five minutes ago. We only spoke briefly. He's working tonight."

Staub smiled. That truck and driver were important.

"Excellent," he told Ito. "How are things with you?"

The man in the warehouse studied the monitors linked to the television cameras sweeping the streets outside. Until the temperature dropped so drastically last week, a skinny prostitute had been working almost every night in a doorway barely twenty yards from the terrorist's covert base. It had been depressing to watch her sell her services again and again. Neither the whore nor anyone else loitered within range of the security cameras tonight, not in this storm.

"It is all quiet," the Japanese said soberly. "There is nothing but snow in the streets."

"It's much more crowded here. A lot of Frank's friends just arrived."

"Is it *uncomfortable?*" Ito tested.

"No way," Staub answered confidently, enjoying his mastery of the American usage. It was one of many phrases and idioms that he had acquired from years of listening to U.S. Armed Forces Radio in several countries.

"I'll catch you later," he concluded and hung up.

In forty-nine minutes, Takeshi Ito thought. Then he studied each of the monitors again and looked around the warehouse. He eyed the bed, lamp, armchair and table . . . the weapons, ammunition and big rack crammed with sophisticated electronics equipment . . . the generator and drums of fuel that fed it . . . and the two large fire extinguishers. Ito wasn't the sort of person who took chances. He wouldn't risk an accidental blaze interfering with his work.

It seemed wasteful to destroy all this, but the plan required total demolition of the building and its contents. He had to stick to the plan, of course. Even before he'd entered high school, he'd learned how *incorrect* it was to deviate. That was not the Japanese way. He was a terrorist out to smash Japan's economic and social system, but a *Japanese* terrorist.

All the charges were in place—incendiary and explosive. The timers were attached, a primary and backup for each. He had checked and rechecked them carefully.

He could set the seven delayed-action fuses in one minute and fifty seconds. By the time they went off, Takeshi Ito would be in a jet hundreds of miles outside U.S. airspace— with three forged passports and a million dollars for the Red Army.

His eyes went to the television screens once more. It looked so peaceful outside, he thought. There was beauty in those fluttering snowflakes. Then he sighed and thought about the prostitute.

In The Cab atop the Kennedy Tower, the printer had been grinding out messages for nearly six minutes. Now it fell silent, and Annie Green walked back to speak to her former lover.

"Frank, the fuel figures on the last four planes just came in. The Concorde isn't the lowest in flying time anymore."

She was frightened.

He could see it.

"TWA twenty-two?" he guessed.

She nodded.

"Assuming that they've been flying at minimum cruise speed to conserve fuel since the jamming started, they're going to run out at about nine forty-seven," she said.

Frank Malone thought of his daughter.

No, there wasn't time for that.

He had to concentrate on facts, not emotion.

He looked at his watch and saw it was 8:49.

TWA 22 Heavy . . . no, *the first plane* . . . would crash in fifty-eight minutes.

# 22

MORE POLICE.

Different ones.

New York City cops, not Port Authority patrolmen.

Staub recognized their garb and insignia at once. He was expert in split-second identification of the various uniformed police in thirty-nine countries. He could pick out each of the five kinds of local or national cops in Paris in the blink of an eye, and knew the multiple uniformed forces of Rome and Madrid equally well. With their fewer police organizations, New York and other North American cities were child's play by comparison.

Looking down from the balcony at the crowded ground floor of the International Arrivals Building, Staub watched the newly arrived cops try to control an increasingly restive and noisy throng. It wasn't only journalists who grasped the significance of the additional police. Almost everyone below understood now.

This was no "routine security exercise."

Something *real* was happening.

Why didn't the cops or airport staff explain what it was?

The people downstairs seemed to be impatient and irate but not frantic. None of them had connected the lateness of the inbound planes with the unusual number of cops—*yet*, Staub thought. The waiting crowd didn't know that not one airliner had landed at or taken off from Kennedy, La Guardia or Newark in fifty minutes. The fools had no idea that the three major airports and the lives of thousands in planes above them were in the hands of ruthless revolutionaries.

They would probably find out soon.

Somebody would let slip a hint or phrase while telephoning a spouse or lover, or perhaps a minor civil servant might tip off a journalist to curry favor.

Once the nasty secret was out, there wouldn't be a crowd downstairs in this terminal. It would suddenly become a mob. Staub had considered calling a radio station himself to put pressure on the authorities. While it might be entertaining to see the arrogant Americans panic, he had decided that a hysterical mob in the terminal through which the liberated prisoners of U.S. imperialism would depart might create *some* sort of problem.

That would be unacceptable.

Willi Staub detested uncertainty.

It meant less than total control, which was unthinkable.

He still had the terrible nightmares about what his father had done to him when he was four and five. Each time the boy had made "too much" noise or broken some other rule, he'd been locked in the closet for hours.

In the dark.

Totally helpless in a situation he couldn't affect at all.

At first he'd beaten at the door until his little hands bled, and he'd screamed and screamed. Then he realized that his father wanted that, so he stopped and sat silent in the blackness. He wouldn't let anyone use darkness, confinement or anything else to terrify him.

Ever again.

Anywhere.

He would have the control, and he would move freely everywhere.

Now the terrified child had come out of the closet to terrify others. He had the control. He did what *he* wanted wherever *he* pleased, and he had no second thoughts. Staub never wondered why he'd chosen a life that forced him to move so frequently and far, one that barred even the idea of a home. As he had told two—or was it three—affectionate women in recent years, he hardly recalled anything about his own youth and home anyway.

Women were often curious about such things, Staub thought as he saw a quartet of cops get onto the escalator. Within a week after the start of the most ordinary sexual liaison, females showed a compulsive interest in a man's past—back to his childhood. They'd been disappointed when Willi Staub explained that he didn't remember his. One long-legged Swedish woman had foolishly suggested that he might be repressing those memories.

Now Staub felt sweat beading on his forehead. It must be that the stupid Americans had the heat turned up too high here as they did in so many public places. Yes, that must be it. That and the effect of the bulletproof vest under his shirt were causing him to perspire.

Sure, he'd wash his face with cold water.

It was probably cooler in the lavatory anyway, and he'd be away from the body heat and cigarette smoke rising from the agitated crowd below. He'd use the men's room on this floor, of course. There was no point in descending into the throng and main group of police.

The counterfeit priest glanced left and right "casually" before he started walking. Some dozen yards to the right was a couple whose clothes suggested a suburban middle-class life. The trim woman had a determined smile, a "good" flannel skirt and a Bloomingdale's shopping bag. Eight or ten years older, the barrel-chested man in the tweed jacket had the hungry wary eyes that Staub knew so well. Their message was unmistakable.

This man was some sort of cop.

And he was working, a detective on stakeout.

She had to be a cop, too, the terrorist reasoned as he walked away from them. He had no reason to believe that they were hunting him . . . and none that they weren't. The prudent thing was to stroll unobtrusively out of sight before they noticed him at all.

When he was safely beyond their view, Staub mopped his glistening brow with a handkerchief. The airliners would start dropping in less than an hour, he thought. Then it would be his enemies who'd sweat.

When the first plane crashed in flames, that high-tech pyre would be a clear signal that Number One was not bluffing. Then the federal government would rush the other four to Kennedy immediately, and there would be no further resistance from the stunned Americans. A nation of weaklings, they would do anything to avoid more loss of human life.

Still damp with perspiration, he made his way to the nearest men's lavatory. Having meticulously reconnoitered every public area of this building three times in preparing his attack, he knew the exact location of each security post, fire alarm, shop, newsstand, snack bar, toilet, stairway and exit. He'd drawn floor plans and studied them again and again until he had memorized every detail. With the help of his undercover agent, he knew the layout of the control tower and Cab just as well.

When Staub entered the men's room, he automatically scanned the chamber in routine self-defense. The door of one booth was closed, and two black men in their thirties were chatting amiably at the urinals. They were speaking French. Their accents had a Caribbean lilt.

Haiti? Martinique? Guadeloupe? St. Martin?

It didn't matter. They finished and stepped forward to the sinks to wash their hands. Staub mopped the sweat from his forehead again and walked slowly to one of the urinals. He should have done this earlier, he thought as he reached for his zipper.

The ebony-skinned men from the Caribbean were laughing as they left the lavatory. Having emptied his bladder, Staub felt more comfortable when he zipped the black trousers closed again. He sighed as he approached the sink.

The cold water felt good on his face.

It was soothing and somehow reassuring. He splashed handfuls of the refreshing liquid across his hot forehead, then into his eyes. The chilled wetness took him away from the total tension for a few seconds. He *almost* relaxed. He was starting to when he heard a toilet flush and a cubicle door unlock *behind* him.

That jerked him back to reality. He couldn't see or cope with whoever was at his back, and he didn't like that. His body reacted more extremely, stiffening as it braced for violence. Sweeping the water from his eyes, Staub forced himself not to spin on his heel in self-defense. With his vision returning to normal, he looked up slowly into the mirror in front of him.

The round-faced man in rimless glasses behind him was dressed in the same black clothes and white Roman collar that Staub wore. With the odds against two clerical impostors meeting enormous, Willi Staub decided that the other man was a genuine priest.

There was no reason to panic.

Staub had successfully impersonated Catholic clergymen several times before.

He'd be pleasant, brief and out the door in fifty or sixty seconds. It would be easy.

So the terrorist smiled.

"Good evening," he said affably and strode toward the paper towel dispenser.

"Good evening," the real priest replied in a sturdy baritone voice. While Staub was briskly drying his hands with a towel, the cleric walked to the sink and turned on the hot water.

"Which parish are you with?" he asked as he soaped his plump hands.

The terrorist was ready for the question. He had created and memorized a complete cover story, right down to where he'd gone to high school.

"I'm at Saint Agnes," the man who liked to kill lied. "Not here . . . in Portland."

"Maine?"

That was too near. The other Portland twenty-six hundred miles away was safer.

"Oregon," Staub parried. "Nice people. You ought to visit us sometime."

Frowning, the priest turned to face Willi Staub.

"I don't understand," the cleric announced.

"What?"

"For the past six years, I've been the pastor of Saint Agnes in Portland, Oregon . . . and I've never seen you before."

Staub smiled again—big.

"Let me explain," he chuckled as he stepped closer.

His left hand was filled with a wad of paper towels. His right was inside his jacket, closing on a black plastic fountain pen in the breast pocket. He was grinning as he took out the writing instrument.

"It's really very simple," the terrorist assured the puzzled priest. Staub pressed the catch on the pen. A five-inch-long ice-pick blade of tempered surgical steel suddenly flicked from the plastic cylinder.

The pastor of Saint Agnes Roman Catholic Church in Portland, Oregon, opened his mouth to scream. He didn't.

Staub crammed a fistful of towels between his open lips at the same moment that the lethal needle penetrated his chest. The terrorist rammed the weapon in with all his strength, plunging it expertly between the priest's ribs into his heart.

Staub knew exactly where to insert the needle. He had read books on anatomy, paying special attention to the head and heart. He knew that a human heart's size varied with the body size of the person, and that the heart usually weighed one tenth of 1 percent of the individual's total. He also knew how to stop a heart—forever.

The priest grunted as the steel sliver tore into him. His body shook and his eyes bulged. The pain was awful. It was pure fire. His mouth opened wider in a frantic attempt to cry out, but only a choked groan emerged. Staub pushed the wad of paper back into his victim's throat.

Deep inside, blood was leaking from a tear in the mortally wounded man's heart. Staub knew that from his anatomy studies, and he knew what to do next—quickly. The assassin drew four inches of the needle out, twisted the grip sharply and rammed the metal back in full at another angle.

This would make another hole in the aorta.

With blood gouting from two tears, the pastor from Portland should be dead within ninety seconds.

Now the priest tottered and moaned, his astonished eyes glazed and his legs failed. He kept making those muffled animal noises as Staub pushed him back, opened the door of a cubicle and shoved him into the toilet. The dying man's vision was blurring, and his head slumped to the right as his last strength leaked away.

Staub looked around and nodded.

There was no blood on the floor.

If the terrorist handled it right, the corpse wouldn't be found until after Staub and the other revolutionaries were a thousand miles out over the Atlantic.

"A *million* to one," Staub thought aloud. "The odds against my running into a priest from Saint Agnes of Portland,

Oregon, here . . . tonight . . . had to be *at least* a million to one. Tough for you, Father."

There was something else to be done.

Willi Staub didn't take chances.

Stepping aside so no spout of crimson from the tiny hole would stain his clothes, Staub removed the ice pick from the priest's chest and plunged it deep into the unconscious cleric's left ear. It wasn't sadism. Staub's target was the brain. This would make sure that the man from Oregon would never tell anyone about the fake Catholic priest at Kennedy.

Now Staub carefully withdrew the needle and retracted it into the false pen. He locked the door of the booth from inside, lowered himself to the floor and tried to slide out.

The dead man's feet were in the way, and it was a struggle to nudge them aside. Now the corpse was shifting on the toilet. Staub had to maneuver warily. One mistake would dump the body on top of him.

Staub was sheeted with perspiration again.

He had to hurry. Someone might come into this lavatory at any moment. Staub had to get out now, immediately. If he didn't, he might be seen by other people—too many to kill. That would put Staub and the whole operation in acute jeopardy.

He had to get away from this corpse, this room, at once.

Every second was crucial.

There wasn't much space between the bottom of the door and the floor—about a foot. It would be a very tight squeeze at best. His attire was far from the best for this. The bullet-proof vest and the black overcoat added an inch and a half or two inches. He had only an inch to spare at the most.

Wriggling and twisting slowly, Staub managed to work his way out of the overcoat. That might do it, he thought. Free of that bulk, he should be able to slide out on his back under the door. Then he'd reach in, pull out the coat and leave the lavatory swiftly.

Even under normal circumstances, when he was alone in

a lavatory cubicle, Willi Staub felt uncomfortable. It was like being in some sort of a cell. Or a *closet*. Confinement in any small space had infuriated him for a long time. Now he was stuck in this goddam booth with the body of some pious fool, barely able to breathe.

There wasn't a moment to waste. He couldn't take much more of this invisible unbearable squeezing. Now he was on his back, drenched in sweat from scalp to toe and panting. He took a deep gulp of air, exhaled and began to slide out under the door.

The first few inches were easy. Then he had to turn his head sideways. He moved forward again. His entire head and neck were beyond the barrier. In another thirty or forty seconds he would be free.

He writhed forward another inch . . . and another.

It would be all right.

He'd be entirely out of the small bad place in a few more moments. The punishment would be over.

Staub slid on—and stopped. He couldn't advance any farther. *Something*—maybe the bulletproof vest—raised his shoulders just a bit too high. Maybe he could wriggle through by very small movements back and forth, the ones you used to park a car in a barely large enough space. He started to try that.

Then he heard the door to the corridor open . . . and voices. He reacted instantly. He began to slide and twist back. He had to be entirely inside before the new arrivals noticed a head and neck—a neck in a white Roman collar—protruding from under the door of the booth.

A little more.

Push just a bit harder.

No, *harder*.

He couldn't move—forward or backward. He was trapped.

In a few moments, the men who had just entered would see him. He struggled with the door—and something else.

Burning up from inside him was a terrible horror of the cell that awaited him, the years of cramped confinement, the helpless rage at being entirely in *their* power.

Maybe it was the dread that did it. Suddenly he was able to slip back—just half an inch. As he tried again, he heard a sound that he couldn't quite identify. Whatever it was, the closet was more important. He wouldn't let anyone put him in *there* again.

Another inch.

One more push. Fueled by desperation, he twisted and strained and slid inside to safety. Soaked with sweat, he lay there gasping. He had made it. No one could see him here. No one could hurt him now.

Then the body fell on him.

Some 190 pounds, dead weight.

It was maddening. Staub wanted to shout, to hit and kick and bite like a small crazed boy. Staub wanted to get rid of this thing that was pressing him down, confining him, making his throat knot and filling his mouth with the bitter taste of bile. Staub knew that it would be senseless to lash out at a corpse, but it took a major effort not to do that.

The terrorist fought down the impulse, and sighed. He could hear his heart pounding. The body on top of him was heavy, but Willi Staub could endure it. He had survived worse, he recalled grimly as he turned his head two inches.

He was peering directly into the dead priest's open eyes.

An inch away, they still showed astonishment and pain. Staub studied them curiously. He had never had the time or reason to peer closely into his victims' eyes before. There wasn't a hint of anything resembling a soul, the man who liked killing noted with satisfaction. He loathed the very idea of souls.

Now Staub heard that sound again. This time he recognized it. Yes, *kissing*. The men whose shoes he could barely discern out of the corner of his eye were *kissing*. Now they were whispering to each other. Staub didn't even try to make out the words, for these lovers were of no interest to him. All he wanted was for them to leave.

When they walked out twenty seconds later, he pushed the corpse up and back onto the toilet seat. Then he pulled a long strip of paper from the roll, dried his face and glanced around for somewhere to dispose of the wad of damp tissue. He couldn't just toss it on the floor. Unlike so many Americans, Willi Staub was no litterer.

So he crammed the balled-up toilet paper into the open mouth of the dead man. That would show his contempt for all religion, he thought bitterly. He listened again . . . heard nothing. He took off his jacket, removed the bulletproof vest and tried again to get out of the booth.

This time he succeeded. He tugged out the coat, suit jacket and protective vest and put them on as fast as he could. He glanced in the mirror, cursed and reached back into the cubicle for the black hat. He donned the fedora, adjusted the angle and strode from the chamber.

When he was thirty yards away, Staub looked at his wristwatch.

He saw that it was 8:56, and nodded in contentment.

They probably wouldn't find the corpse until morning, when he'd be an ocean away.

# 23

THIS WASN'T the worst job in the Soviet Navy, Grilov thought. But it was probably one of the dreariest.

His ears hurt from the headset, his stomach was queasy and he missed his wife back in Leningrad. For two and a half months, the eleven-hundred-ton fishing trawler had been slowly circling a point eighty miles northeast of New London, Connecticut.

Around and around at six knots.

Through choppy seas and steadily deteriorating weather.

Going nowhere.

This trawler wasn't here to fish, and a lot of people in the U.S. Navy knew it. With all the antennas and other electronic gear that adorned the deck and masts, it was obvious that the vessel was one of the scores of "spy trawlers" that the U.S.S.R. operated around the world. Smaller than the other intelligence gathering ships of the Okean, Lentra, Mayak, Primorye and Nicolai Zubor classes, the trawlers did their jobs.

Some of the fake fishing craft tracked NATO naval exercises. Others monitored radio traffic out of major U.S. and British bases or stalked the Western powers' submarines to record their sonar "prints" while studying their speed and tactics. New London was one of the home ports for the most heavily armed American undersea raiders, submersible battleships that could each throw enough nuclear-tipped rockets to kill a dozen cities.

Petty Officer Third Class Sergei Grilov was no missile expert. He wasn't one of the trawler's eighteen electronics warfare specialists either. He was a competent radio technician with a working knowledge of English. His job was to monitor—from four P.M. to midnight, six days a week—the frequencies used in this region by the U.S. Navy and Air Force.

Operating an efficient computer-controlled scanner like those that served the electronic eavesdropping unit at the embassy in Washington, Grilov systematically patrolled the airwaves and taped the American transmissions. The work was strictly routine, often boring.

The significance of the messages was not his responsibility. The trawler carried a team of cryptographers and analysts, all officers of the Glavnoye Razvedyvatelnoye Upravlenie—the Chief Intelligence Directorate of the General Staff. Those GRU specialists decoded and evaluated the transmissions for daily reports radioed home. They were probably being recorded and deciphered by the Americans, Grilov told himself. He was right.

Most of the messages that Grilov's scanner detected did not deal with anything important. Aware that the trawlers were listening, the Americans were cautious. All the U.S. missile submarines and some aircraft operated under radio silence, receiving coded communications but barely replying. Messages were often squirted by ultrafast transmitters in five- or six-second bursts of garbled sounds.

Tonight there wasn't much radio traffic at all.

Another dull evening, Sergei Grilov thought wearily.

There were at least ninety more ahead before a replacement trawler arrived and he could start home. It was wiser to take it step by step. It was now 8:57, so his shift would end in three hours and thirteen minutes. That was easier to face than ninety days.

Then he heard the voice.

"Tomahawk to Hot Rod Four."

Staring at the dial, Grilov saw that he was tuned to this month's U.S. Air Force command frequency.

"Tomahawk to Hot Rod Four. Tomahawk to Hot Rod Four."

The Russian radio operator listened intently, waiting for Hot Rod Four to reply.

Not a word.

"Five seconds to Blue Button," the metallic voice continued. "Commencing countdown. Five . . . four . . . three . . . two . . . one . . . *now*."

All Grilov heard after that was clatter, electronic garbage. Blue Button apparently meant switching to scrambler. After twenty seconds, even that jumble of sound disappeared.

They had changed frequencies.

The trawler's scanner chased and found them. Another torrent of distortion poured through Grilov's earphones, confirming that the American scrambling equipment was still in use. The experts at GRU headquarters might be able to make sense of this noise, the radio operator told himself. They had some very sophisticated machines there.

Suddenly there was silence. Grilov swept up and down the dial, and found nothing. The incident was finished. He glanced at his watch, and saw that it had lasted forty-nine seconds. Tomahawk? *Of course*, Tomahawk was the code word for the headquarters of the U.S.A.F.'s Tactical Air Command, he recalled.

Petty Officer Grilov did not remember what Hot Rod Four was.

It wasn't his fault.

Neither he nor anyone else on the trawler had ever heard of it before.

# 24

*THE STORM* continued to scourge the great city.

In fact, the snow was falling more rapidly now.

Even in good weather, the streets of lower Manhattan around the Municipal Building and City Hall were practically deserted in the evening. Tonight only a few taxis floated by like ghosts, carrying home late workers from Wall Street offices. There were no pedestrians at all.

That was good, the watchers thought.

They didn't want anyone to see what they were about to do.

There were eight sedans near the rear entrance of the modern brick building at 150 Park Row. Six were lined up in the back alley. The others flanked the alley's exit onto Pearl Street. All eight had their headlights out, their motors running. The exhaust fumes swirled in odd stunted curves as the

icy gusts caught them, but the men standing beside the cars
didn't notice it.

With eyes as cold as the night, they were waiting and
watching. Some looked north up Pearl. Half a dozen peered
south. The drivers in the alley stared at the door to 150 Park
Row. No one spoke. The only sounds were the wind and the
rumble of automobile engines.

The men standing near the cars were armed and angry.
Each had a .38-caliber pistol in a shoulder holster, and seven
carried submachine guns. They were FBI agents. Their grim
faces showed concern and bitterness.

They didn't want to be here.

They didn't want to do this.

The building at 150 Park Row housed the Metropolitan
Correctional Center, the New York City facility of the Bureau
of Prisons of the goddam Department of Justice. The Department of Justice of the United States of America, not some
puny banana republic or one of those weak sister govern-
ments in Europe. A major unit of the U.S. Department of
Justice itself, the FBI was supposed to put criminals into jails
like the Metropolitan Correctional Center—not let them out.

This thing tonight was disgraceful.

Every agent in the street and in the cars knew it.

Sooner or later, somewhere, somehow, the terrorists who
were forcing them to do this would pay. No one and no organization could humiliate the Bureau. No matter what or how
long it took, the bastards would be identified and hunted
down. It was more than a question of proper law enforcement. It was a matter of professional pride.

And male dignity, too. More than a little.

The rear door to the jail opened. Two more special agents
stepped out, submachine guns at the ready. After they
scanned the alley for several seconds, they gestured to someone inside the doorway. Now four men—all in handcuffs—
walked out into the snowstorm.

Carlos Arroza.

Ibrahim Farzi.

Arnold Lloyd.

Julio Sanchez.

Another five FBI men hurried out behind them. While several of the agents who had been watching raised their eyes and weapons to cover nearby roofs, others opened the curbside rear doors of four of the sedans. The handcuffed prisoners shuddered under the impact of the snow and cold wind.

"Get in. Get in," an impatient FBI inspector ordered.

Federal agents swiftly separated the prisoners, guided them to the automobiles and nudged-helped them inside. Then the FBI operatives took their assigned places in the cars. It had all been planned in detail. Four sedans would each carry three agents and one of the handcuffed men. The other vehicles would ride shotgun, two in front and a pair behind.

The inspector scanned the alley and walked to Pearl Street. He looked north and south for several seconds before he nodded.

"Seems okay," he said.

"It's *wrong*," the tall agent beside him disagreed harshly.

The inspector understood what he meant.

"The order came from the White House," he reminded.

"It's wrong and you *know* it's wrong."

The inspector shrugged.

"I didn't hear that, Tom," he replied and pointed at the first sedan. The angry operative got into the back as the inspector slid in beside the driver. Then the convoy commander picked up the radio.

"Communications check," he said into the instrument.

Each of the sedans reported in curtly.

"Good. Drive carefully and stay alert. Let's roll."

The drivers turned on their headlights. A few moments later they put their cars in gear and started out for John F. Kennedy International Airport.

Other men were also preparing to go there.

They weren't enthusiastic about the idea either.

They weren't starting from Manhattan. They were fourteen miles on the far side of Kennedy at the Coast Guard air base at Floyd Bennett Field. Trudging through the slashing storm, they approached the twin-rotor H-65 helicopter.

"In this weather?" Ensign Vincent Babbitt asked. "With all those damn jets tearing around up there, blind as bats? You really think it's a good idea?"

"It's a *terrible* idea," Lieutenant Ernesto Saldana replied. "You got a better one?"

Babbitt shook his head.

"I'm not scared, you know," he declared loudly.

"I am, Vince. Anyone with half a brain would be. Get in the chopper."

They climbed up into the search-and-rescue helicopter, brushed the snow from their faces and saw that Aviation Survivalman Luther King was already at his post beside the hoisting gear. When Saldana flashed him a thumbs-up greeting, King nodded and returned it silently. Then the two pilots made their way to their seats up front.

"Shit," Babbitt said gloomily as he began to buckle his harness.

"Cheer up, Vince," Saldana urged. "We're going to be heroes."

"There was a fuel line problem with this bird last week," the uneasy junior officer replied. "Christ, I hope they fixed it."

"Here's where we find out," Saldana answered.

They went through the preflight routine carefully but more quickly than usual. This was a major and acute emergency. When they'd run down the checklist, the senior pilot started the engines. The rotors began to move slowly, cutting swaths through the tumbling snow like giant scimitars.

The roar of the jet engines grew louder.

They could feel the surge of power.

Now the big blades were whirling faster. The Aerospatiale H-65 was a strong and sturdy machine that could handle bad weather. Everything was all right.

"Here we go, Vince," Saldana said.

Suddenly there was a spluttering coughing sound.

Then both engines died.

# 25

*THE SOUND* was unpleasant. It was meant to be. This ugly noise had been selected because it would command immediate attention.

It did. When the special telephone that linked The Cab to the FBI in Manhattan began buzzing insistently, every head in the chamber turned toward the source of the annoying sound. A moment later, Hamilton and the FAA people watched the detective lift the beige receiver.

"Malone," he announced bluntly.

"One moment, please," an unfamiliar voice replied.

As he waited, Malone saw that the others in The Cab were looking and listening. Without animosity, he automatically shifted to face the window so they couldn't hear what he was saying.

Now another voice came from the phone. Malone recognized the accent and the speaker immediately. The voice belonged to the air force general in the command post beneath the Pentagon.

"Is this line secure?" Sloat tested with ritual caution.

"Maybe. Where's the Sentry?"

"We're trying *everything*. We even called Tinker. That's the main nest for these birds."

Frank Malone shook his head angrily.

Typical military by-the-book crap. It was ridiculous to seek help from distant Tinker Air Force Base in Oklahoma just because it was the E-3A wing's headquarters. With those heavily loaded Boeings flying at no more than five hundred and ten miles an hour, Tinker was more than two and a half hours from the besieged New York area airports.

"Can't you get a plane from Langley?" Malone demanded.

"We're working on it," Sloat assured. "One should be taking off very soon."

"How goddam soon? When will it get here?"

"We estimate ten sixteen."

Malone flinched.

Not soon enough.

If Annie Green's numbers were right, TWA 22 would run out of fuel at 9:47. Several other airliners would fall within a dozen minutes after that—well before the E-3A arrived.

"One more thing," Sloat continued quickly. "Some woman phoned from ONI to ask about you. She'd already talked to the FBI, but she wanted to double-check. Gave me a message for you."

ONI—the Office of Naval Intelligence—Sea Sweep.

Had they identified the voice on the tape?

"What's the message?"

"It's short—one word. She insisted on spelling it—twice."

"What word?"

"V . . . e . . . n . . . o . . . m. Venom."

Frank Malone nodded.

It figured.

*Staub.*

Venom was the U.S. intelligence community's code name for savage, tricky Willi Staub, a cunning and meticulous monster whose mind was as dangerous as his pistol. He was responsible for hundreds of deaths.

But Malone wasn't the least bit intimidated.

He nodded again, oddly content.

Number One was no longer nameless, faceless, mysterious.

He had an identity, a size, a shape and a past. There were fat files on Willi Staub. They included more than data on his artificial right eye, known associates and usual weapons. They bulged with details of his methods, disguises, language skills and operating patterns.

There was also a special "personality study." A biographical summary, a psychological profile and a motivational analysis of his political views and target selections filled many pages in that inch-thick dossier. It was one of five classified reports on major terrorists that the FBI had secretly distributed to chiefs of key U.S. counterterrorist units twelve days before the bombing of Libya.

Malone had read and reread his copies carefully. He had learned a lot about Willi Staub. While it obviously wasn't everything, it was enough to make the detective feel better about this duel. He knew much more about Staub than the wily terrorist knew about him.

The odds were changing.

But time was running out. It was 9:03 now. Malone had only forty-four minutes to avert a massacre.

"*Venom*," the general repeated. "She said to call her if you didn't understand."

"Okay," Malone replied noncommittally. "Anything else?"

"Just that I hope our bird does the job for you."

"Me, too," the detective lied.

If Staub had a spy listening, the untruth might convince the eavesdropper that Malone was still counting on the AWACS plane. Maybe an aircraft that couldn't arrive in time would distract or confuse the enemy. Illusion could be just as dangerous as reality in this kind of war, Frank Malone reflected as he hung up the telephone.

Then he saw that Wilber was back in The Cab. Reflected in the window that Malone faced, the FAA executive and Annie Green were speaking earnestly. As the detective turned, they walked toward him.

"Any word from Washington?" Wilber asked nervously.

"Nothing important. Where've you been?"

"My office. Since you think it's safer to phone from there, I went down to call Newark and La Guardia."

It made sense. But that didn't mean it was true.

"Call about what?" Malone questioned.

"The whole situation. Their ILS was blasted at exactly the same time our gear went."

"Of course," Malone said irritably. "Did they get any phone calls?"

"One each. A man who sounded Hispanic said their inbound planes were being held hostage, and he'd get back with his terms. He didn't."

Malone nodded.

Only one call each to Newark and La Guardia—another piece for the puzzle.

Staub was concentrating on Kennedy. JFK International Airport would be the main and final battleground. Malone had suspected that from the moment Staub ordered the getaway jet to be ready there.

Wilber looked at the detective, waiting for curse or comment.

Malone said nothing.

"We've got to do *something*," the FAA official erupted. "When will that Coast Guard chopper get here?"

"I don't know," Malone replied.

Wilber shook his head in frustration, and turned to the nearby cluster of controllers. They didn't look cool or confident anymore. It was the uncertainty in their faces that troubled Wilber the most. No air traffic operation could survive if the controllers didn't believe, totally, in the system and themselves.

"I'll be right back," he told Malone and hurried to speak to the worried controllers.

Malone watched him and wondered.

When Pete Wilber left The Cab, had he phoned only the two airports?

Had he made a *third* call?

And there was the other question, Malone thought with a frown. Annbelle Green saw the clouded look in his eyes.

"What is it?" she asked.

"Nothing."

"You don't lie that well, Frank."

"A lot better than I used to," he replied bitterly.

Maybe it was the terrible stress of the nightmare situation.

It could have been annoyance with his endless free floating suspicion and security obsession.

Whatever it was, her patience and tolerance were exhausted.

"Don't waste your time, Frank," she told him. "I don't treat out-patients anymore, so just tell me what's wrong."

Malone considered her angry demand for several seconds.

"It's the helicopter," he said. "Wilber wasn't here when you sent the request on the teleprinter. How did he know?"

"I told him while you were on the hot line."

The detective frowned again.

"You weren't supposed to tell anyone," he reminded.

"For God's sake, Frank, I've known him for years."

"Not *anyone*," Malone insisted.

"Okay, mark it down to human error," she replied defensively. "Being so damn perfect yourself, I guess you wouldn't know anything about human error."

"I'm a cop, Annie. Human error is my business. As for having all the answers, I don't even know half the questions. Please don't fight me," he appealed. "I need your help."

Maybe he had changed. He was admitting that he was vulnerable, she thought. Suddenly she felt vulnerable herself. She hadn't done that in a long time. In the three hard years since her husband died, she had been wary and safe— and quite alone.

Leaning closer, Malone spoke again in a low intense voice.

"You've helped *so much* already. Please don't stop now."

She looked into his wide blue eyes, and she remembered.

A split second later, she found herself wondering about his wife. Then Annie Green felt embarrassed—and a little afraid. In this situation, such thoughts could be very dangerous.

Who his wife was and what she was like were none of Annie Green's business. Her business was officially defined in a bulky FAA manual under Air Traffic Control: Tower Watch Supervisor. That was all she really was to Captain Frank Malone tonight. And there wasn't going to be any tomorrow for Annie Green and Frank Malone, she reflected. There couldn't be.

Misinterpreting her silence, Malone thought she was resisting.

"*Please*," he pressed.

She forced herself to smile.

"All right, Frank," she sighed a moment before the teleprinter started stuttering again.

Some 180 yards away, Robert Raymond and Jeffrey Raymond were ignoring each other in a public lavatory. It wasn't the usual avoidance of eye contact that prevails in men's toilets around the globe. This was the age thing. Lanky Robert Raymond was nearly sixteen. Peering into the large mirror, he was much more interested in parting his flaxen hair just right than in paying attention to his precocious nine-year-old brother. Their father would arrive any minute now on British Airways's Flight 126 from London, and the teen-ager wanted to look neat.

The younger boy wasn't thinking about his appearance. He was facing the toilet stalls, not the mirror. As usual, he was focused on the calculator he held in his left hand. Now chubby Jeffrey Raymond tapped the device's keys once more. As he considered the numbers, his lips parted just enough to expose the gleaming metal of his dental braces.

"Uh huh," he said.

Then he heard the loud thump.

Something heavy had fallen—nearby.

He glanced around the chamber, saw nothing on the floor and noticed that one stall's door was closed. Whatever fell had to be inside there. He studied the door for several seconds before he called to his brother.

"Robby?"

Humming softly to himself, the teenager continued fine-tuning the part in his hair.

"*Robby!*"

"What is it?" the older boy asked impatiently.

Comb in hand, Robert Raymond turned. He saw his brother pointing at the bottom of the closed door. Something was protruding out from under it. After a few seconds, the teenager recognized it as the tip of a black shoe.

"He's probably had too much to drink," the almost-six-teen-year-old announced authoritatively. "Just sleeping it off. Nothing to *worry* about."

Then he wasn't so sure.

A very thin stream was oozing slowly from the closed booth out onto the tile floor. Recalling his brief glimpse of a gory corpse in the safe-driving film shown at his high school last month, Robert Raymond stared at the dark red rivulet uneasily.

The colors matched.

Yes, this could be blood.

# 26

IN THE COCKPIT of the crown prince's Concorde, Captain Pierre Bersoux studied the instrument panels again, very carefully.

Pressure altimeter *and* radio altimeter.

Horizon and control surface angle displays.

Turbine temperatures, engine horsepower and airspeed gauges.

Rate of turn display and stall warning indicator.

Fuel gauge for the fifteen collector, trim and main tanks.

"*Merde!*" the former Air France pilot whispered tensely.

It wasn't easy here in the cockpit's left seat now. This was the place of command and, of course, responsibility. The thin, forty-three-year-old Parisian usually had no trouble with either, but tonight was different. Guiding a Concorde through a nasty winter storm at only ninety miles an hour above stall speed made him acutely uncomfortable, almost irritated. Cruising so slowly saved fuel, he thought, but this supersonic machine really wasn't designed for *that* sort of flying.

Being so late tonight also troubled Pierre Bersoux—a lot. The Tarmani prince who employed him at $12,000 a month had very rigid ideas about promptness, notions that seemed more North American than Near Eastern. Bersoux suspected that Omar had acquired this attitude at business school in the United States. Wherever he got it, Omar saw on-time arrival as an essential part of the perfect service that was his royal due and he'd accept nothing less.

Insisting on perfect service was a family tradition. Omar's famous and old-fashioned grandfather had ordered that limbs be severed from servants who disappointed him, the French pilot recalled as he eyed the fuel gauge once more. Being a sophisticated modern prince with an M.B.A., Omar simply amputated the offender's salary and comprehensive major medical coverage—firing instantly any employee who didn't do everything as and when expected.

Bersoux had no idea as to where he might get another $144,000 a year job, let alone that excellent health insurance. He also had no way to predict how soon the Concorde could land at Kennedy. What he did know was that he'd never been even half this late before.

The threat to his job was growing every minute.

No, every damn second.

Pierre Bersoux decided that he had to do something *right now*. He had to demonstrate his professional poise and expertise before the prince lost his temper. It must be done adroitly, of course. The pilot silently rehearsed his words twice before he pressed the intercom switch. Some thirty seconds later, Omar's secretary put him through to the prince.

"Yes, Captain?"

"Your Highness, I'm sorry to interrupt you but there's still no communication with Kennedy. Since our radio was re-checked completely only four days ago, it has to be this storm or *their* transmitters."

Blaming the Americans might deflect Omar's wrath.

"Go on, Captain."

"Two things, Your Highness. First, it is not clear when this *unusual* situation might be corrected," Bersoux said. "To buy us flying time, I've been cruising at much reduced speed to stretch out our fuel. But even at this low speed, our tanks have only enough for forty minutes more."

"Second?" the prince asked coolly.

"We are not alone up here, Your Highness. There could be twenty-five or thirty other planes circling within a few miles. In this storm, we can't see them and they can't see us. A pilot in one of those aircraft might make a mistake that could affect us."

"Are we in danger?"

Bersoux paused to recall the words that he had selected.

"Let me put it this way, Your Highness. Being totally committed to your safety," he declared virtuously, "I believe that it might be prudent—*oui, très prudent*—to proceed at once to an airport where weather and radio conditions are normal."

"Which airport?"

"The scheduled alternate in our flight plan is Philadelphia."

Omar weighed the choices for several seconds.

"I'd rather not," he said. "I have a meeting at our U.N. mission in New York tonight, and breakfast with the U.S. delegate at the Waldorf tomorrow at nine. Driving the hundred miles up from Philadelphia at night through a snow-storm might be almost as risky anyway. Let's try it here for another fifteen minutes."

That would be cutting it unpleasantly close, but one did not argue with the crown prince of Tarman. Well, Pierre Bersoux didn't.

"As you wish, Your Highness," the worried pilot replied through clenched lips.

Some half a mile below on a back street in the industrial section of Long Island City, a large truck eased to a stop beside a telephone booth. With the recently-tuned and lubricated engine purring, the driver sat silent in the cab, enjoying the warmth of the heater. He liked it a lot more than the ugly sounds of Ito's jammer spewing from the radio on the seat next to him.

The swarthy man behind the wheel was twenty-seven years old, both strong and determined and quite skilled in techniques of causing death and destruction. He had left dental school in Lebanon to learn covert warfare at the secret South Yemen training camp where he met Willi Staub. The driver's middle-class parents didn't object to his giving up dentistry for arson, explosion and murder. They couldn't. They had been dismembered six weeks earlier by a huge car bomb that massacred fifty-three people.

They were all buried outside Beirut on the day before the beginning of Ramadan, four years ago. The driver had been to many countries since then. This was his first visit to the United States. He despised it, of course, but he was pleased that Hugo had chosen him for this bold operation. He still thought of Willi Staub as Hugo, the name Staub had used while teaching terrorist tactics in Yemen.

The man behind the wheel looked at the dashboard clock, and saw that it was time to report. He shuddered in the winter blast as he got out of the truck, and he shuddered as he hurried through the flailing snow to the booth. He stepped inside a dozen seconds before the telephone bell sounded.

Four rings. Then it stopped, as he expected.

It sounded again a few moments later, and he lifted the receiver.

They spoke in Arabic.

"Early," the driver said.

"Grave," Staub replied in correct countersign.

Then he asked about the truck.

"Operating perfectly," the former dental student told him.

The vehicle and the equipment in its large cargo compartment were important to Staub's plan. Staub didn't inquire about the equipment. They had retested it, briefly, only a week earlier in a rural area 160 miles from Kennedy Airport.

"Good. Continue listening and keep to the schedule," Staub ordered.

When the driver reentered the truck, he started the motor and turned on the special radio tuned to the main JFK Tower frequency. He scowled under the impact of the torrent of endless electronic chaos roaring from Takeshi Ito's powerful transmitter. The man behind the wheel had never heard of either Ito or his jammer. All he knew was what he himself had to do and when he must do it.

He studied the clock again. According to the schedule, it was time to move on. The conscientious young terrorist put his heavily loaded vehicle in gear and set off on the next leg of his journey. He felt quite confident despite the terrible driving weather. The clever and efficient man whom he knew as Hugo had planned the truck's exact route and timetable all the way to the triumphant escape. They had done three test runs with stopwatches in the past ten evenings to check out every detail and possible problem. It all worked perfectly, so there was nothing to worry about tonight.

At the Coast Guard air station, Ensign Vincent Babbitt was much less optimistic. When the Aerospatiale helicopter failed to rise, Lieutenant Ernesto Saldana had led copilot Babbitt and Survivalman King to a second H-65. Now they were completing the preflight instrument check.

Everything *seemed* all right, but that meant nothing.

The motors on this chopper could fail, too.

Either now or, much worse, up at three thousand feet in the storm.

There was no point in arguing anymore with Saldana, Babbitt brooded. Top man in his class at the Coast Guard Academy, the good-looking young Hispanic had as much nerve as he had charm. Even more important, he had the authority, the command, as senior officer.

They finished the checklist.

"I don't suppose that . . ." Babbitt began, then hesitated.

"Forget it, Vince. You can't *really* be scared," Saldana told him. "Coast Guard's not afraid of anything."

"Suppose we find this damn transmitter. How are we going to tell anybody?" Babbitt demanded. "It's got all our frequencies jammed."

"Good thinking, Vince. I'm proud of you," Saldana replied in a cheerful voice.

"You didn't answer my question, Ernie."

"Ready for takeoff," Saldana said briskly.

The conversation was over, Babbitt realized. Some forty-five seconds later, the engines poured power and the rotors began to turn. They were moving faster . . . faster. Finally, Saldana pulled the control to lift the big search-and-rescue machine off the runway.

Saldana took the H-65 up slowly, guiding the machine in a wide arc toward Kennedy as it rose higher. Strong gusts of wind pushed and jarred the helicopter, and the unrelenting snowfall cut visibility to a scant hundred yards.

"You can't fly a chopper in this," Babbitt insisted.

"I know that," Saldana answered.

But he kept climbing, nursing the Aerospatiale with a sure skill through the buffeting storm. When the altimeter showed twenty-eight hundred feet, he leveled off and flicked the radio switch. Then he began to twist the dial.

It was just as Babbitt had warned.

All the FAA and Coast Guard aviation frequencies were jammed.

"*Now* what do we do?" the copilot demanded.

"What we're paid to do: search and rescue," Saldana replied evenly. "Commence search."

Babbitt sighed and shook his head.

Then he turned on the radio direction finder.

The electronic counterattack had begun.

# 27

*IT WAS* a standard "security" formation.

The same one was routinely used to protect Very Important People.

There was, however, one difference.

The four VIPs being escorted tonight were all wearing handcuffs.

The eight FBI sedans rolled through the blizzard in a tight column. They were bunched up with a scant dozen yards between cars so no other vehicle could slip into the convoy. The first and last cars in the column were crowned with flashing lights to warn off anyone else traveling from the city on the Grand Central Parkway tonight.

Seated beside the driver in the convoy's point car, Inspector Barry Kincaid looked out at the billowing storm. There was only one third the usual midevening traffic on this major artery. It was moving at twenty-five miles an hour, half the speed that normally prevailed on this multilane highway.

Going any faster on this slush- and ice-spattered road would be more than risky, Kincaid thought. It would be stupid. Only fools, drunks or people with some extraordinary need to travel would be out on the parkway this night.

Kincaid was a cautious and competent FBI veteran whose intelligence was matched by his self-control. As the column rolled on, he didn't waste a moment on anger or principle or honor. He focused his intelligence on the question of who were the terrorists behind this operation. The prisoners whom the terrorists had demanded represented a variety of interests.

The FALN was skilled with explosives, but the Puerto Rican militants had never used electronic assault before.

The Afrikan People's Army was an urban guerrilla warfare outfit with neither the money nor organization for anything like this.

And the fiery March 13th Brigade was now down to a ragged handful. Recent counterintelligence reports strongly indicated that those few fanatics were on the run.

Maybe it was one of those shadowy Near Eastern groups backed by Iran or Libya or Syria, Kincaid speculated. According to Sea Sweep, those organizations had both ample funds and sophisticated weapons, plus foreign advisors to teach them how to use the gear.

Half a dozen of those outfits had recently been threatening to attack the U.S. mainland. It was hard enough to sort out their grandiose and ambiguous names, the FBI inspector reflected, distinguishing their diverse political causes was even more difficult.

In the next car, forty-eight-year-old Arnold Lloyd wasn't thinking about politics. Since leaving the CIA, he saw himself as a canny businessman, an efficient entrepreneur whose simple cause was Cash. He had sold the poison gas and assassination hardware to Soraq and trained that nation's hit teams purely for money—a great deal of it.

There was $3,410,000 in his secret Swiss account.

He could live nicely on that if he were set free tonight.

Was that what was happening?

Maybe.

The FBI men seemed angry, and the road looked like the Grand Central Parkway—a primary route to New York's major airports. The four prisoners could be on their way to a flight overseas to freedom.

Maybe not.

This ride through the blizzard might be a trick.

After so many years in the treacherous cloak-and-dagger world, Lloyd was instinctively suspicious. The fact that they were on this highway didn't prove anything. The Grand Central Parkway led to many places other than La Guardia and Kennedy.

Where was this convoy going?

Why tonight in such a raging storm?

He might be in mortal danger. His trial was to start in ten days. Maybe he was now being taken from the safety of jail so he wouldn't testify. During two decades with the Agency and four years as an arms and murder merchant, burly balding Arnold Lloyd had lived and learned a lot. He knew many things that *certain people* would not wish him to reveal.

One of those people could be General al-Khalif, Soraq's devious and messianic president-for-life, who had the scruples of a vampire bat and a long history of ordering assassinations. There were quite a few matters and corpses that Arnold Lloyd's biggest customer might not want mentioned in court.

Or the *certain people* might be self-protecting executives in the CIA's covert operations division where Lloyd had worked for so long. In today's political climate, those steely bureaucrats could fear what Lloyd might disclose about dozens of sensitive operations and questions. One was whether those executives had known of and tolerated Arnold Lloyd's dealings with the bloody al-Khalif regime.

Nobody, in or out of any government, would mind if Lloyd and a couple of despised terrorists were slain while "trying to escape." Both the public and the press would be delighted.

Maybe all four prisoners would die when something "happened" to their escape plane five hundred miles out over the deep Atlantic. The pilots—CIA mercenaries— would parachute down to be picked up by a waiting ship. Arnold Lloyd would be silenced—permanently.

There could be some other reason for this unexplained and sudden journey from the city, the businessman who sold death realized. For a few moments he was infuriated that he didn't know. Then he repressed his frustration. Whatever the truth was, he could only watch and wait tensely. He had to be ready for anything at any time, Lloyd realized. His survival was at risk every second now.

Two cars back, Ibrahim Farzi was smiling. He was much younger and less cynical than Lloyd, and full of confidence. He, too, had recognized the highway, and had no doubt that a courageous rescue was being mounted. From the moment of his arrest, the twenty-three-year-old Palestinian had known that his comrades in the holy crusade would not forget him.

It wasn't simply blind faith. The slim, boyish-looking Farzi had been taught a lot about his enemies. These barbaric Western countries were immoral and weak. They had caved in again and again when threatened. Materialist, decadent and cowardly, they had shown themselves willing to pay any price to avoid further bloodshed. Then they lied about it, claiming that they hadn't yielded at all.

The FBI men hadn't said a word about what was happening. Farzi had no idea of what his brethren had done to force his release, and he didn't understand why the other three prisoners were also in the convoy. None of that was important. What mattered was that he'd soon be on his way to rejoin the holy war.

"God is great!" Ibrahim Farzi exulted loudly.

That was when a veteran federal agent and regular church-goer named Heggerty, who was seated to the left of Farzi, controlled an extraordinary impulse to punch him in the mouth.

# 28

IN THE CAB atop the Kennedy Tower, the Port Authority Police lieutenant's radio crackled loudly. Hamilton raised the walkie-talkie and spoke.

"Command Post," he announced.

Then he listened for a dozen seconds. His expression did not change. Only his eyes showed the impact of what he was hearing.

"Where?" he finally asked. "How? No, seal off the room and don't touch anything. Exactly. Not a word about this to anybody—and I mean *anybody*. Say the pipes are broken. I'll take care of that myself. In five minutes."

He put down the radio.

"I think this is for your guys," he told Malone.

"That bad?"

"Worse," Hamilton replied. "It's just what we don't need

tonight. There's a dead priest in a john in the International Arrivals Building. The word is that it looks like homicide."

"*Looks* like?"

"Two small holes in the left side of the chest—maybe an ice pick. Very neat and precise work. Sounds like a pro to me."

Malone nodded before he asked the question.

"Was he robbed?"

"I'll let you know. I'm heading down there now. On the way I'll tell your people about it—unless you'd rather."

"Be my guest," Malone said.

Hamilton thought about the dead priest again.

"This is unusual," he announced. "We normally deal with pickpockets, cargo thieves, loonies or agitated demonstrators. Now and then a gang hits a payroll or a bonded warehouse. It's been years since anyone was *killed* at Kennedy."

"And you're wondering why it happened tonight," Malone guessed.

"Of course. I don't believe in coincidences, Captain. This corpse could be connected with the terrorists."

"Maybe," the detective replied with a shrug.

Now Hamilton picked up the radio.

"I won't be gone long," he assured. "Use this if you need to reach me."

Malone accepted the walkie-talkie silently. As Ben Hamilton started down the stairs, Malone suddenly recalled the priest whom he'd pointed his gun at earlier in the night. That gentle cleric had quietly deplored these "violent times." It would be almost too brutally ironic if he were the victim.

Then Captain Frank Malone remembered someone and something else. One of the lethal tools that Willi Staub had used expertly on several occasions was a long thin blade similar to an ice pick.

But cold-blooded Willi Staub did everything for a reason.

What could make this wary, hunted man risk killing a priest in a crowded public building full of heavily armed police?

If this was homicide, the murderer might well be someone else. Staub wasn't the only killer who slew with such a weapon, Malone reminded himself. Then his thoughts leaped to TWA 22 Heavy again, and his heart beat faster. His only child wouldn't be trapped up there on that plane, minutes from death, if his marriage had not failed.

Or had damn-near-perfect Frank Malone failed?

Had he done enough to keep his family together? There they were again: sins of commission and omission. He had lived with an awareness of them and their blood-brother guilt since the third grade in parochial school. At Harvard, he had discussed and debated them earnestly, many times, with his Jewish roommate. Harry Berger, a judge's son who was now one of Hollywood's senior "baby moguls," had insisted that emotionally healthy and sensible people could deal with any sense of guilt *rationally*.

Sure.

Harry Berger was right, the detective thought.

*Rationally*, it was illogical to blame himself for the fact that his daughter was in terrible danger.

The problem was that he wasn't feeling quite rational.

Not about her.

Not about Willi Staub either.

# 29

*THERE WAS* no warning.

Suddenly the helicopter was being brutally battered in a microburst of fierce turbulence. Clubbed by fists of icy air, the H-65 lurched like a groggy boxer. Then more strong blasts of spinning wind twisted the rotorcraft half around. Straining to keep control, Lieutenant Saldana managed to guide his craft back on course.

But it wasn't over yet.

Ten seconds later, a powerful downdraft abruptly hurled the H-65 toward the ground. The big Aerospatiale, which now weighed more than four tons with its tanks full, dropped like a boulder.

It fell a hundred feet before Saldana could gasp.

It didn't stop.

Two hundred feet . . . three hundred . . . four hundred.

Ernesto Saldana's stomach knotted in instant reflex, but he didn't panic. The aircraft commander grunted and tried to fight back. With one hand he immediately fed more fuel to the two jet engines to increase their thrust. At the same time his other hand worked the control to adjust the "angle of attack" of the rotors.

But the H-65 kept falling.

Down . . . down . . . the moments felt like minutes.

We're going to crash, Saldana thought. We're probably going to die.

Then the large rotorcraft shuddered, shook and broke out of the murderous microburst. Saldana felt somewhat relieved, but not at all safe. This surging storm could strike again at any moment, from any direction, in at least half a dozen ways. Any one of them could be lethal.

His body reminded him of the danger. His shoulders hurt from the seat harness that had saved him from broken bones when the aircraft plummeted. His stomach muscles were still rigid with tension from the very recent crisis as he looked at the altimeter.

Eighteen hundred feet.

The downdraft had dropped the H-65 a full thousand feet. Damp with perspiration, Saldana held the helicopter on search course and considered his options. He wanted to find that transmitter, but he didn't wish to die in the process.

He decided not to climb back to twenty-eight hundred feet. A number of big fast airliners were circling nearby in the storm at altitudes between two thousand and four thousand feet. With visibility so poor tonight and no air traffic control radar to help, there was a genuine risk of collision if the helicopter rose again.

He'd take the H-65 even lower.

Fifteen hundred—that ought to do it.

Saldana slowly moved the control forward. Beside him in the right seat, the copilot was cursing. It had nothing to do with the change in altitude. Vincent Babbitt had been swearing steadily for five minutes. The river of obscenities—none of them either original or colorful—had begun well before the microburst nearly killed him. He wasn't aware that he was cursing. The stream of oaths was like some exotic litany, a bizarre tribal chant to appease nameless and terrible gods who might protect him.

Both pilots wore hard plastic flying helmets, brightly colored and equipped with built-in earphones. Saldana had tuned his to the rotorcraft's intercom channel so he might stay in constant touch with his crew as the blizzard pounded the H-65. Babbitt was listening for something quite different. He was looking for it too—urgently.

Leaning forward toward the instrument panel, he was utterly focused on the round glass face of the radio direction finder. Only four inches in diameter, the compact electronic device probably meant life or death for the thousands of people in those airliners.

And perhaps for Vincent Babbitt, too, the copilot thought.

If it worked, this desperately dangerous flight might end soon and the helicopter could return to the safety of its hangar. But if the direction finder didn't locate the jammer quickly, the H-65 would have to continue battling the massive storm—a chilling prospect.

The visual display part of the direction finder resembled a compass. It had a rotating needle that was supposed to point toward the transmitter being sought. When the device detected the transmitter, the crewman operating the finder would hear a signal in his headset. As the search-and-rescue craft flew where the needle pointed and got nearer to the transmitter, the sound in the operator's earphones grew louder.

So far nothing was happening with the needle. There was no sound signal either. Maybe the storm was somehow playing havoc with the machine, the tense young ensign worried. Perhaps the terrorists' powerful jammer was blinding the direction finder with ECM transmissions—electronic counter-measures such as those used to confuse radar scanners.

Or the damn thing could just be broken.

It didn't matter what the problem was, Babbitt reasoned. If the usually reliable DF equipment was not functioning, there could be no hope of locating the jammer and no dishonor in returning to base. They might as well start back now.

Babbitt reached over and tapped Saldana's shoulder. When the aircraft commander turned his head in response, Babbitt pointed at the dormant direction finder and shook his head. The he gestured emphatically with his right hand—twice—toward their squadron's home airfield.

Saldana studied the direction finder soberly for almost fifteen seconds before he spoke into the minimicrophone connected to his helmet. When he realized that the copilot didn't hear him, Saldana hand-signaled Babbitt to switch to the intercom setting. The junior officer complied at once.

"Can you fix it, Vince?" the aircraft commander repeated.

"I don't even know what the hell's wrong with it. I'm a chopper pilot, not an electronics expert."

"There has to be *something* we can do," Saldana insisted.

"Not *us* . . . not up here tonight. Maybe *God* can fix it," the copilot said cynically.

There was a bolt of lightning and thunder boomed. More lightning flashed by only yards from the helicopter. Then Vincent Babbitt swore again.

"Son of a bitch!"

The needle on the radio direction finder had moved.

It was pointing to the northwest.

The startled young ensign wondered what had happened. Was this another form of mechanical malfunction or was the machine performing at last? There was one way to double-check. Babbitt swiftly turned the dial to switch his headset to the direction finder's audio location channel. His eyes widened and beamed five seconds later.

"It's really working!" he exulted. "We've got the sound too. It isn't very loud, but it's there."

"Let's make it louder," Saldana replied with a smile as he turned the H-65 in the direction to which the needle pointed.

Then he increased the fuel flowing to the pair of jet engines. They produced 750 horsepower each, and the standing orders were to fly these rotorcraft at 150 or 160 miles an hour. The outside limit for safe operations was 180. That was the speed at which Lieutenant Ernesto Saldana was now pounding his helicopter through the dangerous storm.

And the sound did grow louder.

At 180 miles an hour, the H-65 was closing quickly on the target. It was three, four, maybe five miles at most. Both pilots listened intently as the signal got stronger and stronger. The aircraft comander began to reduce speed.

"Two minutes—max," he said.

It grew still louder. The level of sound was annoying now, but the Coast Guard fliers didn't care.

"*One* minute," Saldana estimated.

He was wrong. Just forty seconds later they were staring at the direction finder when it happened. Without warning, the needle swung completely around and pointed in the opposite direction.

"Bingo!" Saldana called out triumphantly.

"We did it! Son of a bitch, we did it!" Babbitt celebrated.

As the sound level of the signal in their earphones eased a tiny bit lower, Saldana turned the H-65 in a tight circle. He was heading back to the place where the needle had abruptly spun. That was the site of the terrorists' transmitter. Despite the massive snow and powerful winds, despite the first H-65 that wouldn't fly and the microburst and downdraft that nearly destroyed the second, despite the finder that wouldn't work, despite *everything*, they had found the jammer.

Now it was time to finish the job.

They had to pinpoint the exact building, and that couldn't be done from eighteen hundred feet in this storm.

"I'm going in closer for a good look," the aircraft commander said as he inched the control forward.

The helicopter descended rapidly. It was down to nine hundred feet by the time it flew over the warehouse that concealed Ito's transmitter. The needle swung around again once more before Saldana guided his craft into another curved course. The H-65 was only five hundred feet above the streets as it approached the warehouse this time.

"They might hear us," Babbitt warned.

"Not in this storm," Saldana disagreed.

As if on cue, a booming barrage of thunder began to fill the night with more than enough noise to cover the sounds of the H-65 engines. Encouraged by this, Saldana took the helicopter down to 350 feet and reduced the airspeed to seventy miles an hour.

With histamines flooding his bloodstream, the tense aircraft commander calculated the risks at near computer speed. There were two major dangers. First, several tall smokestacks and a microwave relay tower rose unpleasantly close to the target. A very small error in flying through here could be fatal.

Second, the terrorists might have human or television camera guards on the roof. If Saldana brought the Coast Guard chopper in too low, they could see it even if they didn't hear it. Once they knew they had been spotted, they might do anything.

But Saldana *knew* that he had two things to do.

He had to find out what was on top of that building.

Then he must tell the police what he had seen so they might smash in quickly with minimum loss of life in a surprise attack.

There was only one way to examine that roof now, and he had to succeed on the first try. A second, low-flying pass was almost certain to be noticed and understood by the terrorists below. If Ernesto Saldana didn't do this exactly right, a lot of people would die—soon.

He couldn't delay.

The building was directly ahead.

He'd have about three or four seconds over it, and he had to see the roof clearly. Saldana pointed at a switch on the instrument panel to warn Babbitt what he meant to do. As the copilot nodded in comprehension, Saldana pressed the switch. The helicopter's powerful main searchlight instantly stabbed a big bright beam down through the falling snow.

"Everybody check the roof," Saldana ordered as he expertly banked the H-65 and slipped the rotorcraft even lower so all three crewmen could get a better look at the target.

A wire fence, several feet high, ran around the top of the building.

Antennas, complicated-looking, three . . . no, *four* of them.

And what the hell were those things jutting out halfway up the sides of the smokestack?

Now the helicopter flashed past the target and the needle spun full circle again. With his eyes swiveling left and right, Saldana scanned the sides of the escape route and pulled back the control to regain altitude.

There was the damn microwave tower two hundred yards ahead, seven or eight seconds at this speed. Saldana swiftly turned the H-65 sharply to the left and missed the tower by fifty feet. Ignoring the oath that exploded from his copilot's lips, the aircraft commander brought the helicopter up to seven hundred feet in a steady climb.

As the H-65 leveled off, Saldana turned on the radio to find out whether he might now report to the Coast Guard base. All he heard was Ito's man-made static. The frequency was still jammed.

"Now what do we do?" Babbitt asked.

Saldana unzipped a pocket in his flying suit, reached in and pulled out a twenty-five-cent coin. He knew, though, that the call would be free.

"What do you say?" Ernesto Saldana asked.

It was a startling idea, and a dangerous one.

But the risk didn't seem that important to Vincent Babbitt now. Something had changed in him when the direction finder began to function. He had suddenly realized that it *was* possible. Despite the short time and long odds they faced, they *could* win. A boyish and naive American sense of coming from behind, a sentimental and preposterous conviction that Good would triumph, an irrational belief that he could survive any hazard and blind faith that nothing would defeat this helicopter crew tonight had obsessed him since the radio locator needle "miraculously" came to life.

"Let's go for it!" Babbitt replied.

Then the aircraft commander told Aviation Survivalman Luther King, who was manning the winch behind them, what he was about to attempt.

"No shit, Lieutenant?" King blurted.

"No shit. Keep your eyes open."

Saldana swung the helicopter in a circle and took it down to four hundred feet once more. The searchlight helped as they studied the buildings and streets below. It was only fifty seconds before Saldana pointed down and adjusted the rotors so the H-65 shifted from "forward" to "hover."

"Here we go," he announced.

Then, quite carefully, he prepared to land the helicopter in a parking and loading area behind a small factory. The open space was only sixty by ninety feet and a large metal trash bin occupied some of that. There was a strong wind to fight, too. As he struggled to hover the craft over the center of the small safe area, jarring gusts pushed and bumped him off course.

The winds stopped.

Saldana immediately seized the opportunity. Maneuvering as carefully as a surgeon, he managed to guide the H-65 to the middle of the "landing zone" and started to descend. The big machine would stay on the ground here until the storm ended, he thought. He wasn't stupid enough to defy the odds any further tonight.

Three hundred feet . . . two hundred . . . one hundred . . . fifty.

He reduced power steadily as he prepared to land.

A powerful gust of wind jolted the helicopter and another followed immediately before Saldana could compensate in his steering. The H-65 lurched. Then Ernesto Saldana heard a sound like a rifle shot, and he *felt something*.

With no time to think about it, he guided the Coast Guard craft back to the middle of the open space and held his breath as he eased the machine down.

"I do believe we hit something, Lieutenant," King said from his seat near the winch.

"That building, I imagine," Saldana replied and pointed at the factory a dozen yards away.

As soon as he turned off the engines, he asked Babbitt and King what they had seen on the roof of the target. They hadn't noticed anything more than he had. They didn't know what was protruding from the high chimney either. Saldana opened the hatch, climbed down from the helicopter and looked at it through the tumbling snow.

All of the eleven small blades of the tail rotor were intact.

One of the main rotor's four big blades—each eighteen feet long and made of very strong Kevlar plastic—was not. When the wind had slammed it against the factory wall, a three-and-a-half-foot piece had been snapped off by the impact.

That was what he had heard and felt.

The aircraft commander, who normally detested clichés, found himself recalling Murphy's Law: Anything that can go wrong, will. Well, just about everything had and he was still alive. He hoped his luck would hold a bit longer.

It did.

Running through the swirling storm, he only stumbled

once before he found a telephone booth two and a half blocks away. Since there weren't many people in this industrial section of Queens, thieves hadn't ravaged the instrument yet. It still worked. Delighted by the dial tone, Saldana dialed 911. A woman answered.

"Police Operator Seven," she said crisply. "What is the emergency?"

# 30

"*HE WASN'T ROBBED*," Hamilton announced as he reentered The Cab. "Your guys found $191 in his wallet—*and* an airline ticket back to Portland."

"Oregon?" Malone asked automatically.

"Oregon," the handsome ebony policeman confirmed. "Father Patrick O'Connor of Saint Agnes there, aged forty-one—according to the ID he was carrying."

"What else was he carrying?"

"No weapon, no drugs—just the regular stuff a regular priest would have."

Frank Malone frowned and shook his head.

"Why would anyone kill a regular priest?" he wondered.

"And stash the body in a locked cubicle in the toilet," Hamilton added.

"To buy time by delaying discovery of the corpse," Malone calculated.

"So the creep who did this could be miles from here."

"Maybe, but we still don't have a motive. I don't think this was a planned hit," Malone reasoned. "You don't plan to kill somebody in a public toilet. Even the Mafia doesn't work like that anymore."

Now Hamilton looked uncomfortable.

"I suppose . . . well, you know who sometimes hang out in public toilets. It might be a sex thing," he said. "This could get very messy."

"It already is," Malone answered. "This priest? He wasn't the one we talked to downstairs, was he?"

"No."

Hamilton saw the detective's glance swing to the telephone—the instrument on which Number One called.

"Yes, I expect to hear from him any minute," Malone said in reply to the unspoken question. He has to maintain the pressure to keep us intimidated. That's a standard tactic in this kind of war, and . . ."

The antiterrorist professional didn't finish the sentence. Malone had been about to say "he's good at it." That would have been a serious mistake. He shouldn't utter a word to suggest that he knew anything about Number One. Annoyed that he had almost made such a naive error, Frank Malone avoided Hamilton's eyes by looking back at the phone.

It did not ring.

But the teletype began to clatter.

Annie Green scanned the incoming message for fifteen seconds before she gestured to Malone to come to the machine. He read the succinct message from the Coast Guard air base swiftly.

They had found the transmitter.

Some lieutenant named Saldana was at a phone booth a few blocks from the building. Malone recognized the address where the Coast Guard officer was waiting. It was about six and a half miles from Kennedy.

Now Malone thought about the assault—and Willi Staub. The son of a bitch would have the building entrances rigged with alarms. There would be heavily armed terrorists inside to protect the jammer for as long as possible before they fled. It was all in Venom's file. A wily professional, he always planned some clever escape route so his fighters could slip away to do battle another day.

But those defending the building didn't matter.

Time, not their machine guns, was Willi Staub's deadliest weapon now.

Minutes, not bullets, would determine whether the legion of people on TWA 22 Heavy and the other airliners lived or perished.

Anything like a normal police siege would destroy them as well as the terrorists. Recognizing this, Frank Malone chose his strategy. It was a gamble, but the others were sure to bring disaster.

"Let's go downstairs," he said to Hamilton.

"But what if Number One phones, Frank?" Annie Green asked.

"Tell him his seven friends will be here very soon and their plane's ready," the detective answered.

Then he led Hamilton from The Cab. Malone didn't ask the question until they strode off the snowswept bridge into the International Arrivals Building.

"Is your armored car here?"

Hamilton nodded.

"Is there some back way we can get to it without going through that mob in the lobby downstairs?"

The Port Authority Police lieutenant nodded again and led him to the service stairway. The armored car was parked by the side of the terminal, just out of sight of those inside.

"You found the bastards, didn't you?" Hamilton said.

"Some of them."

"I'm coming with you."

"Go inside and grab the commander of the Emergency Services Unit team," Malone said. "Tell him to load twenty of his men—full assault gear—into vehicles and meet me in the armored car up the service road a bit. I'll lead them from there."

"That it?"

Malone shook his head.

"You're not coming," he announced. "They need you here, and you know it."

Hamilton glared at him, angry because Malone was right. Barely controlling his wrath, he pounded on the armored car turret.

"This is Captain Malone," he told the driver. "He's in command."

Then Hamilton hurried back into the building. In a few minutes, the armored car was leading the ESU truck and three police cars toward the airport exit. They were almost there when Frank Malone realized what was wrong with Staub's list.

There was one name that didn't fit.

And there had to be a reason it was on the list.

There was something special about the person. Suddenly the detective realized what this operation was really about, and who had to be behind it.

And who had to pay for tonight. No matter what happened in the next hour, Malone thought grimly, that person would pay. It was more than a decision. It was a commitment.

Malone leaned forward to tell the driver to speed up now. The man at the wheel looked ahead through the slit in the armor, saw the ice-glazed road and blowing snow, thought about the danger and obeyed. By the time the armored car reached the highway, it was moving at fifty miles an hour.

# 31

ON THE GRAND CENTRAL PARKWAY, Mitchell Hoffman guided his new Mercedes 420 SEL sedan east through the gusting snow. The storm didn't bother him at all. He felt absolutely wonderful.

It wasn't just the "high" of the five glasses of twelve-year-old Chivas and the four lines of top-quality cocaine that he'd had at the corporate Christmas party earlier.

It wasn't the ego rush effect of the $310,000 bonus that he had received two days ago either.

It was a lot of things.

He'd had an enormously successful year. The chairman had said that intense, quick-witted Mitchell Hoffman was "one of the shrewdest traders" the Wall Street firm had. It had taken an effort not to correct the chairman. Mitch Hoffman knew, beyond any doubt, that he was *the* shrewdest and *the* most brilliant. He was the most skillful, the most insightful, the toughest—the *best*.

He was nearly twenty-nine, and he'd have his first million before thirty.

No, *two* million.

He was on a roll. Nothing could stop him—in business, on the squash court, anywhere. Mitch Hoffman would have it all. He was heading straight for the top. He thought about his glamorous blond wife, and grinned. He'd be on top of her in about half an hour, and he'd make fantastic love to her until she screamed in ecstasy. Not just once. Masterful Mitch Hoffman would have her shrieking and moaning all night.

He looked at the speedometer and scowled.

This was ridiculous.

Maybe thirty goddam miles an hour was all right for the uneasy mediocrities behind the wheels of the other vehicles, but a superb driver such as Mitch Hoffman didn't have to creep along with them. He didn't have the time to waste with these nervous nonentities. He had a terrific car, complete control of it and no fear of the snow or anything else.

He began to accelerate.

The maroon Mercedes glided past the other cars easily.

No problem at all.

Then he saw the fork in the multilane highway directly ahead.

He was almost upon it. This was where he had to veer right to get onto the Van Wyck Expressway that ran past Kennedy out toward Cedarhurst. His wife was waiting for him—hungrily—in his big waterfront house in Cedarhurst.

Dammit, a cluster of cars was crawling along, all bunched together. They were blocking his way. He wasn't going to put up with that stupidity. Hoffman stepped on the gas contemptuously, speeding to sweep past the FBI convoy.

He was flashing by the fourth sedan when he hit a patch of icy slush. The heavy Mercedes slid, swerved and bucked as he struggled for control. Then it spun and crashed into the left rear of the car carrying Arnold Lloyd.

The impact at fifty miles an hour knocked the FBI sedan out of the tight security formation. The government car lurched off to the right, careening at an angle before it rolled over onto its roof and slid forward. Sparks flew as the metal top scraped along the highway.

It was the FBI sedan behind it that smashed into the rear of the Mercedes. The drivers of the other six federal cars were slamming on their brakes, and the agents beside them were shouting into their radios.

"Wagon Train! Wagon Train!" the convoy commander called out immediately.

That was the code phrase for an ambush. Kincaid thought they were under premeditated attack by some heavily armed and fanatical force. He didn't have any idea as to who or how many of the raiders there were, but he knew that the bastards weren't going to take any of *his* prisoners.

"Wagon Train! Wagon Train!" he repeated.

While the drivers of civilian vehicles swung wide into the left lane to avoid ramming the suddenly stopped group of unmarked government cars, determined FBI agents poured from their sedans with their pistols and submachine guns at the ready. They swiftly took up defensive positions behind their cars, prepared to do battle.

Hoffman was not aware of this. His three-week-old Mercedes had whipsawed off the highway into a large boulder. Aglow with whiskey and cocaine confidence when he'd entered his car thirty-nine minutes earlier, the almost but not quite perfect stock trader had made one error. He had not bothered to fasten his seat belt. As a result, part of his face was smeared across the inside of the expensive West German windshield and all of him was dead.

Arnold Lloyd was alive. Everyone else in the turned-over car was either unconscious or badly injured. Lloyd had a broken left shoulder and was bleeding profusely from a two-inch face cut, but he wasn't hurt nearly as seriously as the government agents beside him.

The pain didn't affect Lloyd's mind one bit.

He was totally alert.

For a moment he wondered whether someone had staged this to break him loose. He immediately decided that it didn't matter. This was his one opportunity to defeat them all.

He took it.

The broken shoulder hurt terribly as he forced open a door and wriggled from the ruined car. Lloyd didn't cry out though. As a veteran professional, he realized that he could not afford to do anything to draw the attention—or the fire—of the other FBI agents nearby. Forcing himself to stifle any normal sound of pain, he crouched low as he circled the smashed sedan.

They didn't see him.

He had to get away from here—at once.

Maybe the billowing snow would shield him. The FBI men would probably be watching this side of the divided multilane highway. He'd make a run for the other side and the cars heading back to the city.

Not exactly a run. He was too battered for that. He jogged and staggered and stumbled toward the divider, dodging civilian vehicles as he lurched toward escape. He was panting from the shock and the agony. It felt as if something inside him might be broken, too.

He was struggling over the divider when one of the FBI men saw him. The agent pointed at him, and swung up his submachine gun.

"Don't shoot!" Kincaid shouted. "Get him!"

Four special agents ran out into the flow of traffic. They were young, strong, bold. They hadn't been in an auto smash-up, and they were in much better physical condition than Lloyd was after his months of incarceration. They were at the divider in seconds.

They were about to vault the low barrier when it happened.

Lloyd was almost across the other side of the highway when the wood-paneled station wagon hit him. It really wasn't the fault of the woman behind the wheel. Visibility was awful, and no one would expect somebody to dash out onto a highway a mile from any exit.

She saw him at the last moment, and twisted her wheel sharply in a frantic effort to avoid him. She almost succeeded. She shrieked as she felt the impact. The sound of that thump of human meeting metal was terrible. His body flew through the air like some discarded toy, hurtling forty feet before it dropped onto the side of the road.

She stepped on the brake and began to shudder. She was still shaking a minute later when a group of men carrying guns suddenly appeared.

"I'm sorry," she managed to say. "Oh, my God. I'm so sorry. I didn't see him. I'm sorry."

Then she began to cry.

"It wasn't your fault," Kincaid assured her. "We know that."

He saw that she was staring at the pistol in his hand. He slid it into his shoulder holster and took out his official identity card. He held it open for her to examine.

"We're the FBI," he said. "I'm Inspector Barry Kincaid. The man who ran in front of your car was a federal prisoner trying to escape."

She was still shuddering.

"Nobody's going to blame you," he told her as he put away his ID folder. "You couldn't have seen him in time, not in this weather. Nobody could. It was an unavoidable accident."

She began to cry.

"Stay with her," Kincaid ordered one of the agents and walked toward the body. As he trudged through the falling snow, he thought about tomorrow. He might well be held responsible for the death of Lloyd—and any airline passengers who perished because the terrorists' demands were not fully met.

He stopped to glance across the highway at the FBI cars and the Mercedes. There had been no assault by armed fanatics, just one bad driver who lost control of a heavy $45,000 sedan in a raging storm. The security formation and the well-trained special agents with machine guns could have dealt with almost anything—except that.

Kincaid reached the body, and looked down at it in anger.

He couldn't believe what he saw.

One of Lloyd's eyes was open . . . staring at him hatefully. The "corpse" was gasping. The impact of being hit by a car doing twenty-five or thirty miles an hour had injured him gravely, but—against all odds—Arnold Lloyd was still alive.

# 32

*IT WAS HOT* in the armored car.

Malone was sweating profusely, and so were the Port Authority cops. There was barely enough room for the four men inside the steel-plated vehicle. Malone felt cramped and uncomfortable wedged into the small space beside the driver, and the nasty stench of gasoline fumes added to his annoyance.

It was noisy in there, too.

The sound level was ten times as loud as that inside an ordinary car. The naked metal walls magnified the mechanical growl of the engine. With narrow steel slits instead of the big rubber-sheathed windows of civilian vehicles, almost none of the noise escaped.

Malone peered through the small opening, and tapped the driver's shoulder. The detective pointed left. He had worked this area in a patrol car when he was two years out of the Police Academy. He knew these streets. Well, he hoped he did. It had been a long time ago.

The armored vehicle swerved as he'd ordered. It was eleven blocks to the intersection where the Coast Guard pilot waited. Finding him wasn't going to be difficult. Getting into the building that concealed the transmitter would be much trickier, Malone realized.

There had to be a quick way in.

Quick and sure.

He saw it—dead ahead—a minute later.

"Stop him," he called to the driver. "*Stop him!*"

The startled man behind the wheel swung the armored car directly across the path of a motorized snowplow that was moving slowly down the street. Malone opened the door beside him, scrambled out and ran to the big Department of Sanitation truck.

"What the fuck is this?" the irate driver yelled.

"Police emergency," Malone replied and pointed at the plainly marked Emergency Services Unit van and the blue-and-white radio cars behind the armored vehicle.

The Sanitation man opened his mouth to ask a question. Malone spoke first.

"Follow us—right now!" he ordered.

Then Malone hurried back to the armored car. When it reached the phone booth, he got out as a young man in an orange jumpsuit stepped from the shelter. Eyeing the heavy fabric and the outfit's design, the detective reasoned that it could be a flier's winter gear.

"You the chopper pilot?"

The Coast Guard lieutenant nodded.

"How far is it?" Malone demanded.

"Five or six blocks," Saldana replied and pointed west.

"Let's go."

With Saldana and Malone leading the way on foot, the vehicles moved quietly through the deserted streets. None of the police in the ESU van said a word. They put on their steel battle helmets, checked the clips in their weapons and wondered whether the terrorists might have armor-piercing ammunition that could penetrate their police flak jackets. Those bulky garments were *supposed* to stop almost anything under 50 caliber, but who knew what the terrorists might be using?

Suddenly the Coast Guard flier stopped.

"I think it's around this corner, near the far end of the block," he said.

Malone turned and held up his right hand. As the armored car and other police vehicles slowed to a halt, Malone walked to the ESU van to talk with the team's commander. When the wide-shouldered man in the flak jacket stepped down to the street, Frank Malone recognized him. Six years ago—before Anthony Arbolino made lieutenant, Malone had barely defeated him for the department's pistol championship. Arbolino was more than a fine shot, he was a damn good cop.

Neither man wasted a moment on amenities.

"What have we got?" Arbolino asked bluntly.

"Let's take a look."

Arbolino gestured to thè driver of the van. Looking larger than life-sized in their bulky body armor, the ESU cops climbed out as Malone and their commander hurried to join the helicopter pilot. With only his head extending beyond the corner, Saldana was warily peering up the block. He stepped back as the two police officers reached him.

"I think it's the third building from the end—the other side of the street," he told them.

"*Think?*" Frank Malone asked.

"I only saw it for a couple of seconds as we flew over. There are four antennas on the roof . . . and something's projecting from the side of the chimney. None of us could figure out what it was."

"Is that all?"

"There's a wire fence—maybe four or five feet high—running all around the roof."

"What about the building itself?" Malone questioned.

"It seems to be a small warehouse."

The antiterrorist specialist leaned forward past the edge of the building, studied the third building from the end on the other side of the street and then stepped back.

"Looks like a small three-story warehouse all right," he confirmed.

It was then that the ESU team commander shook his head.

"I'm listening, Tony," Malone announced.

"Who's inside that building?" Arbolino asked.

"Armed terrorists."

"How many?"

Malone shrugged.

"What kind of weapons do they have?"

"Assume the worst. These bastards probably have everything," Malone said.

"What bastards? Who are they, Frank?"

"They could be West Germans. Their leader is. He's a goddam monster. That's all I can say about him, Tony. Hope you don't mind."

"Let's see," Arbolino answered. "We're not sure it's the right building . . . and we don't know what the hell's rigged to the chimney . . . and we have no idea how many bad guys are in there. We don't know whether they've got bows and arrows or poison gas. You're not sure who these creeps are . . . and you won't trust me enough to say who their leader is. How could any reasonable police lieutenant *possibly* mind taking his men into a terrific situation like that?"

Malone ignored the sarcasm.

"Tell your guys to bring their gas masks, Tony," Malone said evenly. "We're hitting that warehouse as soon as you've got all the exits covered."

It was a flat statement of fact—nonnegotiable.

"Be nice if we knew it was the right building," Arbolino pointed out. "Can I borrow the fly boy for five minutes?"

"Three would be better."

Arbolino turned toward the van, punching the air in a signal that the men beside it understood. An ESU sergeant rushed to him, listened to the orders and went back to tell the others. Then Arbolino led the pilot around the block to the rear entrance of the building on the north side of the warehouse. Pushing Saldana back, Arbolino drew his pistol. For a moment he considered the court decisions and departmental regulations about search warrants and legally justified entry.

He shrugged, swung the gun and smashed a glass panel in the door. After he reached in and opened it, he pulled a small flashlight from his rear pocket before they entered the building. There were tables heaped with fabric, sewing machines and racks of dresses all over the room. It was a small clothing plant.

Advancing behind the narrow beam of his flashlight, Arbolino led Saldana through the clutter to a freight elevator. They stepped out onto the roof twenty-five seconds later. The pilot pointed at the top of the adjacent building.

The roof was ringed by a barbed-wire fence that was nearly five feet high.

Three . . . no, four large antennas . . . unusual ones. Arbolino had never seen anything like them.

And there was the tall smokestack. The police lieutenant stared through the snow for several seconds before he realized exactly what was jutting out halfway up the chimney.

"*Christ!*" he whispered as he jerked Saldana back inside the clothing factory.

In the warehouse next door, Takeshi Ito blinked.

Then he rubbed his eyes and looked back at the television monitor again.

There were six video screens facing him. Each of the half dozen was linked to a different closed-circuit camera. These state-of-the-art cameras were equipped with light intensification devices to provide superior night vision.

Ito studied the monitor displaying what one of the roof cameras "saw." Everything seemed normal. For a few seconds he had thought he was looking at a human figure in some kind of bright orange garb, but there was clearly no one on the roof now. It must have been some kind of optical illusion, perhaps one caused by the flashing lightning.

Orange clothing in New York in midwinter?

What a strange idea, Ito reflected. It was almost surreal, like those dreams in which a naked two-headed woman was choking him. Neither head had a face. Ito had never quite figured out what this unusual recurring fantasy represented.

Now he saw something move.

On the monitor linked to the camera scanning the street in front of the warehouse, a large white vehicle was approaching through the storm. It was difficult to identify. Ito squinted as he peered at it intently. After several seconds, he smiled and sighed.

It was just a snowplow.

With a major snowstorm battering the entire metropolitan area, it was natural for New York to send out its Department of Sanitation plows to clear the streets. This was both realistic and rational.

No visions of imaginary men in bizarre orange attire.

No nightmares of homicidal and faceless female freaks.

Just a standard, nonmilitary machine being operated by some unarmed and ordinary civil servants—a routine activity anywhere.

It was almost time to depart. He would be glad to get out of this building, this situation, this country. He wasn't exhausted, but he had endured enough of the confinement and growing stress. He stood up, walked to the delayed-action bombs and deftly set the timers.

Then he took another look at the bank of video screens. He saw the snowplow lumber around the corner and disappear. It hadn't really cleaned the street thoroughly, but that came as no surprise to Takeshi Ito. He understood that few Americans were committed to perfect work.

He studied the clocks once more. This would be the last time. It was half past nine. In three minutes, he would descend to his car in the garage below and start for Kennedy Airport.

# 33

*STAMPING THEIR FEET* in the cold, the police in the steel helmets and heavy flak jackets watched silently as the snowplow rumbled to a halt beside the armored car. There were two men in the front seat of the Sanitation Department vehicle. The one behind the wheel wore coveralls. Lieutenant Anthony Arbolino hurried forward to speak to the other one.

"It's the right building, Frank," he told Malone. "Antennas on the roof like he said, and those items on the chimney are goddam T-fucking-V cameras."

"There's another one near the front door," Malone replied. "Your people in place?"

"I've got three men on the top floor of the clothing plant next door. As soon as they get the word on their walkie-talkies, they step outside to cover the warehouse roof. Two

radio cars are about to plug the other end of the block, and
two more are sealing the back alley."

"How about the building on the other side, Tony?"

"Three more of my guys are inside, ready to hit the roof
on command. One of them's my best shooter."

"We'd prefer prisoners, not stiffs, if possible. There's just
one thing more important than prisoners: knocking out the
transmitter. That's our primary target," Malone explained.

As he spoke, an ESU sergeant approached carrying a flak
jacket and steel battle helmet.

"We're all gonna be *their* primary targets, Frank," Arbolino reminded Malone. "Put this stuff on."

Malone stepped down to the street, donned the combat
gear and quickly climbed back into the municipal vehicle.

"This is where you get out," he told the driver. "I'll take it
from here."

"Wait a minute! This is my plow!" the man behind the
wheel protested.

"It could be *your hearse*," the detective warned. "Don't
argue. *Go*."

The Sanitation Department driver went, and Frank Malone immediately slid over behind the wheel.

"Keep the armored car and your people out of sight until
I'm about twenty yards from the warehouse," he said to Arbolino. "When you see me accelerate, come on in like gangbus-
ters."

Arbolino understood just what Malone had in mind.
Aware that it would be useless to oppose the plan, he simply
made a thumbs-up gesture to signal "good luck." Malone
returned it, and started the engine.


In the warehouse, Takeshi Ito put on his overcoat. Then he
scanned the video screens again. Everything outside looked
peaceful, safe. He put the silenced MAC-11 submachine gun
and clips in the Pan American flight bag, slipped it over his

shoulder and walked to the doorway. Just outside the threshold, he paused to activate the booby trap before turning toward the stairs.

The snowplow swung around the corner.

Malone stared down the block at the warehouse some seventy yards ahead. With the white flakes tumbling down and the windshield wipers slogging back and forth across the soot-smeared glass, it was difficult to see that far on this black winter night. That would not affect his plan. Frank Malone knew exactly where he was going and what he must do.

Within the next forty-five seconds.

When Ito got down to the second floor, he reached under the banister one step below the landing. He switched on another booby trap. This flat, one-pound charge of plastic explosive was rigged to a pressure plate beneath the grubby runner of industrial carpeting. That done, he resumed his descent.

Less than fifty yards to go.

The heavy metal plow was pushing the snow aside steadily. Malone's eyes shifted from the street to the rearview mirror for a glimpse of the armored car.

Not yet.

Any moment now, he thought.

He fed more fuel to the engine to start building speed.

Ito reached the ground floor, entered the garage and flicked on the light. Turning to the video monitor on the wall, he saw a large white vehicle—another snowplow. It would pass by before he drove out, helpfully cleaning the street he'd use only moments later.

Pleased by this good luck, he turned off the antipersonnel mine that guarded the garage door. Then he got into the Jeep, placing the flight bag with the submachine gun on the seat beside him.


Malone glanced at the mirror once more.

He saw the armored car turn the corner.

Then he looked ahead at the warehouse barely twenty yards away.

It was time.

He stepped harder on the gas pedal, forcing it to the floor. As the plow accelerated, cool Harvard-educated Frank Malone realized that he was probably doing precisely what his unsophisticated aggressive father would have done. In spite of everything, the worldly detective captain was, irrationally and irrevocably, very much the son of the tough street cop known as Big Mike Malone.

Suddenly it all came back.

For an instant, the thirty-five-year-old man in the snow-plow was a twelve-year-old boy at that funeral twenty-three years ago. He felt the pain—and something else. It was fierce primitive pride.

"Hang on Mike," Frank Malone said as he began to twist the steering wheel.


In the garage, the efficient electronics terrorist was confident as he put the key in the ignition. The Jeep had four-wheel drive, snow tires, a strong new battery and a full tank of fuel. Having driven to the big international airport on three test runs, he knew the route to Kennedy well. He'd join Staub there in eleven or twelve minutes.

He started the engine.

Malone spun the wheel all the way. The snowplow veered sharply to the right. It hurtled right at the warehouse.

Ito opened the glove compartment. He took out the remote-control device, and pressed the button to send the radio signal that would open the door.

The door didn't open.

It exploded.

The steel prow of the heavy Sanitation Department truck hit it like a bomb. The impact blasted the metal slat door into scrap, spraying jagged chunks and razor-edged slivers like shrapnel. The video monitor screen and three overhead fluorescent tubes shattered into flying shards.

Pipes on the rear wall were gashed open in a dozen places. Water spouted from two of them. Jets of scalding steam erupted from another. A yard away, a ruined burglar alarm crackled and spat sparks.

Liquid dripped from multiple punctures of the Jeep's oil, fuel and hydraulic lines. Almost every square inch of the safety-glass windshield was defaced by a dense cobweb of cracks and scratches that reduced visibility drastically. The headlights were totally destroyed. Bits of the glass faces and inner workings were strewn around the floor.

When Takeshi Ito first heard the sound of the collision, he had thought that it was some sort of explosive charge or perhaps a shoulder-fired rocket such as the U.S. Army's M72 tank killer. He reacted immediately . . . realistically . . . defensively.

He didn't believe in accidents.

Whatever it was, it was deliberate . . . hostile . . . dangerous.

He had a very brief look at the front of the snowplow as it

smashed through the door. The driver's strange headgear puzzled Ito for two or three seconds before he recognized it as a metal combat helmet. He was right. The Americans were attacking.

And they'd caught him by surprise. It was his own fault. He should have suspected something when he saw a snow-plow sweeping this street in an industrial area twice within five minutes. He'd been as stupid as they'd been clever.

All this flashed through his mind in an instant.

That was all the time he had.

The snowplow was almost upon him.

In another ten seconds, the Jeep and Takeshi Ito would be crushed.

He dropped the remote-control unit. Grabbing the flight bag that contained the silenced submachine gun and five extra thirty-two-round clips, Ito jerked open the door beside him and hurled himself out of the vehicle. He felt the heat radiating from the plow's motor as he rolled away.

Now the massive steel front of the thirty-five-thousand-pound machine smashed into the Jeep. With the garage walls confining the sound, the crash of metal against metal was deafening. And the plow didn't even slow down. It slammed ahead like a tank, driving the maimed Jeep back into the rear wall. There was a terrible grinding noise as the Jeep began to buckle. Within a few moments, it was a broken compacted wreck.

Pistol in hand, Malone turned off the engine and jumped down. As his feet touched the floor, he saw a crouching figure open a side door. The detective raised his weapon.

"Freeze!" he shouted.

When Ito spun, Malone saw the automatic weapon that the terrorist held. Malone took cover behind the big truck barely an instant before a scythe of 9-millimeter slugs slashed the air where he'd stood. Then Takeshi Ito bolted through the doorway into the warehouse.

Seconds later, Malone warily peered out from behind the

plow. Pistol in hand, he slowly scanned the garage for the shooter or other hostile gunmen. He saw none, but knew that meant nothing. There could be a dozen heavily armed fanatics in the building—perhaps just beyond that open portal.

"You okay, Frank?"

It was Arbolino. Framed in the space where the wide garage door to the street had been, the snow-spattered ESU lieutenant and four of his men eyed the devastation. Arbolino looked at the gasoline pouring from the mangled Jeep's fuel tank, the spreading puddle of oil and the sparks sputtering from the shattered burglar alarm. The threat of fire was obvious.

"This place could go *anytime*," Arbolino warned.

Frank Malone nodded.

"I only saw one of them," he said evenly. "Asian—and working a machine gun rigged with a silencer. He went *that* way."

Malone pointed at the exit that Ito had used.

"You coming?" he asked.

"As soon as I take care of something," Arbolino replied. He raised the walkie-talkie and told his teams covering the rear alley and the roof to start their assaults in twenty seconds with heavy firing. Malone understood the sound strategy at once. The noisy attacks would distract and divide the defenders. That would reduce the number of terrorist guns pouring bullets at the force breaking in from the garage.

"Get ready," Arbolino said to the men beside him.

They waited tensely in the silence. Then the shooting began. It continued for more than a dozen seconds before the ESU lieutenant spoke again.

"Let's do it!"

Arbolino and Malone were the first through the doorway. Neither wanted to be a hero; they were simply professionals doing their job. Since the days of the cavemen, the field commanders of small units automatically led the charge.

Takeshi Ito was waiting for them. Crouched on the first-floor landing, he stared down at the doorway intently. His finger was on the MAC-11's trigger, and his face was grim. He had heard the firing on the roof and in the back alley. He understood what it meant.

There was no way to escape.

He had to shoot it out, here, now.

For a moment he wondered how they had found him. Then he squeezed the trigger. The first burst punched half a dozen holes in the wall before four 9-millimeter slugs slammed into the bigger American's middle. They hammered Arbolino back reeling. The ESU lieutenant yelled in pain.

But he didn't die.

He didn't even bleed.

The heavy protective garb was damaged, but the slugs didn't get through to his flesh. As Arbolino staggered under the impact, Ito swung his machine gun to slay the second attacker. Since that man also wore body armor, logical Takeshi Ito raised the MAC-11's muzzle to aim for his throat.

Malone shot first.

He fired three rounds before Ito could chop his head off with the rapid-fire weapon.

One .38-caliber slug blasted a chunk of wood from the banister. The second broke the terrorist's left arm an inch above the elbow, and the third obliterated his left ear. Jolted by the searing pain, he wasn't even aware of the crimson fluid pouring from the wounds.

The injured arm throbbed fiercely, but that wasn't the worst of it. The whole left side of his head felt as if it was on fire. The hurt was almost dizzying, but he had too much pride and hate to collapse. He'd show them that Takeshi Ito wasn't finished yet.

He'd make them pay for what they had done to him. He'd make them pay in the only way left to him now. He would keep them from the transmitter—*his* transmitter—as long as he could. Every extra second would be a small victory. Every minute would ensure that more airliners crowded with imperialist racists would crash. He might not be alive to see it, but knowing that it was coming would make dying easier.

Screaming a Japanese Red Army slogan defiantly, Ito squeezed off another burst that passed only inches above Malone's head. Then the bleeding terrorist stumbled toward the stairs to the next floor. When he reached them, he turned and fired down toward the Americans to discourage pursuit. Suddenly he heard a metallic click that meant his weapon was out of ammunition. With his injured left arm hanging useless, he managed to snap out the empty clip and insert a full one.

Slowly and doggedly, he forced himself up the stairs—each step a mountain and a personal triumph. Though he was alone, wounded and ringed by enemies in a depraved foreign land, *he was winning*. Exhilarated by that knowledge, he shouted the militant slogan again.

The six policemen below heard him, but they didn't understand Japanese and they weren't interested in revolutionary rhetoric. Five of them were concentrating on how they could shoot him down with minimum risk to themselves. The sixth—a Harvard-educated captain—was thinking how useful it might be to interrogate this terrorist or others about the jamming equipment.

"If we can take a couple of them alive . . . " Malone began.

"*Sure*," a sergeant replied briskly as he checked the shells in his 12-gauge shotgun. Malone recognized the tone of a pragmatic man humoring a stupid superior. He'd used it himself. The sergeant's attitude didn't surprise Frank Malone. He understood how the idea of trying to capture a fanatic armed with a machine gun might seem both naive and foolhardy.

But that was Malone's way.

That was how he had to do it.

"Cover me," he told Tony Arbolino and started up the stairs.

The ESU lieutenant did not wait on the ground floor. Gesturing for his men to follow, he was barely a yard behind Malone as the detective climbed to the next landing. Expecting terrorist bullets or bombs at any instant, Malone watched and listened tensely every step of the way.

He saw no one.

He heard nothing but the sounds of the other ESU teams pressing their diversionary attacks.

*Where* were the terrorists?

Now there was a different noise—from above. It sounded like a human in profound pain, Malone judged. But he knew that it could be a trick to lure the police into some murderous trap. Life-or-death time again, Frank Malone thought grimly.

Stop or advance? His instincts and the watch on his wrist made the decision. There was no time to spare. With his eyes sweeping back and forth for a gun muzzle or trip wire, Malone made his way to the end of the short corridor. When he looked up the stairwell, he saw Ito nearing the second-floor landing.

The terrorist's gait seemed unsteady. His left arm dangled limply, but his right hand still grasped the terrible little MAC-11. Malone had to act effectively and immediately to prevent him from using it. There was no margin for error, the twelve-hundred-rounds-per-minute weapon could totally dismember Frank Malone in a few seconds.

Aiming carefully, Malone fired. One bullet ruined Ito's right wrist, wrenching a scream from his throat and making him drop the machine gun. The next round shattered the electronics expert's right ankle like a blow from a sledgehammer. Whirling in agony, weaponless and disabled, Takeshi Ito began to fall.

We've got him—*alive*, Malone exulted silently.

As Ito crumpled, his cry changed abruptly. It was no

longer one of shock and pain. Now it was an awful noise that Frank Malone had heard so many times—the sound of stomach-wrenching fear. Staub had probably told the man that Americans butchered captured revolutionaries, the detective reasoned.

But it wasn't any abstract lie that terrified Takeshi Ito.

He was afraid of something real and tangible.

Malone saw him struggle desperately to catch hold of the banister. He failed. From the instant he hit the stairs, he twisted and strained in a frantic effort to get up . . . to get away. Bleeding badly and half dazed by the agony of his wounds, he somehow rose to one knee.

That was when the booby trap he'd hidden beneath the worn carpet exploded. The blast hurled the short slim terrorist over the railing, and he tumbled down the stairwell. He wasn't screaming anymore.

Ito dropped like a sandbag. There was a loud thump as his body hit the ground floor. Two newly arrived patrolmen rushed forward, pointing their guns at his head. Aware that he might have a concealed weapon, they were ready to shoot if he made any threatening move.

He didn't move at all. He lay there facedown and utterly still. After a few seconds, one of the police reached down and warily turned over the apparently unconscious terrorist. With an ear destroyed, his nose broken by the impact of a two-story fall and his mouth distorted in a grimace of panic, he looked terrible.

He didn't seem to be breathing. Aiming his pistol between Ito's eyes, a black policeman bent down slowly to check the electronics expert's wrist for a pulse. Some twenty seconds later, the officer straightened up and shook his head.

The cunningly concealed bomb had killed the clever man who installed it. The bloody thing on the floor was a corpse. Takeshi Ito was dead.

# 34

*BUT* his powerful transmitter was still alive.

It had to be somewhere overhead, and it had to be stopped.

Malone pointed at the steps leading up to the third floor.

"There could be more booby traps," Arbolino warned.

"Bet on it," Malone replied harshly.

Arbolino frowned in concern.

"My guys aren't explosives experts, Frank," he said. "I think we better call the Bomb Squad."

"No time. We've got to knock out that jammer *now*."

"We could cut off the power in the basement," the ESU lieutenant suggested.

"That's probably booby trapped, too," Malone said, "and the odds are they've got a backup generator. No point in going downstairs. We've got to hit them from above."

Arbolino stiffened as he thought of the armed terrorists and hidden bombs to be challenged. Even in body armor, policemen would be maimed or killed.

"*Way* above." Frank Malone continued. "You said your best shooter's on the roof next door. Get on the radio and tell him to blast the antennas."

"At night in a snowstorm?"

"He can use a machine gun. Tell him, dammit!"

Arbolino took a walkie-talkie from one of his men, and warned the police on the roof opposite the "shooter" to take cover. Then he radioed the order for the marksman to attack the antennas with an automatic weapon. A husky sergeant handed the expert "shooter" a submachine gun, and repeated the lieutenant's command.

"I don't think it'll work, Sarge," the younger cop said.

"Don't think, Caplan. Shoot."

Some thirty yards away in the warehouse, Malone picked up the MAC-11 and flight bag that the terrorist had dropped.

"Call the Bomb Squad," he told Arbolino, then he ran down the stairs.

The "shooter" peered through the swirling snow, brushed the melting flakes from his face and took a deep breath of the cold air. Then he raised his weapon, squinted and began to fire.

His first short burst didn't hit anything. Sparks flew as his second struck one of the antennas. It bent under the impact but it didn't fall. Silently cursing the stupidity of his orders, he fired again.

The slugs broke off a piece of the antenna—a small piece. The next burst amputated a two-foot section. Four fifths of the antenna stood intact. Now the marksman was angry— angry at the impossible orders, at the goddam target that defied him, at himself.

"Shit!" he swore and squeezed the trigger again.

The top three feet of the mast drooped like a broken wing of a bird, but the main part of the antenna did not fall.

Now the clip was empty. Furious, Caplan slammed in a fresh one.

When Malone reached the front door of the building, he found it locked. The ESU men had come in through a rear entrance. Malone shot the lock off, kicked in the door and charged up the stairs.

The "shooter" resumed firing. Now he aimed at the middle of the antenna, one . . . two . . . three bursts. More hits, more sparks like fireflies in the night. The battle had become personal to Caplan, the marksman and his pride against the goddam antenna.

He won.

After emptying two thirds of the clip, he saw his enemy lean over and drop to the roof.

"Nice shooting, Caplan," the sergeant encouraged.

The man with the machine gun wiped the snow from his face again.

"It won't work," he said. "There are still three standing, and half my ammo's gone."

"I've got plenty," Malone announced as he strode onto the roof.

Caplan pointed at another antenna.

"Fine," Malone agreed. They fired together at the lower part of the metal mast. Defying the cold wind and endless snow, they poured slugs at the second antenna. Battered and shattered by four bursts, it fell.

"*That* one next," the detective proposed.

"I'm dry," Caplan said and tapped his empty machine gun.

Studying the marksman's weapon, Malone saw that it wouldn't take the 9-millimeter bullets in Ito's clips. Malone looked into the dead terrorist's flight bag. There were only two full magazines left, and two totally undamaged antennas to kill.

It took one and a half clips to knock down the third one.

MAC-11 clips came in two sizes. These were the bigger ones with thirty-two rounds, and Malone estimated that he had about sixteen or seventeen bullets left. He had tried to count the shots when he began firing this final magazine, but he wasn't sure. There might be only fourteen or fifteen rounds remaining. Whichever number was correct, it would be almost impossible to wreck the last mast with so little ammunition.

But he had to—immediately.

They had done the "almost impossible" in finding the jammer and these antennas in a major blizzard, and Frank Malone wasn't going to let Venom and his gunmen and their booby traps defeat him now.

Then he thought about the booby traps.

*Maybe.*

It was logical, and his only hope.

If the bastards had booby trapped the inside of the warehouse, it was possible that they'd rigged the antennas with explosive devices to protect them.

Antipersonnel weapons to delay or slay intruders.

That would fit vicious and methodical Willi Staub's pattern.

Malone stared at the last antenna, but the December night and heavy snowfall drastically limited what he could see. He walked five yards to the left to try from another angle. It wasn't any better.

Right or wrong, he had to shoot now.

Where would the terrorists put it? Somewhere very low on the mast, he reasoned. Of course, that would explain why the earlier bursts hadn't found the charges. If there were any, he thought grimly as he raised Takeshi Ito's weapon.

Now he noticed that Caplan was standing a few feet away with a regulation policeman's .38-caliber pistol in his right hand. Still angry, the "shooter" wasn't giving up either.

They began firing. It was extremely difficult to limit the

MAC-11 to very short bursts, but Malone tried. They scored a dozen hits, but there was no explosion. Then Malone heard the sound that announced that his last clip was exhausted.

Maybe there was no booby trap anywhere.

There *had* to be.

Malone drew his own .38 from its shoulder holster. How many rounds had he fired at Ito? Five? No, six. He pulled out the chamber and reloaded.

The two stubborn policemen resumed firing.

And the booby trap blew up.

The antenna swayed, hung in the wind for several seconds and dropped. The goddam jamming machine was dead.

Now the planes, including TWA 22 Heavy, had a chance.

With his heart pounding, Frank Malone reached out and shook hands with the marksman. Then Malone slid his pistol into its holster, took off the bulky flak jacket and the battle helmet and ran down to the street.

He kept running until he reached the ESU van.

"Come on," he said to the Coast Guard pilot.

When the van reached the helicopter ninety seconds later, Frank Malone told the copilot to turn on his radio. Malone had to be sure.

"It's been on for five minutes," Babbitt answered. "I've been trying to reach our base."

"Trying?" the detective asked.

"And getting nowhere," the young copilot complained.

"But the jamming stopped a couple of minutes ago."

"For ten seconds. Then it started up again."

So it wasn't over.

The son of a bitch had a backup transmitter.

That would be typical of methodical murderous Willi Staub, and exactly what Malone should have expected.

"They've got *another* jammer," Malone told the Coast Guard fliers, "and we have to find it *right* away. I'm coming with you."

Ernesto Saldana pointed at the broken rotor blade.

"I don't know if we can even get the bird up with that damage," he said. "And if we do, it's going to be real hairy with a busted blade in this kind of storm."

"Your extra weight won't help," Babbitt told the detective.

"I'm sure you guys are right," Malone said. "Where do I sit?"

The pilots looked at each other.

"My daughter's in one of those planes," Malone said.

The fliers glanced at each other again. They considered the severe penalties they might face for violating specific Coast Guard safe-flying regulations. They thought about the acute immediate danger to themselves. Then they both nodded.

"Get in the back," Saldana told Malone, "and pray."

They took their places in the big H-65, and the pilots rushed through their preflight checklist. Malone waited impatiently behind them on a jump seat near the winch operator while Babbitt and Saldana completed their required ritual.

"*You* can pray, too, Vince," the aircraft commander said. "Here we go."

He fed power to the turbines. Everything sounded all right, Saldana decided, but he knew that all four of them could be dead in sixty seconds—or hideously burned for life. Pushing those realities from his mind, Saldana cautiously increased the thrust.

The jet engines whined loudly. They seemed almost deafening to Frank Malone, who had no headset to keep out the thunderous noise. Now the helicopter began to vibrate. Four . . . five . . . six seconds later, it left the ground.

Saldana was taking no unnecessary chances in his takeoff. He guided the Aerospatiale away from the wall that had broken the rotor blade, and he took the large search-and-rescue machine up slowly. Shielded from the storm's gusts by the buildings that surrounded it, the H-65 was relatively safe for the moment. What troubled Saldana was what might happen when his damaged machine was up higher and out in the open sky.

The helicopter continued to ascend. Saldana fed it more fuel as it passed the roofs, building power and momentum to resist the might of the blizzard. The two pilots watched the altimeter: one hundred . . . two hundred . . . three hundred feet. Saldana listened carefully for any sound of rotor problems.

Nothing.

Four hundred . . . five hundred . . . six hundred.

Then a blast of wind hit the helicopter like a hammer. The H-65 lurched and tilted at a 90-degree angle. Blaming the storm, the missing piece of rotor blade and himself in soft sibilant Spanish, Ernesto Saldana skillfully adjusted the rotor pitch with one hand and guided the machine higher with the other.

The storm struck again.

It slammed the Coast Guard craft to the left, and then it pounded the machine with another blast of wind from the opposite direction. The H-65 bucked and jumped, but Ernesto Saldana kept putting it back on course.

Seven hundred . . . eight hundred . . . nine hundred.

Suddenly there was less wind. Neither of the pilots had any idea as to why, or whether this patch of meteorological peace would continue. They realized that they had to start the electronic search immediately.

Babbitt turned on the radio direction finder.

Within seconds the needle spun and he heard the sound. Saldana adjusted the helicopter's course, flying south toward the source of the signal. Some thirty seconds passed before the two pilots saw the needle move.

There could be but one explanation.

Moments later, the hoist operator gestured for Malone to come to his post. When the detective got there, the crewman handed him his headset. Malone put it on immediately.

"Good news and bad news, Captain," the aircraft commander announced.

"Have you found their transmitter?" Malone asked urgently.

"That's the good news. The bad news is that the damn thing seems to be moving."

Very professional . . . very cunning . . . very Staub.

The master terrorist's backup jammer was in a vehicle that was slowly cruising along the snowswept city's half-deserted streets. It was probably an ordinary-looking truck, utterly inconspicuous and driven carefully by some disciplined armed fanatic who was complying with every traffic regulation.

"Can you catch up with it?" Malone asked.

"I think so," Saldana answered. "Our direction finder's working fine. With a little luck and full power, we can probably be over that thing in about three minutes."

"Do it," the detective told him.

In the cockpit, the aircraft commander hesitated. Full power could move the helicopter at 180 miles an hour—under ideal conditions. With a truncated rotor blade, it might also cripple the main propulsion unit. Saldana decided to fly at 140 miles per hour. That would be safer, and the extra half a minute *couldn't* be that crucial anyway.

As the H-65 accelerated, Malone thought about Staub's mobile jammer. Power probably came from an efficient portable generator running on diesel oil from an extra tank beside it. The system wouldn't need a ton of fuel. Two hours' worth would be enough to massacre the thousands of people in the trapped airliners.

Now his concentration switched to something much more urgent. In another 110 or 120 seconds, the helicopter would be directly above the enemy's transmitter. From two hundred or three hundred feet up, how could the men in the H-65 identify and stop a truck moving through a blizzard?

They didn't know its size, color or configuration.

There might be several other trucks nearby.

How precise was the damn radio direction finder anyway?

And if they did pinpoint the terrorists' vehicle, they would need powerful weapons to attack it effectively. The few rounds left in the .38-caliber pistol under Frank Malone's arm would hardly halt a large moving truck—if he hit it. There was also the likelihood that the men in the truck had automatic weapons that they'd turn on the helicopter.

Malone looked around, but saw no guns mounted.

He turned to the winch operator.

"What kind of weapons do you carry?" Malone asked over the noise of the turbines.

"I don't carry anything," Luther King replied, "and the pilots don't either."

"I mean the aircraft," Malone said impatiently.

"We're not a navy fighter-bomber, Mister," the winch operator told him. "We're Coast Guard search and rescue. We don't chase dope boats. We save lives. This is *my* weapon."

He patted the hoisting device beside him.

The detective looked at it, and decided that it would be no match for either a moving truck or a 9-millimeter submachine gun. At that moment, he heard Saldana's voice through the earphones Malone was still wearing.

"Target has turned toward us. We are closing rapidly. Estimated time of intercept—about ninety seconds."

"Do you have anything—any kind of gun or bomb or *anything*—we can use to stop that mobile jammer?"

Saldana thought for several seconds.

"I'm afraid not," he finally answered.

"Sound rising sharply," the copilot announced. "Distance to transmitter about half a mile."

"Taking her down to two hundred," Saldana said.

The H-65 lost altitude rapidly.

"Max sound. Max sound. Target dead ahead," Babbitt reported.

"Searchlight," the aircraft commander ordered curtly.

Babbitt flicked the switch, stabbing a powerful beam down through the storm.

There was a large truck beneath them, about forty feet ahead.

It was difficult to make out the truck's exact color or type through the falling snow, but one thing was clear: None of the other moving vehicles nearby on this street was big enough to contain the jammer, generator and fuel tank.

Staub's backup unit *had* to be in that truck.

They had found it, but that wasn't enough.

They had to destroy it.

"Let's get a better look," Malone said.

"Descending to one hundred," Saldana responded and eased the altitude control forward.

In the truck cab, the former Lebanese dental student was suddenly aware of a strange whining-thumping noise. He couldn't quite identify it. With the windows shut tight and the storm pounding outside, the sound that he heard was not clear.

Peering ahead, he saw nothing unusual in the light traffic. His rearview mirror showed a couple of ordinary civilian cars. It didn't occur to him to look up. He couldn't have done that anyway.

He decided to ignore the odd noise. He would concentrate on doing his job. He had listened intently as Hugo had told him to, and he had turned on the jammer in the truck when he heard the other one fall silent. Now all he had to do was to continue to follow the plan—and be careful.

He eyed the rearview mirror again. The street behind seemed unusually bright. One of the stupid drivers back there must have turned on his "high beams." Then the man from Beirut looked at the street ahead.

No police cars. No road blocks. Nothing could stop him now.

"I think it's *green*," Babbitt said as he stared down at the truck.

Beside him, Saldana strained to maintain the rotorcraft's position. The terrorists' vehicle was moving at fourteen or fifteen miles an hour, and at that speed it was difficult to keep the H-65 in place in the surging storm. Then the truck suddenly stopped. So did the rest of the adjacent traffic.

"Looks like a red light," Saldana said as he halted the helicopter's forward movement.

Frank Malone recognized the danger immediately. Every instant that H-65 hovered over the motionless truck increased the risk that the terrorists would detect the defenseless rotorcraft and shoot it down.

"Take her up! Take her up!" Malone called out urgently.

As the helicopter began to rise, Malone spoke again.

"Kill the light!"

Babbitt complied at once. The Coast Guard craft ascended for another twenty-five seconds before Saldana halted the climb.

"We're at four-fifty," he said. "That's high enough?"

"I hope so," the detective answered. "Down again when they start to move."

Then the copilot asked *the* question.

"To do what?"

At that moment, the winch operator pointed at a metal box bolted to the inside of the fuselage a few feet away. Malone read the two small words stenciled on the lid, and felt a surge of hope.

"It's not exactly a weapon," King said.

"Don't apologize," Malone replied. "How many in there?"

"Four or five."

"It'll have to do," the detective said. Then he explained his plan to the three airmen.

"My God!" Babbitt gasped. "If you do that, a whole bunch of people might get killed."

"A lot more will die *for sure* if I don't," Malone answered.

"Our only chance is complete surprise. Use the light as little as possible until we're alongside."

The headlights below were moving. Traffic was flowing again. Saldana started to guide the H-65 down in a smooth descent.

"We're gonna have a major damn accident," Babbitt warned.

"*At least*," Saldana agreed coolly. "Give me ten seconds of searchlight, Vince. . . . *There* she is. Okay, kill it."

Half a dozen feet behind the pilots, Malone opened the metal box. He removed the fat-mouthed flare pistol, took out one of the rockets and put it in the stubby signaling gun.

"Ready back there?" Saldana asked.

Malone pointed at the wide door beside the winch operator, and King opened it. The two men shivered in the rush of icy air.

"Ready," Malone answered.

"Good. When they stop again at the next red light, we'll whip right in."

The detective looked at his wristwatch.

"Do it *now*," he said.

Some twenty seconds later, the man in the truck noticed that the whining-thumping noise was back. It was much louder than before, and seemed to come from somewhere directly behind him. A glance at the rearview mirror showed nothing unusual. It was very different when he looked ahead.

Facing the mind-boggling threat of an imminent head-on collision with a helicopter, bug-eyed drivers of vehicles coming toward the truck from the opposite direction twisted their steering wheels in panic. Some made sharp turns to escape up a side street. More frantic, others drove up onto the sidewalk. One slammed his compact Toyota into the side of a parked delivery van, breaking most of the bones in his body.

None of this automotive anarchy made any sense to the terrorist in the truck, who couldn't quite believe what he was seeing. The noise grew deafening, and a moment later he couldn't see anything.

Babbitt had turned on the H-65's searchlight, carefully spearing its powerful beam into the truck's cab. Momentarily blinded, the driver instinctively raised his left hand to shield his eyes as his right hand spun the wheel to get away from the dazzling pain.

He had to find out what was happening. Squinting between cupped fingers, he looked over his shoulder and saw something huge and blurry for a few seconds. Then he couldn't face the bright brutal thing anymore. He turned his head away from the glare, blinking as he faced forward again.

As he did, he realized that he was being stalked by a helicopter. Suddenly he felt better. He knew how to fight helicopters. The Israelis and other imperialists used them a lot, so tactics to defeat such aircraft were part of basic training at the camp where he had met Hugo. He would not let Hugo down, the determined driver resolved.

Hugo had taught him that helicopters were vulnerable from behind. If he could get in back of this one, he could wreck its tail rotor with gunfire and it would spin out of control. The compact Beretta M-12 submachine gun on the seat beside him should do the job, he thought as he rolled the window down five inches.

Then he stepped on the brake—hard.

The trick worked.

The helicopter pilot was caught by surprise. The rotorcraft began to sweep past the truck. Now out of the blinding beam, the driver saw someone framed in an open side door. The terrorist took his foot off the brake, lowered the window another five inches and picked up the machine gun.

Malone fired the flare pistol. The signal rocket flashed through the open window, spewing acrid, colored smoke and sparks as it dug into the dashboard. Coughing in the choking fumes that billowed around him, the terrorist frantically tried to pull the missile loose.

The skin on his hand blistered as he clawed at the sizzling flare, but he couldn't stop. He realized that he must get the thing out of the truck before its fumes overcame him. He knew he had only fifteen or twenty seconds before he lost control.

His estimate was incorrect.

He didn't have any time at all.

Malone fired his second rocket. This one plunged into the driver's left shoulder, ripping muscles and charring flesh as it stabbed three inches into him. He screamed. It was a howl of both hurt and horror. Through the chemical fumes of the colored smoke, he could smell his body burning.

He was a courageous and stubborn man, but he had a low threshold for pain. He was still trying to rip the missile out when he slumped forward over the steering wheel, unconscious. His foot slid from the gas pedal, but the big van kept rolling forward on momentum. As it slowly lost speed, the uncontrolled vehicle began to drift to the left.

Inexorably.

Right across traffic from the opposite direction.

In the endangered vehicles, the men and women behind the steering wheels shouted, prayed and swore as they tried to avoid a fatal collision. Moving at them like a four-ton battering ram, the truck cut diagonally between the bucking zigzagging cars and swept through a red light. It missed a bus by inches.

Then it crashed into a massive self-propelled crane. Parked in the street beside a half-finished apartment house, the large piece of heavy construction machinery stopped the runaway vehicle like a stone wall. The impact caved in the whole front of the truck, ruptured the fuel line and burst open the door beside the unconscious driver.

He fell out of the truck.

The sputtering flare embedded in the dashboard didn't. Tiny flames were flickering as the padding and plastic ignited, adding another foul smell to that of the colored smoke still pouring from the rocket.

Some one hundred twenty feet overhead, the helicopter circled slowly with its bright searchlight beam never leaving the terrorists' truck.

"Let's get in closer," the detective said.

"That might not be a good idea," Saldana warned.

"Why?"

Suddenly the flames in the cab leaped higher. The fuel tank exploded a moment later, leaving the broken vehicle a blazing hulk. The fire shot high in the air, and so did a twisting pillar of acrid black fumes.

"*That's* why," the helicopter commander told Malone. "Now let's check our radio. I'll tune you in."

The pilots and Malone listened intently.

There was no interference of any kind on any of the six civilian or military aviation frequencies that Ernesto Saldana tested.

"All clear," Saldana said.

For how long?

Calculating, obsessive Willi Staub could have a third jammer—or something else.

Even if the airwaves were open for the moment, there were very few moments left. Malone realized that he had to return to Kennedy at once. That was where the final battle of this war would be fought—probably within the next twenty minutes. The H-65 could get him there in less than five, Malone estimated.

"Can you take me to JFK? *Right away?*" he asked urgently.

The helicopter commander thought of the danger of flying into the airport in a heavy snowstorm, with all those big jets circling blindly and no radar or air traffic control to keep them from smashing into the Coast Guard rotorcraft. Then he thought of the people in the airliners.

"No sweat," he lied and guided the H-65 higher.

He leveled off at six hundred feet. Since the airliners were probably circling well up above one thousand, an altitude of six hundred would be relatively safe. Well, it *ought* to be.

Standing beside the winch a few yards away, Frank Malone was busy with his own calculations. The seven prisoners whom the terrorists had demanded would reach JFK at any minute. So would Staub and his team, if they weren't there already. No, the shrewd wary man code-named Venom had probably been there for some time, spying on his enemy's strength and positions. Collecting up-to-the-minute intelligence about his foes was part of Staub's pattern and a reason that he was still alive.

But his information was incomplete, Malone calculated as he looked out at the snow. Staub didn't know that Malone had learned Number One's identity, or that the detective had figured out what was behind the entire operation. Six prisoners on Staub's list belonged to revolutionary groups that generally used basic conventional weapons.

The seventh was *different*. That had been the clue.

The seventh wasn't a revolutionary at all. He was a greedy merchant who sold high-tech arms to an immensely rich dictator. There could be but one reason why rabid leftist terrorist Willi Staub would rescue capitalist Arnold Lloyd—a lot of money.

Enough to fund this complex electronic assault.

Enough to fund years of Staub's future operations.

Lloyd couldn't provide that much cash, but General al-Khalif had billions and good reason to keep the amoral ex-CIA man from going to trial. That must be it, Malone reasoned. Sleazy Arnold Lloyd was the key card in this barbarous game.

The odds were shifting.

Two terrorists and their transmitters had been taken out of the war. Malone now shared one of Willi Staub's vital secrets, and the terrorist chief didn't know it. At the right time, Frank Malone would use that secret . . . would use Lloyd . . . against him.

But there was almost no time left. The detective studied his watch. If Annie Green's estimate was right, TWA 22 Heavy would exhaust its fuel in about one and a half minutes.

She must be wrong, Malone told himself. She had to be.

# 35

*HE WAS WATCHING* her again.

The pretty woman in the nun's habit didn't dare turn her eyes to look at him. She didn't have to. She knew it.

From the moment she boarded the Aerovias 767, she had been aware that the chief steward was paying special attention to her. His oily pretense that it was respect for a member of the clergy didn't fool her. He was probably an informer for the secret police. There would be nothing surprising about that; the airline was owned by the government and the government had spies everywhere.

The people who had given her the package to deliver at Kennedy Airport hadn't prepared her for this. She didn't know what to do, and it was so noisy in the plane now it was hard to think. She wasn't the only one who was afraid. Many others were frightened by the unexplained delay and the storm.

You couldn't tell by listening to them, she thought. Raised in the macho tradition of never showing doubt or distress, most of the Latin men were speaking even more loudly than usual. Radiating exaggerated assurance, some told jokes and laughed boisterously. The women nearby were quieter, concentrating on reading, repairing their nails and wondering whether there really was an afterlife.

Now the sly steward was coming directly to her.

"It's just a minor technical problem," he lied with an ease that reflected years of airline employment. "There's nothing to worry about, Sister."

"Why should I worry?" she responded evasively. "We're all in His hands, aren't we?"

"Of course," the dapper steward agreed with much more sincerity than he felt. His earnest expression changed as he walked away a moment later. He was smiling as he thought of the men and money—so much money—waiting for him in New York.

In the British Airways 747 cruising a mile away, the buxom blond stewardess was also smiling—dutifully, not joyfully. British Airways had made it quite clear that she owed it to the company and the passengers to be cheerful at all times, especially in stressful situations.

It was a damn sight more stressful on BA 126 tonight than most of the passengers realized, she told herself as she worked diligently to keep her smile in place. So far only the crew knew about the extraordinary situation, though there were signs that a number of travelers were getting increasingly uneasy. Most of the worried ones had stopped speaking altogether. Sitting stiff and silent, they didn't even ask any questions. A number of them avoided eye contact with her completely.

They were controlling their tension for the moment, but she suspected that it wouldn't last much longer. Somebody—

probably not a British passenger—would get a bit difficult soon. It might be one of those emotional *foreigners*—perhaps a person back in Economy Class, she thought. It certainly wouldn't be anyone such as Sir Brian, she reflected as she eyed the poised and patrician diplomat admiringly.

Then a passenger seated six rows behind the U.N. delegate stood up and stepped into the aisle. It was the young man with the black attaché case. He was still holding it as he spoke.

"I don't want to die," he announced loudly.

A well-dressed London barrister nearby looked away, pretending he hadn't heard.

"I don't want to die," he insisted in tones tinged with hysteria. "Tell the pilot to go back."

"Now, sir—" the stewardess began soothingly.

She didn't finish her sentence.

"I'll tell him!" the wild-eyed man with the leather case screamed. "I'll make him do it!"

Shouting incoherently, he began running forward toward the cockpit. When the stewardess tried to block his way, he hurled her aside. He knocked a gray-haired Nashville newspaper publisher down with one stunning blow of the case. Three seconds later, Miss Ellen Jenkins of the Foreign Office rose and struck the hysterical passenger in the pit of the stomach with the stiff extended fingers of her right hand.

He gasped and staggered. Then he collapsed.

The cabin crew rushed forward to deal with him, and Ellen Jenkins smoothed her skirt as she sat down again beside her boss.

"You never cease to amaze me," Sir Brian Forsythe said.

"It seemed like the right thing to do, Ambassador," she told the man she loved.

"It was. Now where did you learn *that*?" he asked.

He seemed genuinely interested as she began to tell him. He leaned forward to listen. Unaware of the fact that BA 126 would run out of fuel in minutes, she enjoyed the closeness.

Some two thousand feet above the British jumbo jet, several passengers on the TWA L-1011 were making it clear that they weren't enjoying anything. Three movie studio executives and the "young hunk" star of this season's least obnoxious situation comedy series on ABC-TV complained aggressively about the outrageous lateness. The surly young man traveling with the Styrofoam box was even more irate.

"If this thing doesn't get to New York soon," he told the Chinese-American flight attendant as he tapped the plastic container, "you're going to be murderers. A man's going to die because of this dumb airline."

Suppressing a desire to set him on fire, footsore and bone-tired Samantha Wong assured him that she would communicate the urgency of the situation to Captain Pace immediately. In the cockpit, the senior pilot didn't need any reminder that he was in a life-or-death emergency. One look at the fuel gauges told it all.

Swallowing another antacid pill to cope with the pain in his stomach, Pace decided to try the radio for the hundredth time. He grinned when he heard a human voice—loud and clear.

"This is Kennedy Tower. Stand by for instructions."

Then Pace felt the tingling sensation zigzag up his left arm, and the cockpit temperature seemed to escalate dramatically. His arm hurt. Now the pain coursed over to his chest, and he knew. This didn't have anything to do with financial worries or spicy food.

It was what every pilot feared most.

He was having a heart attack—in flight.

He was covered with sweat and his arm was burning, and something was hurting his chest intensely. This was no minor cardiac "incident"—the veteran pilot realized that. He was aware that he needed immediate help, but there was something else that came first. Woman-chasing, tax-beating, autocratic and *totally* professional Lawrence Pace had to protect the passengers.

That came before medical care for himself.

That came before anything.

"Don . . . Don," he appealed hoarsely to his copilot as he released his harness. "You've got to—"

Then he lost consciousness, falling forward against the controls. Before the copilot could intervene, the big jet went into a steep dive. There was chaos in the passenger cabin as the packed transport dropped swiftly.

It fell a thousand feet in seconds. Screaming through the winter wind, it hurtled straight toward the Japan Air Lines cargo plane. The cool and experienced senior pilot on the freighter responded quickly and professionally. With scant moments to react to the threat, Captain Shigeta expertly turned his plane sharply right and avoided the L-1011 by barely a hundred yards.

It was a masterpeice of flying, copilot Kenyi Tokoro thought proudly. His wise and skillful captain had saved hundreds of lives. Why there was no telling how many people might—

There was *another* airliner directly ahead.

It looked like a twin-jet, perhaps one of those one-hundred-and-ten seaters used on some U.S. carriers' hourly shuttle services. Stunned, copilot Kenji Tokoro caught only a very brief glimpse of the other plane before he died.

An instant after the freighter and the shuttle plane collided, an explosion that could be heard ten miles away boomed across the sky. A huge fireball rivaling the moon suddenly blossomed over a residential area near Kennedy Airport.

And things began to fall from the heavens.

White-hot things.

Twisted things.

Scorched and broken things.

Metal and plastic. Bone and flesh.

In addition to the crews of the two aircraft, fifty-seven people traveling on the passenger plane perished. So did three bowlers en route to their weekly game when an engine from the freighter dropped on their car. Flaming debris set four houses ablaze as TWA 22 Heavy finally leveled off at thirteen hundred feet.

Still dressed in clerical attire, Willi Staub had stepped outside the International Arrivals Building to see whether the seven prisoners on his list were arriving. He saw three of them, under heavy guard, emerge from city police cars. He was wondering about the other four—the ones in federal hands—when the fireball flashed. Then the blast of the collision thundered through the night.

He understood immediately.

He knew exactly what had happened, and he was glad.

It would teach them a lesson, he thought.

Now they wouldn't dare resist. Freeing the other six would make Willi Staub a hero to the whole world of revolutionary fighters. Getting Lloyd out would bring the funds to take the armed struggle everywhere. The FBI should be delivering Lloyd and the other federal prisoners at any moment, and the DC-10 was ready to take off immediately.

Knowing what the enemy was doing had been a great help, Staub thought smugly as he turned to start for the rendezvous. It had been vital in making this operation such a success. His meticulous planning—right down to using fighters from different groups with weapons made by various countries as a smokescreen—had worked perfectly.

Tonight was only the beginning, of course.

Willi Staub would be back.

Warmed by this prospect, he continued toward the far end of the building. He was halfway there when he heard something overhead. It sounded like the whine of a small jet engine.

# 36

*THE SNOW* was falling even more heavily now, but that didn't bother Babbitt. The lights of The Cab did. He flinched when he suddenly spotted them.

Not below.

At the same altitude as the jet-powered rotorcraft, barely a hundred yards to the left.

Not much more than that ahead.

"*Jeezus*," the startled copilot reacted loudly.

"I see it, Vince," Saldana assured as he turned the H-65 sharply to the right.

The helicopter landed behind the International Arrivals Building half a minute later. Malone leaped out, crouched under the whirling rotor and ran on past a parked DC-10 to the terminal. When he reached The Cab, he saw the control-

lers speaking into their microphones again. Despite the fact
that the jamming was over, their faces were as grim as before.

"Midair collision," Wilber said angrily and pointed
north toward a dim glow.

Annie Green answered the question before Malone could
ask it.

"Your daughter's plane is still up there, Frank."

He resumed breathing again.

"Are you bringing them down?" the detective asked.

"We can't. Radar and ILS are still out," Wilber replied.

"But the radio's working."

"We're using it right now to divert as many planes as we
can to alternates. That's the best we can do," Wilber told him.

"Why not all of them?"

"Some don't have enough fuel to go anywhere else," the
FAA executive explained. "If the wind hadn't changed, a
couple would have run out already."

TWA 22 Heavy had the least fuel left.

It must be one of them.

"You did the numbers, Annie," Malone said. "How much
longer can they stay up?"

"It's hard to say. There are a lot of variables."

"*Five* minutes? *Three?*"

"I don't know. I'm not God, Frank. I'm a watch supervisor. Look, we're talking to the pilots about it. They *could* try
to land without radar."

"And there could be another midair collision," he
responded harshly.

Then Hamilton hurried into The Cab, walkie-talkie in
hand.

"All seven are here," he reported. "Just got word the FBI
convoy arrived with its four. Now what?"

Before Malone could answer, a telephone rang.

It was the outside line.

"This is Number One. Are you ready to make the delivery?"

"Yes, as soon as you stop jamming the radar," Malone replied.

"*After* we're outside U.S. airspace. Don't try to bargain with me, Stupid. You've got nothing to bargain with," Staub taunted. "What about our long-range jet?"

Malone pointed down at the big airliner on the apron near the Coast Guard helicopter.

"Is that their plane?"

Wilber nodded.

"Set to go?"

"Full tanks and the flying crew's in the cockpit."

"There's a DC-ten waiting for you about sixty yards from the International Arrivals Building," Malone told the terrorist. "It's ready for immediate takeoff."

"Pilots and navigator on board?"

"In the cockpit."

"Tell them to start the engines," Staub ordered.

He hung up the phone and walked quickly from the terminal. As he strode through the snow to rejoin the Puerto Rican brothers in the white van, he smiled.

"We've won!" Willi Staub said triumphantly to the storm.

It hadn't gone exactly as he wanted, but that didn't matter much. The fact that the men assigned to operate the two jammers were not here wasn't important. They had obviously made some errors, deviated from his perfect plan. That was annoying, but Staub certainly didn't need those fools anymore. Like everyone else he knew, they were disposable. They had served their purpose.

And he had done what he had set out to do.

He had outwitted the reputedly impregnable air traffic control system, massed local and federal police forces and total military might of what was supposed to be the greatest power on earth.

One man—Willi Staub—had defeated the United States.

Delighted by that thought, he chuckled. He was still grinning when he reached the van. Juan and Paco Garcia stared at him curiously as he opened the right front door. The older brother was behind the wheel, and Paco Garcia was looking through an opening from the rear compartment. Neither brother had ever seen this cold and domineering man smile before.

"Good news?" Juan Garcia asked as Staub settled into the front seat beside him.

"*Of course.* Let's go."

As always, Staub had considered every fact and possibility in shaping his plan. He'd expected that there would be crowds of civilians filling the International Arrivals Building. He'd also anticipated that there would be many police in the terminal by this phase of the operation. He didn't want to deal with either group, so he had decided to avoid the building.

He had worked out another way to get out onto the airfield. Using a map and photographs, he had drilled the Garcias on exactly what to do and say. The two young FALN members had carried out his instructions efficiently in blowing up the key microwave relay towers right on schedule. Now he would make sure that the brothers performed with similar precision here.

As Juan Garcia started the motor, Staub took out his 9-millimeter pistol and screwed on its silencer. He put the weapon on his lap, carefully covering the gun with part of his raincoat. The van cruised slowly down a curving service road for more than half a mile before it turned off at a gate marked AUTHORIZED VEHICLES ONLY. Juan Garcia stopped the small truck beside the guard post.

"Your pass?" the security man asked from his booth.

"Medical emergency. We're from Queens General," Juan Garcia told him. "Some Delta mechanic's had a heart attack. Father Shanley's with us to give the last rites."

QUEENS GENERAL HOSPITAL was neatly stenciled on both sides of the white van. The driver wore the equally white uniform of a paramedic, and the sober-faced man beside him was garbed in the black attire and stiff white collar of a priest.

"You're supposed to have a pass," the guard said.

"*Please*," Staub appealed earnestly as he reached for the pistol. "We're told the poor man doesn't have much time."

His fingers closed around the gun butt.

He released the safety catch.

Peering through the swirling snow, the guard hesitated, thought about his own uncle in the oxygen tent at Bellevue and opened the gate.

"Bless you," Willi Staub sighed with a well-practiced hint of piety a moment before Juan Garcia stepped on the gas pedal.

The van rolled through the portal onto the airfield.

Within seconds, it was out of sight in the storm.

# 37

''*I WANT* to ask you something,'' Hamilton said to Malone as the tower elevator descended.

"Ask."

"I hear a lot of people died in that damn collision. At least seventy."

"Is that the question?"

The Port Authority lieutenant shook his head.

"The question is whether you're really going to do this," he said. "Are you *really* going to let the bastards who murdered seventy people fly out of here?"

"What would you do?"

"I'd take a rifle with a scope onto the roof and blow those bastards away," Hamilton replied vehemently.

"That wouldn't help all the people still up there. There are a lot more than seventy . . . maybe twenty times that. To answer your question, I'm going to do whatever it takes to get that radar working again. That's their only chance."

"So the bastards walk?"

"Unless something changes," Malone replied as the elevator door opened. As they stepped out, Malone recognized the face of the man walking toward them. It was Inspector Barry Kincaid of the FBI's local antiterrorist unit. Concisely and swiftly, Frank Malone briefed him on the urgent situation.

"Okay, we'll take it from here," Kincaid said.

The FBI was asserting its authority.

"No way," Frank Malone said quickly. "They've been dealing with me, and there's no time to change players. It would be too dangerous."

"Better let the captain finish this," Hamilton advised.

"Who the hell are you?"

"Lieutenant Benjamin Hamilton, Port Authority Police. *I'm* in charge of security at this airport tonight, Mister."

"Federal law says terrorism's ours," the FBI inspector reminded.

"*All* yours—the minute those planes up there land," Malone proposed. "If anything goes wrong before then, I'll be responsible."

And the Bureau wouldn't be blamed.

"Okay," Kincaid agreed.

"Good. We're delivering the seven prisoners on the apron behind the International Arrivals Building," Malone told him. "Bring your four around there—on the double."

"We have a problem," Kincaid replied. "There was an accident on the way out. Some idiot slammed his car into one of ours. A prisoner was seriously injured."

"Bring him out on a stretcher, if you have to. We need all seven."

The federal agent shook his head.

"I'm sorry, Frank. About five minutes ago, just as we reached the terminal, he died."

Malone tensed.

"Who was it?"

"Arnold Lloyd."

Now he really had nothing to bargain with.

With Lloyd dead, there was no telling what the homicidal Willi Staub might do.

Or not do.

Denied his prize, the frustrated terrorist might not turn off the radar jamming at all.

"We've got a problem all right," Malone said.

He thought . . . he made his decision.

"We promised seven and we'll deliver seven," he announced. "Here's what I want you to do."

Kincaid listened, and left to carry out the instructions. As he walked away, Malone tapped Hamilton's walkie-talkie.

"Pass the word to bring the other three to the apron," the detective said. Hamilton lifted the radio and swiftly relayed the message.

"Tell the cops it's an order," he concluded. "Right, Captain Malone . . . I'll tell him. . . . Anything else? . . . You're sure? . . . You better let The Cab know."

He was visibly troubled as he turned to Malone.

"Men from your own unit are on the way from the terminal," he reported.

"But that's not what's bothering you."

"No. There was a radio message from the Jersey State Police. They found one of their patrol cars off the highway near a microwave relay tower. The two cops working the car were shot to pieces, and the tower blasted into scrap. Then they found another one wrecked. I'd bet there are some more blown-up towers in New York," the Port Authority lieutenant said harshly.

"What does it mean?"

"Those towers relay radar signals for miles from sensors to the controllers' screens at airports," Hamilton explained.

"No microwave towers, no radar images in The Cab, no air traffic control."

"And no way he can turn the radar back on," Frank Malone reasoned inexorably. "The bastard never intended to. He *meant* to kill them all."

The door to the bridge from the terminal opened, and nine plainclothes policemen from Malone's antiterrorist unit entered the tower lobby. Two officers carried submachine guns, another held one of the very accurate scope-equipped M-14 rifles used by snipers and a third grasped an automatic shotgun. Malone nodded to his team, walked forward and took the rifle.

"See you later," he said to Hamilton evenly.

Then he gave him the rifle.

# 38

"*TWA TWENTY-TWO HEAVY* to Kennedy Tower. Our cardiac patient is hardly breathing now. Is that medical team we requested ready?"

"Kennedy Tower to TWA twenty-two Heavy. Ambulances, fire engines and other emergency service units are standing by to assist."

The two men pacing the apron behind the International Arrivals Building were both dressed in dark overcoats. Properly attired in accord with Bureau policy, the FBI inspector also wore a neat gray fedora. Malone walked bareheaded beside him, indifferent to the snow.

"Where are they?" Kincaid asked uneasily.

"They'll be here."

"How will they get out on the apron?"

"He'll do something *cute*," Malone predicted. "It's Venom, Barry. He's always cute."

"*Venom?*" Kincaid erupted. "Why didn't you say so?"

Malone pointed off to the left. Through the snow, they could see the lights of a vehicle moving slowly toward them. It stopped about fifty yards away, engine throbbing and headlights beaming. Peering through their glare, Malone made out the boxy shape of a white panel truck or van.

Now the lights flared to maximum strength.

The driver had turned on his high-intensity "brights" to blind them.

*Very* cute, Frank Malone thought as he waited for the terrorists to emerge from the dazzling beams.

They didn't.

Instead, a voice boomed out over an electric bullhorn.

"Where are they?" Staub demanded in Number One's fake Hispanic accent.

Malone pointed to the terminal a dozen yards away.

"Bring them out," the terrorist ordered. "No tricks."

The detective gestured, and eight members of his antiterrorist unit emerged from the building. They lined up carefully, four on each side of the door. They stood at least five yards apart, spread out to offer minimum targets for automatic weapons.

Then another half dozen people came out.

They all wore handcuffs.

There were five males and one female.

"Power to the people!" the woman shouted enthusiastically.

Despite her sincerity, no one else on the apron paid any attention to her. Willi Staub couldn't. He was counting.

"I only see six," he said menacingly over the bullhorn.

Malone waved at the glass door behind him again, and two uniformed policemen pushed out a wheelchair. The middle-aged male it carried was wrapped in a blanket up to his shoulder. The top of his head was swathed in a bandage.

Staub studied the man through his night binoculars. It was Lloyd.

"What's wrong with him?" Staub challenged.

"He had a stroke. Fell down and hurt his head," Malone yelled over the whine of the DC-10's engines.

Staub assumed that this was a lie, but he wasn't angry.

The tortures that the American had undoubtedly inflicted on the renegade were irrelevant to this operation. The sole issue was the terms of the deal.

Dead or alive, the Soraqi ruler had said.

General al-Khalif would pay the second half of the fee without argument so long as Lloyd was "spared the indignity" of a trial in an operation that could not be linked to Soraq. Staub had accomplished that, and in a way that would humiliate the Americans, whom al-Khalif hated. There might even be a bonus, the terrorist told himself as he stroked the reassuring grenade in his coat pocket.

Now it was time to finish the operation.

"Unlock those handcuffs," he commanded over the bullhorn.

Malone nodded, and the uniformed police took out keys to comply.

"*TWA twenty-two to Kennedy Tower. We're showing empty. Repeat, empty. Number Four engine has just died, and we've shut down Number One to stretch the last few gallons. I think we'll have to come in blind.*"

Free of the handcuffs, the six terrorists rubbed their wrists and looked toward the DC-10 some fifty yards away.

"Everyone to the plane," Staub ordered.

As the newly liberated revolutionaries started to walk, most of the police watched them. Frank Malone's eyes remained fixed on the headlights. Then he saw what he was waiting for. Three figures emerged from the glare. Two were in white, the third in darker clothes. Malone watched the trio advance toward the airliner.

Which one was Staub?

Malone had to get closer to find out.

"I'll take the chair," he said. The uniformed police who had rolled it out stepped aside, and Malone got behind and began to push it toward the airliner. Moving nearer to the big jet, he glanced furtively to the left.

There were still only three men coming from the direction of the van. This was it—Staub's entire force. This was all Willi Staub had left.

They were getting closer now.

Thirty yards.

Twenty.

Light was streaming from the airliner's window. Staub could barely control his elation as he looked up at it. He had done it. Another fifteen steps and he'd be at the stairs. He'd lead the six up, and the Garcias could carry the motionless body of Arnold Lloyd into the plane.

In another two minutes the DC-10 would start rolling down the runway. Six or seven minutes after that, they would be out of U.S. airspace—safe. The trapped planes would come tumbling down behind him. The whole world would be stunned.

He glanced at the steps, then up at the open door.

That was when Frank Malone knew.

The shaft of light pouring down had made something gleam in the face of the man in black.

His right eye.

It wasn't real.

This man in clerical garb, the "priest" Malone had spoken to a little more than an hour ago, was Willi Staub.

The detective took out his pistol.

All the other police nearby immediately drew their weapons.

Resisting panic, Staub forced himself to smile.

"I wouldn't do that," he said. "If you want that radar turned on—"

"It won't work," Malone interrupted. "We know about

the towers. Now you're the one who has nothing to bargain
with. It's over, Willi."

No, it wasn't, the terrorist told himself.

It couldn't be.

His fingers touched the grenade for strength, but this time
it didn't come.

He felt his heart pounding. Desperately, his eyes swung
back and forth—and then he regained control. He didn't
need the damn grenade. Willi Staub didn't need anyone or
anything. He'd show them all. They would pay for this—and
soon. The planes would start falling any minute. That would
be his victory.

"Frisk him and cuff him," Malone said.

A sergeant stepped forward with the metal bracelet. Staub
shrugged and put out his hands. The he lifted both fists
swiftly to smash the policeman under the chin. As the cop
reeled, Staub dove to the apron and rolled under the airliner.
He was on his feet seconds later, running.

He heard the shouting and then gunfire. He hoped the
Garcia brothers were trying to get away. They might distract
the police for a minute or two before they were shot down.
That could buy him time to reach the van—his key to escape.
Once he got out of the airport in that van, they would never
find him in this major storm.

More gunfire.

Someone cried out in agony.

Another three shots.

Staub was panting as he ran around the DC-10's tail and
raced toward the vehicle that would save him. Avoiding the
beams of its headlights, he felt invisible in the snowy night.
He wasn't. A man at an open third-floor window of the terminal was watching him intently. Looking down through the M-
14's telescopic sight, Lieutenant Benjamin Hamilton
squeezed the rifle's trigger.

The 7.62-millimeter slug slammed into Staub's bulletproof vest, pounding his chest like a hammer. He staggered, stumbled, then regained his balance and kept running. The van was barely a dozen yards away. He was only a step from it when the pistol champion of the New York Police Department fired twice.

Aware of body armor, Malone didn't aim at Staub's torso.

He broke both of the terrorist's legs, just below the knees.

Staub screamed as he fell. He was still screaming when he pulled the grenade from his pocket and jerked out the pin. He looks like a rabid animal, Frank Malone thought as he shot Staub in the forehead. The detective dropped flat on the concrete apron an instant before the grenade exploded in the dead terrorist's hand.

"*TWA twenty-two Heavy to Kennedy Tower. Three engines are out and the fourth is sputtering. Correction: it's gone. All engines dead.*"

"*Can you see the field?*"

"*Negative. Airspeed falling . . . Losing altitude . . . sixteen hundred . . . fifteen hundred . . . Get those crash trucks ready. We're coming down!*"

There was silence in The Cab.

Then one of the Federal Aviation Administration's most efficient watch supervisors began to cry.

# 39

*IT HAPPENED* five seconds later.

Everyone listening to the frequency was startled.

"Hot Rod Four to TWA twenty-two. Hot Rod Four to TWA twenty-two. I have you on my screen. Bear left, thirty degrees."

"What screen? Who are you?" the surprised airline pilot blurted.

"U.S. Air Force airborne warning and command aircraft," the stranger replied in tones as Southern as pecan pie.

Mature, dignified Peter Wilber jumped to his feet.

"It's the cavalry!" he shouted in an uncharacteristically loud voice. "Goddammit, he did it!"

The E-3A Sentry—the AWACS plane loaded with Top Secret radar gear that Frank Malone had demanded so stubbornly had arrived.

"Move your ass, Boy," the controller on the air force plane pressed. "Left, thirty degrees, *now*."

Wilber grabbed a headset and microphone.

"This is Kennedy Tower. Do it!" he pleaded.

"Left, thirty," the TWA pilot agreed. "Losing altitude."

"Our screen shows you're at eleven hundred."

"Your screen's right. Now what?"

"Now I know which one of the blips is you, Boy. That turn just told me. New heading: fifty degrees right."

"Fifty, right. Down to nine hundred. How far from the field are we?"

"Not far. Maybe a mile."

"Seven hundred feet. Airspeed falling . . . I don't think we can make it."

Listening in the cockpit of Aerovias 16 three miles away, the captain looked at his own fuel gauge and wondered whether you'd really go to hell for sleeping with your sister-in-law.

"You're gonna make it, Boy," the radar officer said firmly. "Ten more to the right."

"Five hundred feet."

"Hang in there. You're doin' fine."

As the British Airways stewardess announced that an emergency landing was imminent, Sir Brian Forsythe did something quite unusual. He reached over and took Miss Ellen Jenkins's hand.

"Approaching stall speed . . . three hundred feet . . . controls getting mushy."

"You're right on the money," the lushly Southern voice assured.

"Water! I see water! My God, we're over the bay!"

"*Easy* now. Runway's just a spit ahead."

"I see the lights . . . one hundred feet. . . . We're going into the water. Send out the boats!"

"You got it made, Boy. Ten more seconds and you're home."

The TWA pilot saw the water looming closer . . . closer
"We don't have ten seconds," he said.

At that instant, the wind over Jamaica Bay grew stronger
A powerful gust suddenly lifted the falling L-1011. Its air
speed jumped fifteen miles an hour. The awed pilot stared a
the indicator incredulously.

"Maybe we do," he said.

Like the hand of God, the wind was still carrying the L
1011, providing lift. The big jet was twenty feet above the
water when it reached the shoreline. The airliner's from
wheels touched the Runway Four-Right a scant yard from
where the grooved-and-crowned asphalt strip began. Blink
ing into the high-intensity lights that framed his path, the
sweating pilot guided the plane along the runway silently fo
several seconds before he could speak.

"TWA twenty-two on the ground and rolling. Thanks a
lot, Hot Rod Four—and one more thing. Knock off that *bo*
crap, will you?"

Everyone in The Cab had been rigid with fear.

Now they all stood up and cheered.

"Just doin' my job, *Boy*," the air force officer replied
cheerfully.

Then he began directing the other planes down to safety

# 40

THE BIG L-1011 had to be towed in slowly. That was why a much faster ambulance was sent out to the runway to collect the heart attack victim and rush him to a hospital. It was also why people on planes that landed after TWA 22 Heavy reached the terminal first.

Waiting for his daughter in a corridor through which those arriving would pass, Frank Malone puffed on a cigar and listened to the noise. There had been instant uproar when the media mob and others in the lobby heard about the bloody little battle on the apron. It had grown louder when they learned about all those held hostage in the sky until a few minutes earlier.

Now it was the press pack making most of the noise—for solid journalistic reasons. The first major terrorist attack inside the United States . . . scores of corpses from a midair

collision and the airport confrontation . . . notorious Will
Staub putting thousands in peril.

Prominent people—a prince and the British member of
the United Nations Security Council, important Hollywood
figures and the newly celebrated Kiev Grandma—snatched
from death by the handsome son of a dead police hero, the
FBI and a secret and sophisticated U.S. Air Force plane that
cost $150 million.

Photo opportunities, gory details, touching accounts of
courage and drama, interviews with poignant quotes and
misquotes, pungent rehashes of the crimes of those Staub
tried to free, word and picture accounts of the master terrorist's own gruesome deeds, speculation on air traffic and airport security—there was enough sensational material for a
week.

And not a moment to waste. Pending arrival of the passengers and crews, hard-working journalists were briskly inter-
viewing Senator Joseph A. Bono, FBI Inspector Barry Kincaid, New York City's articulate and well-dressed police
commissioner, who always gave great quotes, and Lieutenant
Benjamin Hamilton. After the 128th "probing question,"
Hamilton excused himself and walked away to rejoin Malone.

He reached him as people began to come through from
Aerovias Flight 16. Among the first was a shining-eyed young
nun, as pretty as the actresses who played such parts on the
screen. Sister Teresa wasn't playing. She was intensely serious about the photos and microfilmed reports in the envelope
taped under her breasts. In a few minutes, she would give
them to the assistant head of her order, who was waiting in
the lobby. In a few days, this hard evidence of the jungle
massacres of defenseless Indians would be released to the
world.

The Aerovias steward was thirty yards behind her. He
walked with a confident gait, unaware that a dozen employ-

ees of the Drug Enforcement Administration were nearby, eagerly anticipating his delivery of the cocaine. Two of the biggest narcotics importers on the East Coast and a lot of other people would be in jail before morning.

"Those reporters want to talk to you," Hamilton said to Malone, and waved the cigar smoke away.

The detective puffed on the Don Diego and shook his head.

"Why don't you go out for just a minute?" Hamilton suggested.

"Because I've got something more important to do. Tell them I'm invoking my constitutional right to free speech."

"Free speech?"

"Yeah, I'm free not to talk to anyone I please," Malone explained. "It's a great country, isn't it?"

"Terrific. Listen, they're not going to give up," Hamilton warned.

"Let them talk to the commissioner. He speaks very well. I think he took elocution lessons."

"They want *you*. You're the guy who took out Staub, dammit."

"That's one of the things I don't want to talk about. Here comes another bunch."

It was the British Airways passengers and crew. The blond stewardess was escorting the old Russian woman. Behind her two male flight attendants had firm grips on the arms of the man who had gotten hysterical.

"I'm not mad, you know," he said firmly. "I'm just utterly terrified of flying. Please let me go. I must delivery my case to the CBS chaps immediately. It contains the master tape of the next album of a *very important* rock group. I'm not at liberty to mention the name."

"Is there a policeman about?" one of the stewards asked and nodded toward the still distraught passenger he held.

"About fifty-six of them—out there," Malone replied.

The frazzled courier was still protesting volubly as they led him away. Another score of passengers passed by before Malone recognized a familiar face.

"Good evening, Frank," the British member of the U.N. Security Council said brightly.

"Good evening, Brian. You're in pretty good spirits for a gent who almost got killed."

Sir Brian Forsythe smiled.

"I'm in *excellent* spirits," he confided.

"That's more than I can say for one of your countrymen," Malone joked. "He seemed—may I say *agitated*—when the stewards took him by ten seconds ago."

"Say anything you please," the diplomat replied. "Excuse my manners, Frank. I'd like to introduce Ellen Jenkins. She's the person who disabled that odd gent with one blow."

"I'm impressed, Miss Jenkins," Malone said politely.

"She's very impressive," Forsythe declared.

"Sir Brian's terribly generous," she demurred.

"And grateful," the senior diplomat added. "I hear that we owe you a great deal, Frank. A first-class dinner at the very least."

Then he took her arm.

"Not *tonight*, of course," Sir Brian Forsythe said briskly. "I'll phone you, Old Boy."

"That's the U.N. guy," Hamilton said a moment later. "He called you *Frank*."

"You can call me Frank, too, *Ben*."

More passengers from BA 126 . . . and still more.

Then the police commissioner of New York City came up from the lobby, smoothing his tie as he hurried. He stopped abruptly and showed a low of perfectly capped teeth—his version of a sincere smile.

"Ah, Your Highness," he said in a cloud of expensive and refined after-shave lotion, "Welcome to New York."

Malone turned the other way. He saw six male Arabs.

Four carried West German MP-5 submachine guns. The fifth wore a military uniform with the fancy gold epaulets of an aide to somebody senior. The sixth was clearly that person. Hawk-faced and radiating power, he even looked like royalty.

"Prince Omar, I'm Bruce Allan Shaw, the police commissioner of New York City."

Then Omar said something in Arabic.

"His Highness thanks you for your kindness in coming to meet him," the aide translated.

"He might also want to thank one of the outstanding members of *my* department—a man who did a great deal to smash this terrible plot and save His Highness's life. He personally killed Willi Staub. Yes, I can safely say that Captain Malone is one of *New York's finest*."

As Omar spoke again in Arabic to his aide, Hamilton saw something change in Malone's eyes. Now they looked like the muzzles of pistols—steely and dangerous.

The aide nodded deferentially, reached into the leather dispatch case he carried and took out a small rectangular box.

"His Highness has asked me to present this modest token of his profound indebtedness," the aide announced as he held out the box to Malone.

"No, thanks," Malone said harshly.

Everyone else looked startled.

"But, Captain," the commissioner protested.

"It's a watch, isn't it?" Malone said. "A solid gold Rolex."

"As a matter of fact it is," the aide replied.

"I've *got* a watch," Frank Malone announced.

Shaw was sweating visibly.

"If Prince Omar wants to make this very friendly gesture, Captain," he began.

"There is something else he can do for me," Malone broke in bluntly. "I think he knows General al-Khalif of Soraq."

"They are acquainted," the aide admitted cautiously.

"And the general is coming here next week for the U.N. meetings."

"I believe so."

"Would Prince Omar be kind enough to let the general know that it could be a very serious mistake to come here?" Malone asked.

"Might I tell His Highness why, Captain?" the uneasy aide wondered.

"Because some people think that he was behind this thing tonight . . . and *somebody* might put a fucking bullet in the general. Maybe *two*."

"The captain means that there could be an *attempt*," Shaw intervened smoothly, "and he'd rather avoid such an incident. If the general comes, we'd certainly be able to protect him. We have an excellent police department with a topnotch antiterrorist team. Captain Malone's in charge of that unit himself."

"I'll be on vacation next week," Malone said. "My daughter just flew in from California on TWA, and I'll be on vacation in about five minutes when she walks through that door."

The crown prince of Tarman nodded in comprehension.

He understood *this* even better than he knew oil and banking.

It was something he'd learned—absorbed—as a child.

Blood feud.

The blue-eyed policeman was saying that al-Khalif had endangered the life of his child, and he would be held accountable. That was as it should be, Omar thought.

It was a simple matter of family and honor, two subjects that Omar knew were nonnegotiable. There was no way to argue with the law of blood feud. It was more than a tradition. It was a fact.

The military aide put the watch away before he spoke.

"I'll give your message to His Highness," he promised.

"You don't have to," Malone said. "He spoke perfect English at Stanford not so long ago."

Prince Omar smiled.

"What if the general comes here next year, Captain?" he tested.

"I could be on vacation then, too," Malone answered.

Then a small tanned girl ran down the corridor with her arms outstretched. Malone swept her up and kissed her.

"Your daughter?" the prince guessed.

Malone nodded and kissed her again.

"Kate, this is Prince Omar of Tarman," the detective said a few seconds later after he put her down.

"I'm pleased to meet you, sir," she responded courteously.

"The pleasure is mine," he told her. "It was a pleasure to meet you, too, Captain. It is always a pleasure to meet a man of honor."

Now he saw the question in Frank Malone's hard eyes.

"You have my word that your thoughtful advice will reach General al-Khalif within twenty-four hours," Omar pledged.

He turned to Shaw.

"And I'll be sending a contribution to your fund for widows and orphans, Commissioner," the heir to the throne announced.

"That would be splendid," Shaw responded enthusiastically as he visualized the press conference. "Well, we'd better go now. If you'll come with me, Your Highness, there are some press people who'd like to talk to you."

"Of course. Good-bye, Captain. We shall meet again."

"*Inshallah*," Malone replied.

"Yes, if Allah wills it," Omar of Tarman agreed.

Then he walked away with Shaw, the aide and four bodyguards following. Frank Malone introduced his daughter to Hamilton, and she began telling them, in an eight-year-old's breathless detail, what had happened on the flight and how passengers had reacted.

"Then they told us to take the sharp things out of our pockets, and one of the motors stopped about a minute later. I wasn't scared, Daddy, but a lot of grown-ups were."

"I'd have been scared," Benjamin Hamilton told her.

"I was a *little* scared," she admitted.

Now she remembered—relived—those terrible minutes when the situation looked hopeless and death seemed imminent.

"People were screaming when the other motors stopped," she continued. "Not everyone . . . but some people."

She paused for a moment before she took her father's hand.

"I was a *lot* scared, Daddy."

Malone picked her up again, held her close.

She felt him struggle to suppress a shudder.

"It's all right, Daddy," she said. "Let me tell you the rest of it."

Her father kissed her, put her down and listened. As she recounted the dramatic events—with gestures—more people just off TWA 22 Heavy were moving down the passage. A bearded young man carrying a large Styrofoam box relentlessly pushed and bumped other passengers aside as he strode forward.

"Out of my way! Out of my way!" he ordered imperiously.

He was bulling ahead, just a few steps from Kate Malone, when he saw a stocky Hispanic man in a rain slicker walking toward him. The slicker was marked MOUNT SINAI, and the ambulance driver who wore it was being escorted by two uniformed Port Authority police.

"*There* you are!" the man with the Styrofoam box accused. "Took your own sweet time, didn't you?"

Before he could continue his diatribe, a sleekly attractive TWA flight attendant who looked oriental tapped his left shoulder lightly. He turned and glared at her.

"I told you," he snapped. "It's a kidney."

"Okay. Are you really a doctor?" Samantha Wong challenged.

"I'll have my doctorate in biochemistry next year," the courier announced haughtily. He brushed past her and resumed his verbal assault on the ambulance driver as they marched off to the parked vehicle.

"He's not a doctor-doctor at all," Samantha Wong said in a tone of outrage. "Hell, he's just a *creep.*"

"I hear there's one on every flight," Hamilton told her.

"Sometimes *more,*" the chic flight attendant confided. "I'd give this job up if I weren't so good at it," she announced, and strode off purposefully to keep her date with a highly talented and sexually indefatigable sculptor.

She was still in sight when Hamilton remembered.

"Good Lord!" he said and pointed at a pair of pay phones on the wall. "I *never* called my wife. I was due home almost three hours ago. She probably thinks I smashed up the car in this storm."

"Not if she's got the radio or TV on," Malone said as they began walking to the telephones. "You're the good fellow who was interviewed. Word of your heroism must be flooding the airwaves."

Hamilton groped in his pocket, and took out the coin he needed.

"Not a chance, Frank," he replied cheerfully. "My mama brought me up right. I told them all the whole thrilling truth about what *you* did. *You're* the hero, Frank."

He didn't give Malone a chance to answer. Hamilton reached the telephone, pushed in the quarter and dialed his home number. He was talking to his wife when Frank Malone guided his daughter to the adjacent phone.

"I already called Mom to say your plane was down safely," the detective told his daughter, "but I suspect she won't breathe right until she speaks to you."

That happened thirty-five seconds later.

Kate Malone was still talking to her mother in Malibu

when Hamilton hung up the other phone and walked across the corridor to join the detective.

Both men heard the eight-year-old girl say it.

"He's a hero, Mom. . . . Yes, he is. . . . He *is*. Turn on the radio!"

Hamilton saw Malone flinch.

"It's perfectly normal for a little girl to love her father, Frank," the Port Authority lieutenant declared.

"That's not what's bothering me."

"What is?"

"She's going back to her mother in California in ten days. I don't know *when* I'll see her again. She may not even *want* to see me again," Malone said.

"You divorced?"

"Separated. We're about to get a very civilized annulment," the detective explained bitterly. "Kate could have a new stepfather in a few months. *That* bothers me."

"I can see why," Hamilton answered compassionately.

"And there's still the nasty loose end here," Malone continued.

"What loose end?"

"We haven't finished with this operation tonight, dammit," the detective declared.

"Staub's dead, his people are in custody and all the planes have landed safely. It's over, Frank."

Malone shook his head. There was a fierce look in his eyes, and Hamilton wondered whether the detective might be confused by exhaustion.

"It won't be over till we nail Staub's spy in The Cab," Frank Malone insisted. "Don't argue with me! It isn't over at all!"

# 41

IN THE CAB, the watch supervisor hung up the telephone, the instrument over which Willi Staub had made his demands. She looked at it for several seconds.

"I think we'd better tell Captain Malone," she told Pete Wilber slowly. "He's got a right to know."

"Take your break now," Wilber said. "I'll come with you."

A Port Authority policeman on the balcony of the arrivals terminal used his walkie-talkie to find Hamilton, who said that he was with Malone at the baggage carousels waiting for the child's suitcase. When Annie Green and Wilber got there, they saw Hamilton first.

"He's over there," Hamilton said and pointed. Wilber and the watch supervisor turned in time to see Malone pick up a twenty-six-inch valise of blue nylon. With his blond daughter at his side, he walked over to Annie Green and sighed.

"In case you're wondering why my friend is so down," Hamilton said to her, "it's because he thinks we haven't won the whole ball of wax. He's got no proof, you understand, but he's convinced that the late Mr. Staub had a spy in The Cab. Wild idea isn't it?"

"Absolutely," Wilber answered. "Wild—and *right*."

"And there's proof," Annie Green added. "You weren't being paranoid, Frank. I suppose we owe you an apology."

"I'll settle for the facts," Malone responded.

"A police lieutenant named Arbolino found the spy, not us. He called us over a phone in some warehouse. He said to tell you that the Bomb Squad had cleared out the charges, and he was up in the main control room with the electronic equipment."

"What about the spy?" Malone asked tensely.

"I'm coming to that, Frank," she replied. "Lieutenant Arbolino explained that he was standing beside a loudspeaker. He then proceeded to recap everything we'd said in The Cab in the previous three minutes. He'd heard it all over the speaker!"

Now she held out her right first and opened it.

Malone recognized the object in her palm immediately.

"In your phone?" he asked.

"In the outside line. We had some noise on that line about two weeks ago, and a man came to fix the instrument. He must have put this in the mouthpiece, turning it into a round-the-clock listening device."

"So Staub's people heard everything said in The Cab for two full weeks before the attack . . . and everything else until we hit that warehouse," Frank Malone analyzed. "Very cute."

"It still isn't over," Hamilton announced. "How did Staub screw up the phone in The Cab, and how did the terrorists slip a phony repairman with fake ID through our security?"

"Maybe your security is like the air traffic control system," Malone said softly. *"Nearly* perfect."

"Our system's fine," Wilber defended loyally, "and it'll be even better when OMB releases the eight billion dollars and we get the advanced equipment."

"The federal government's warehousing eight billion dollars collected in user's fees from airlines," Annabelle Green translated. "The Office of Management and Budget won't let us spend that money because it wants to make the national deficit look smaller."

"That's crazy," Malone said. Then he noticed that his daughter was whispering something to Annie Green.

"Excuse us, Frank," the watch supervisor said. "We have to wash our hands. We'll meet you at the main door out front."

As they walked away, Wilber spoke again.

"Thanks for what you did tonight, Captain," he said sincerely. "Don't worry about our system."

"Couldn't happen again, right?"

"Let's say that we understand what happened, and we know how to prevent a repeat," Wilber declared.

"Let's say I certainly hope you're right," the detective replied as they shook hands.

The FAA official started back to The Cab, and Frank Malone nodded toward the lobby. The music that he'd been hearing from there seemed to be getting louder.

"Somebody's having fun," the detective said to Hamilton as they walked toward the sound.

"I wanted to talk to you about that," Hamilton replied. "That's the Hassidim. It's their music."

"Not the music. Fun. You were just having fun with the prince, weren't you?" the Port Authority lieutenant asked.

"Omar?"

"He's the only damn prince we met tonight."

"Seemed like a decent guy," Malone said and relit his cigar.

"I'm talking about the other guy, that al-Khalif," Hamilton announced as they zigzagged through the crowd.

"He's definitely indecent."

"You wouldn't really shoot him, would you? It was just a threat to scare him, right?"

Malone's head was bobbing to the powerfully rhythmic music.

"Catchy, isn't it?" he said.

"You didn't answer my question."

"Cultural diversity," Malone said warmly. "One of the things that makes America great."

"For God's sake, Frank!" Hamilton protested.

Now they entered the lobby. Everything was happening there. Everything and a half. Families were weeping in relief. People were shouting in joy. Reporters were yelling questions over the uproar. Police were cursing the blinding lights of the television news crews. Politicians were beaming as they basked in the attention, and the Kiev Grandma looked happy but a bit bewildered.

And the music was very loud. The Hassidim were singing, dancing, celebrating this night's divine deed as they had celebrated all the others. It wasn't only the Hassidim. A dozen Haitians had joined the passionate dancing, three booted Texans, a score of other people. Malone grinned as he saw Senator Bono pile into the line. There were the two Coast Guard helicopter pilots, several Asians, a blond woman in $18,000 worth of mink, four nuns, and Samantha Wong. Even the earnest Associated Press photographer whom Malone had avoided earlier was out there, doing his best with the unfamiliar steps.

Now a TV news producer spotted Malone, shouted in triumph.

Then he pointed and yelled to his crew.

"There they come, Frank," Hamilton warned.

"Here we go," Malone replied.

The camera team surged forward and hit a wall of people.

And more people.

And still more.

Dancing, hugging, sobbing, laughing—and utterly indifferent to the possibility that Western Civilization might collapse if that television crew didn't reach Frank Malone.

Two other people did.

His daughter and Annie Green worked their way around the outer edge of the joyous crowd and reached him at the door from the building. Malone pushed the portal open, and they all slipped out into the night.

"Kate's been telling me about California, Frank," Annie Green said.

Malone realized that she knew.

She was aware of the separation, maybe more.

"There's no snow in Malibu, Daddy," the child said.

Malone looked out at the storm.

"I think it's slowing down," he judged.

"But we'll still have a white Christmas," Kate Malone said hopefully.

"I guarantee it," her father replied.

Annie Green couldn't help smiling.

"I'd better get back to The Cab," she said.

"Now it's my turn to thank you," the detective said. "I'll do it more thoroughly on Saturday, of course."

"Saturday?"

"We're having lunch on Saturday," he announced. "Pick you up at twelve thirty sharp."

"You don't know where I live."

"I'm going to find out, Annie," he said meaningfully. "Twelve thirty, don't be late."

Then Captain Frank Malone put down his daughter's suitcase and kissed an FAA watch supervisor. When she stepped back she was glowing.

"Saturday," she agreed.

"And I'll see you whenever you have that critique," he told Hamilton.

"Listen, Frank," the Port Authority lieutenant appealed.

"You're a good cop, Ben," Malone said.

"You're not so bad yourself," Hamilton answered.

They grasped each other's hands in silence.

Then somebody came from the terminal, releasing another burst of infectious music into the winter night.

"Definitely catchy," Frank Malone said as he picked up the suitcase. He began to hum the melody as they started for his car. By the time they reached the vehicle, his daughter was humming it, too. As he started the motor, Frank Malone thought about what had happened this cold and stormy December night.

The terrorists' perfect attack on the perfect system.

The AWACS plane that arrived from some secret mission over the North Atlantic that the air force still wouldn't discuss.

And Annabelle Green. Oh yes, Annabelle Green.

It was going to be one extraordinary Christmas.

He guided the sedan out of the parking lot, and when they reached the highway he accepted his daughter's suggestion that they go on to songs whose words she knew. They sang the carols all the way into the city.

# Author's Note

The author wishes to thank the individuals at the Federal Aviation Administration, the U.S. Air Force, the Coast Guard and public relations staff of Pan American Airways who provided so much factual assistance and helpful advice.

The technology described in this novel is based on their knowledge and guidance. Air traffic control experts have told the writer that there are, in addition to the equipment described in this book, other "systems" that should prevent the sabotage and crisis set forth in this work of fiction from happening.

I would certainly hope so. To add a minor contribution to air safety, these "systems" and how they work were not included in *58 Minutes*.

w. w.

# THE BEST IN SUSPENSE

☐ 50105-5   CITADEL RUN by Paul Bishop     $4.95
    50106-3                           Canada $5.95

☐ 54106-5   BLOOD OF EAGLES by Dean Ing     $3.95
    54107-3                           Canada $4.95

☐ 51066-6   PESTIS 18 by Sharon Webb     $4.50
    51067-4                           Canada $5.50

☐ 50616-2   THE SERAPHIM CODE by Robert A. Liston     $3.95
    50617-0                           Canada $4.95

☐ 51041-0   WILD NIGHT by L. J. Washburn     $3.95
    51042-9                           Canada $4.95

☐ 50413-5   WITHOUT HONOR by David Hagberg     $4.95
    50414-3                           Canada $5.95

☐ 50825-4   NO EXIT FROM BROOKLYN by Robert J. Randisi     $3.95
    50826-2                           Canada $4.95

☐ 50165-9   SPREE by Max Allan Collins     $3.95
    50166-7                           Canada $4.95

---

Buy them at your local bookstore or use this handy coupon:
Clip and mail this page with your order.

Publishers Book and Audio Mailing Service
P.O. Box 120159, Staten Island, NY 10312-0004

Please send me the book(s) I have checked above. I am enclosing $_____
(please add $1.25 for the first book, and $.25 for each additional book to
cover postage and handling. Send check or money order only—no CODs.)

Name _____

Address _____

City _____ State/Zip _____

Please allow six weeks for delivery. Prices subject to change without notice.

# BESTSELLING BOOKS FROM TOR

☐ 58341-8  ANGEL FIRE by Andrew M. Greeley $4.95
☐ 58342-6 Canada $5.95

☐ 58338-8  THE FINAL PLANET by Andrew M. Greeley $4.95
☐ 58339-6 Canada $5.95

☐ 58336-1  GOD GAME by Andrew M. Greeley $4.50
☐ 58337-X Canada $5.50

☐ 50105-5  CITADEL RUN by Paul Bishop $4.95
☐ 50106-3 Canada $5.95

☐ 58459-7  THE BAREFOOT BRIGADE by Douglas C. Jones $4.50
☐ 58460-0 Canada $5.50

☐ 58457-0  ELKHORN TAVERN by Douglas C. Jones $4.50
☐ 58458-9 Canada $5.50

☐ 58364-7  BON MARCHE by Chet Hagan $4.95
☐ 58365-5 Canada $5.95

☐ 50773-8  THE NIGHT OF FOUR HUNDRED RABBITS $4.50
☐ 50774-6  by Elizabeth Peters Canada $5.50

☐ 55709-3  ARAMINTA STATION by Jack Vance $4.95
☐ 55710-7 Canada $5.95

☐ 52126-9  VAMPHYRI! by Brian Lumley (U.S. orders only) $4.50

☐ 52166-8  NECROSCOPE by Brian Lumley (U.S. orders only) $3.95

---

Buy them at your local bookstore or use this handy coupon:
Clip and mail this page with your order.

Publishers Book and Audio Mailing Service
P.O. Box 120159, Staten Island, NY 10312-0004

Please send me the book(s) I have checked above. I am enclosing $_____
(please add $1.25 for the first book, and $.25 for each additional book to
cover postage and handling. Send check or money order only—no CODs.)

Name _____

Address _____

City _____ State/Zip _____

Please allow six weeks for delivery. Prices subject to change without notice.

# THE BEST IN SCIENCE FICTION

# THE TOR DOUBLES

Two complete short science fiction novels in one volume!

---

# ELIZABETH PETERS